Sir
Coffin
Graves

ENJOY!

LEINAD PU

Sir Coffin Graves

Book 1

A Novel

Leinad Platz

Mill City Press, Minneapolis

Mill City Press, Inc.
322 First Avenue N, 5th floor
Minneapolis, MN 55401
612.455.2293
www.millcitypublishing.com

ISBN-13: 978-1-63413-764-5
LCCN: 2015916627

Printed in the United States of America

Dedication

This book is dedicated to both my grandmothers, Jean Holtz and Sara "Sally" Morgan-Davis; to my cousin (who passed way too young) Michael "Mickey" Fejnas, and to my superstar father David W. Platz. Their memories have deeply touched and shaped my soul. I love and miss them with all my heart.

Acknowledgments

First and foremost: Thank you God, for your Son, and for blessing me beyond comprehension.

Thanks also to: Eric Dalen, my super badass ghostwriter/editor, whose sharp editorial eye, friendship and creativity shine. Susie DePinto, graphic artist, who designed a hauntingly beautiful cover. I am so grateful to have two people like you in my corner.

To everyone at Mill City publishing for putting the final touches together.

My brother "Big D" David W. Platz II and his family—wife Mary Ellen, children Molly, Matthew, Taylor and Ben—for their support and endless love that means more to me than words can ever express.

To my mother Terry K. Ross, for encouraging me to be myself even if it meant failure at times. To my sons Christopher and Danny, and grandchildren Trenton and Allison. May your lives be full of happiness.

Cheers go out to my Colorado friends and to my "Limaland" Lima, Ohio inner-circle friends.

Also, to all the wonderful hardworking sales people, managers and owners that I've had the privilege to work with across America. (Way too many to list everyone's name . . . but you know who you are.)

I attended high school with a wonderful bunch of people. But I would like to particularly thank Mrs. Brigham-Schmuhl, my art teacher for inspiring me and believing in my creativity.

Props go out to the Canadian band Rush, for providing my music soul with meaningful lyrics and legendary music. Rock-on!

Prologue

"No one ever told me that grief felt so like fear."—C. S. Lewis

People think graves are six feet deep. They're not.

I stomp the shovel into the earth again, having already excavated most of what I needed. It is a struggle to keep focused. I've dug dozens of these, but never for someone I knew.

36 inches wide, 48 inches deep, and 96 inches long . . . 36 inches wide, 48 inches deep, and 96 inches long . . . 36 inches wide, 48 inches deep, and 96 inches long . . .

I chant this over and over in a feeble attempt to keep my mind off who I'm digging for, and why.

I don't know why. I just knew I couldn't sleep and had to do something.

The fog is settling in, dawn will come soon, but I don't know how soon. I just need to finish.

It looks like I'm pretty close.

I yank the tape measure off my belt and begin measuring.

36 inches wide, and 96 inches long . . . 46 inches deep. Almost there.

It hurt bad enough that she was gone, but that she was gone for no apparent reason . . . that's what is so confusing and disturbing. No reason for her to be dead. No blood, no marks, no sign. It was just like she went to sleep and never woke up.

But that doesn't normally happen to a 21 year old.

Was she killed?

I scoop more earth out of the grave.

If it wasn't natural causes, then it was unnatural.

I measure again and find it's just right. I level off the bottom as best I can with the shovel, then work to square the corners properly. Using my bare hands, I make them the best 90-degree boxed-off edge I can. Even dad would be proud, if such a feeling existed in him.

I lift myself out and eye my work from above. It looks just about perfect, as it should be.

For her.

Except for one thing. I can't believe I left the shovel at the bottom.

I jump down, but between the slick dirt and my slippery shoes, both feet go out from under me, and I land face-first into the shovel.

* * *

The dreams came and went. They didn't make any sense. They rarely did. But she was in them, and that was what mattered.

She was smiling. Head cocked, listening. Swinging a baseball bat. Slipping a tooth into her pocket. Washing the red-head woman's hair. Screaming.

They weren't always pleasant images, but I couldn't look away.

* * *

I slowly came around. The musky smell of the earth. The feeling of light rain on the back of my neck. The taste of dirt.

I was facing the wrong way. Not up. My head throbbing.

I manage to move my arms up and roll myself onto my back,

eyes open but not seeing very well.

A large black cloud looms. But then the cloud coughs.

My eyes clear. Harold is looking down at me.

I raise an arm up, hoping he will lean in and help pull me up.

He slants himself slightly, then spits on me. I feel it plop on my left cheek and slide down towards my ear.

Why the hell did he do that?

Then he just walks away.

I lay for a few more minutes, the drizzle tickling my skin, the spit stuck near my earlobe, my forehead feeling tight. It might seem weird, but I find a calming peace in here. Death wouldn't be so bad if I could be with her.

I raise up into a sitting position, fighting the dizziness, then slowly get to my feet.

The grave is four feet deep, so my body rose two feet above ground level . . . but I feel so much smaller. I don't know if I have the energy to lift myself out of the hole. But I try, and I do.

I slowly walk towards the house, gingerly feeling the three-inch line over my eyebrows where the shovel had tried to scalp me. The gash felt like the Grand Canyon.

And I still left the damn shovel in the bottom of the grave.

Chapter 1

"May the love hidden deep inside your heart find the love waiting in your dreams. May the laughter that you find in your tomorrow wipe away the pain you find in your yesterdays." —Unknown

January 10

Sometimes I think I'm bi-polar, or maybe even schizophrenic. I'd like to tell myself that the occasional random voice I think I hear is not me. That's probably just a cop-out. I mean, I just turned 19—technically an adult, but I don't feel much like one. Some of the things that cross my mind don't seem much like me, but who else would it be?

Don't be late.

Don't be late? I'm already pulling in the parking lot. It's 8:55. The store opens at 9. Even Patrick, the chronic tardy, is standing by the side door, finishing his cigarette in the cold.

"Hey," I say as I get out of the pickup.

"Hey yourself. You're looking extra dapper."

"You're not."

He shrugs, taking a drag on his smoke. "Chicks dig it."

"Yeah, I can see that."

Patrick is my age, but where I'm white and nerdy, he's mulatto and street cool. If his laid-back-yet-wary attitude didn't telegraph it, the white tank top he usually wore showing off the tattoos did. I often wonder why we became friends, but I shouldn't question the only one I have.

"You ready for another day?"

"Nah, but I need some bills to pay some bills." He puts out his cigarette, rubs his hand over his shiny shaved head and opens the door. "Let's get to it."

We go inside, clock in, take off our coats, and begin our set-up. I head up front for sales, Patrick to the back for repairs. At least he'd have something interesting to do while I wait for the first customers show up. If they show up. They don't exactly form a line outside a furniture store drooling over a 40% discount on an ottoman.

I know Chauncey is upstairs, watching. As the boss/owner, he liked to make sure we were giving him his money's worth because sweeping clean floors and straightening perfectly straight *On Sale* signs is better than nothing.

Greg, the other salesman, unlocks the door a whole two minutes early. He already appears disheveled, shirt half-untucked, greasy hair askew. He wants to be here less than me, having a background in IT and now reduced to this. At least this is my first job, so I have an excuse.

He no sooner steps away than the door opens and a stunning young woman walks in. I shouldn't say that, not very professional and all, but *dang*. Label me horny, or shallow, or whatever, but . . . *dang*.

She sees me—completely missing Greg, who is standing six feet away—and smiles. I think I smiled back. She is older than me, but not a lot, all fresh-faced and perky.

"Hi!" she says. "I hope you can help me, I don't have a lot of time."

I only nod, probably not capable of speaking if I could think of anything to say.

"I'm looking for a curio."

I nod again, probably still smiling like a goofball, and turn, heading towards the corner where the two curios we had on display are sitting.

"Oh, this is nice," she says, pointing at one as her cell phone goes off. "Excuse me."

I nod. I could be drooling, but wouldn't know.

"Now?" she says to the phone. "Okay, I'll be right in." She hangs up and turns to me. "I have to run. Do you have a card?"

I nod, something I'm quite good at. I pull a card out of my breast pocket and hand it over.

She looks at it. "Thank you, Jacob Davis! I'll be back!"

And off she goes, gliding out the door.

"Dude," Greg says. "You know who that is?"

I shake my head—another one of my talents—afraid my voice would revert to sounding like a fifth grader.

"That's Jill Stone, the reporter on Channel 6."

I blink at him. I didn't watch the news, much less Channel 6. They usually seem to play infomercials. I don't need nor want a blender that turns broccoli into a milkshake.

"She had her eye on you," Greg says, pulling a half-eaten Snickers bar from his back pocket and stuffing the last half into his mouth. "Yoush mah neeooh aller."

I have no idea what he said, and don't care. I'm still smiling.

* * *

At lunch, I go to the nearby fast food place for some of tacos and surprise Patrick with a couple. He calmly looks at me with those light brown eyes.

"What's this for?" he says, cigarette dangling from his lips.

"I don't know, I probably owe you for something."

He takes them and nods. "Yeah, you probably do. Thanks."

"You ever going to quit smoking?"

He stubs it out and blows a plume of smoke in my general direction. "I'll quit when you get a tat."

I think about this a few moments. "So, you want me to permanently scar my body so you can live an extra thirty years?"

"Sure. Why not?" He takes a bite of a taco.

Greg comes out and tries to get in on the conversation, telling Patrick of my close encounter with the feminine kind.

"She was sweet," Greg says, wiggling his eyebrows. "The hottie on Channel 6."

Patrick stares at him in brief disbelief, then turns to me. "You get her number?"

"No. I didn't think of it." I don't bother to tell him that I'd had trouble even forming words at the time.

"Dude, how you ever gonna get some if you don't plan ahead?"

Greg looks at me. "You're a virgin?"

I take a bite of taco to avoid answering.

"Look who's talking," Patrick says.

"Hey, I was married."

Possible. He's in his mid-30's, had made a lot of money in computers, got caught hacking, spent a year in jail, and now sells recliners to retirees for something slightly north of minimum wage, plus commission.

"Jake went to an all-boys school," Patrick says, smirking at me.

I eat more taco.

"Hey," Chauncey Phillips says from the doorway and pointing at Greg. "You already had your lunch break—get back on the floor."

Greg slinks away.

Chauncey checks his watch to make sure I'm not taking advantage of my thirty minutes, then leaves.

"I gave her my card," I say.

Patrick beams. "There's hope for you yet."

* * *

My normal darkish mood is gone for the rest of the day, and when I get home, I turn on the TV. Channel 6 is on a commercial, so I head for the kitchen to make dinner. More specifically, a sandwich.

While it is easy to understand why the girl bypassed Greg—most girls do—I couldn't shake the feeling she sought me out. My ego's not big enough to believe it was based on my Midwestern good looks, mop of black hair, or tall lanky frame. There had never been a girl, ever, who seemed to show any interest in me. I just found it weird that a young, attractive TV reporter would be the first. If there was any truth to my fantasy.

"The West Side Chicago Kennel has an overabundance of pooches," the middle-aged woman anchor says after a Honda commercial. *"Channel 6 reporter Jill Stone paid a visit to get details on how you can adopt one."*

The picture switches to a cute little yappy dog wagging its tail and jumping around.

"Max is a two-year-old mixed breed found wandering the streets," a female voice-over says. *"And he's got a lot of company."*

I watch the report, which was long on dogs, short on Jill, but there is finally a shot of her at the end, holding Max, and telling people how they can adopt their own special pet. She looks better than I remember, and I remembered everything.

But it ends, and they go to the weather. I finish my sandwich, change clothes, and head out to take care of Ginger.

Harold, the groundskeeper, is waiting for me.

"You seen your dad?" he asks. He looks as grimy as he usually does, unshaven, overall making Greg look like a male model.

Truth is, I haven't seen my father in three months, and only then it was from a distance. We live on the same property, but I moved out to the old, vacated mortician's house on the far side of the cemetery. Sometimes I felt it wasn't far enough.

"No. Something wrong?"

Harold harrumphs, heaves a healthy wad of spit on the ground, and lumbers off.

I watch him for a bit, making sure he is gone before I head to the barn.

Ginger is somewhat annoyed, apparently because I am a tad late in visiting her. She snorts and whinnies, and looks at me with an accusing eye. I pat her mane and promise I'd take her on a good ride over the weekend. This evening, it would be the usual short loop.

I tell her about my day as we go around the cemetery, coming right along the backside of the Meadows Polo Club and Resort. Ginger always seems to move a little faster through this area, and I have to hold her back until we're away so she doesn't get into a gallop. Back at the barn, I brush her, feed her, fill her water and wish her a good night. She snorts in return. She sounds happier.

The rest of the evening is spent reading, and I go to bed early. It wasn't much of a surprise that I dreamt of Jill.

I only wish I hadn't.

Chapter 2

"Dreams are today's answers to tomorrow's questions." —Edgar Cayce

January 11

I walk into a room and see Jill Stone on the other side. I'm about to say something when I notice she's got her ear to a door, listening. Then she opens it slowly and slips through. I walk over and peek in.

There's a woman, mid-50's, in a bathtub. I feel both embarrassed and intrigued by her large breasts. She has her head back, a washcloth over her eyes. She has the reddest red hair I've ever seen.

Jill is sneaking up to her. I'm thinking at first she's going to surprise her, but as Jill gets behind the woman, she takes a towel off a rack and, in one swift move, pushes the white terrycloth against the woman's face, shoving her underwater.

The woman's arms come up, hands grasping Jill's wrists, but Jill is forceful, holding her down.

I try to say something, but either she doesn't hear me, or nothing comes out. I stand frozen, watching Jill drown the naked woman, doing nothing to stop it.

Finally, the woman stops thrashing, and Jill waits another minute before letting up.

Jill turns and looks at me, smiling.

"Collin, that felt so good," she says. "You should try it some time."

* * *

I wake up not feeling very rested. I don't put much credit into my dreams, even if they are often quite vivid and sometimes even come true. So I try to do that this time. But one little thing keeps bugging me, even if I know it's nothing.

Why did she call me Collin?

Truth is, Collin is my middle name, and few know that. I'm not even sure my father remembers.

I hop in and out of the shower, get ready for work, and then go out to check on Ginger. Immediately, I'm greeted by Gizzi—a Tibetan Pekinese—who happily runs to me, jumping up and down for me to hold her. I pick her up and she licks my face as I look around for her owner.

Sylvana comes around the corner, appearing much the same as she always does—both stunning and a little odd. Mid-60's with a shock of white hair, hazel eyes that seemed to look through me and into me at the same time. One is slightly darker than the other, adding to the strange effect. She became my nanny after my mother died when I was four, and still manages to keep an eye on me.

"Good morning. What are you doing up and out so early?"

"I am always up early, Collin." She smiles calmly, but a chill goes up my spine.

Collin.

She must have noticed my discomfort. "I was hoping you could do a favor for me. I need to go out of town for a few days, and was wondering if you could watch Gizzi for me."

"Sure. Where are you going? Somewhere nice, I hope."

"I'm moving away." She says this with finality, watching my

reaction. "My time is finished here."

"Wow. Okay. I thought you would stay on to help father."

A small twitch of a smile. "I have arranged for someone to come by to help around his house a couple of times a week."

"Alright. I . . . I will just have a hard time not having you around."

She nods as if she understands. "We'll keep in touch. It's been a pleasure watching you grow into a fine young man, and I'm looking forward to see what you'll accomplish in life." Sylvana takes the wiggling Gizzi out of my arms. "I will bring her by before I leave. Thank you so much for taking care of her."

"Sure," I say, then turn to the barn to check on Ginger, still a little stunned Sylvana would be leaving. She had been like a mother to me, especially since mine had died. Now, fifteen years later, she was . . . well, she wouldn't be here. Sylvana and Ginger had been the only two stable things in my life.

* * *

At Phillip's Furniture, my dark mood hangs heavy. Few customers, none buying. No commissions. I don't really care. Money, no money, it's all the same.

Stop it.

I wish I could. I wish I could stop the voice. Sometimes it whispers, sometimes yells, sometimes is judging and sarcastic. Once in a while it's pleasant, but not often. There are times I wonder if it's my conscience, or something more meaningful, more relevant, trying to tell me something.

The weird thing is . . . it's usually right.

"Jake, line one . . . Jake, line one."

Chauncey from up in his lair. I resist looking up to see his pudgy face peering down at me to make sure I take the call.

I walk over to the service counter where the customers get written up, pay for their furniture, arrange for delivery. Holly is sitting there, chomping on gum, going through a gossip magazine, not even bothering to look up when I approach. She was 17 or 18, had a baby at 16, her mom watching the toddler while she sat and did nothing.

I pick up the phone and punch the blinking button.

"Jake Davis, how may I help you?"

"Hi Jake, it's Jill Stone. I stopped by yesterday to look at the curios you had on display. I was wondering if I could stop by around one—you still have it, right?"

"Oh, yes," I manage to say. I don't tell her that it had been here when I started almost a year ago, and would probably be here for generations to come.

"Great. I'll see you then."

And she hangs up.

I smile at Holly as I put the phone down, and she continues to ignore me.

I check the time. 11:10.

If time went slow before, it practically crawls from this point on.

* * *

"What are you doin' this weekend?" Patrick asks before taking a bite of his sandwich.

"Usual. I got a couple of graves to dig."

"You're one exciting dude."

"Hey, it's five hundred bucks a pop. Hard to pass that up."

"Five bills? I want a piece of that. Your daddy must like you."

I pause, not sure what to say. I have no idea what father thinks of me. Or if he thinks of me.

"Maybe he's grooming you to take over." Patrick pops a potato chip in his mouth.

"I doubt it." I leave it at that.

Patrick probably senses my discomfort, and changes the subject.

"I'm goin' to the Cannonball Friday night, if you'd like to

come."

"That bar?"

"You got somethin' against it?" He smirks.

"I don't know, never been there. Seems to always be a police car or ambulance blocking the parking lot."

"Yeah, they are known for their fights—but it's Ladies Night. The low-lifes act nicer and smell better."

"Yeah, maybe I will." I pause. I want to tell him, but thought I'd sound dorky.

Then I thought *Hey—you are dorky.*

"She called this morning."

His passive expression doesn't change, he just nods. "Sounds like you sold a curio."

I think this over, getting his point.

Don't get your hopes up.

* * *

If it wasn't exactly 1 o'clock straight up, it's close enough to not matter. The door opens and Jill Stone, reporter for WCBC Channel 6 Chicago, walks in wearing black workout Capris, a purple tank top, and a black headband holding back her chestnut brown hair. She sees me and her face blossoms into a smile.

"Hi, I hope I'm not late."

This time, I somehow manage to find my voice. "No, not at all." I smile back, seeing Greg out of the corner of my eye, leering. I turn and lead her to the curio.

"Sorry I had to run off yesterday. It was supposed to be my day off, but someone called in sick, so I had to cover their assignment."

"Did anyone adopt Max?"

Her head snaps around in surprise. "Well, I don't know. I hope so. He was a cutie."

We chat about the curio, I show her the features and let her check it out.

"When can it be delivered?"

"Would this afternoon be okay?" I turn towards the service counter.

"That would be great."

I step behind the counter and grab the paperwork, Holly giving me a look that was either disdain or relief that I was doing her job for her. Hard to tell.

"Could be delivered after three?" Jill asks. "I'll be home then."

"Going to work out?"

She tilts her head. "Yeah, Better Body Fitness."

"I have a membership there too." Which is true. I just haven't gone in . . . a while.

"Well, cool. Maybe I'll run into you sometime," she says as she signs the paperwork. She slides the contract back and hands me the pen. "Like tomorrow evening?"

*   *   *

I hate to admit that I did a little research on Jill Stone, but I did. There wasn't much to find. There seemed to be a million girls with that name on the social networks, and none looked anything like her. The bio on the cheesy WCBC ("Windy City Broadcasting Company") website was anemic, saying only she joined the station right out of college and liked movies, music and good food—who didn't? It looked like I would have to learn about her the old fashioned way.

There's a rap at the front door, and I open it to find Sylvana holding Gizzi in one arm and a bag of something in the other. I wonder how she managed to knock.

"Hey." I pluck the wiggling dog from her as she enters.

"I brought some of her food, snacks and toys—and dinner for you."

"Aw, you didn't have to do that."

"Yes, I did. A man should not live by sandwiches alone." She says this without humor, but her eyes twinkle.

"I had tacos yesterday."

"Those are just Mexican sandwiches." She sets the bag down on the coffee table and sees the laptop with the screen showing the WCBC photo of Jill Stone. She stares at it for a moment, then turns to me with a smirk. "You have good taste, Collin." She pats my cheek. "Thank you for taking care of Gizzi—I will be back in a couple of days."

"No problem."

She stops at the door, then turns and gazes at me for several moments. With her white hair and eerie hazel eyes . . . if she did that to someone else, they might have not appreciated it. But I've known her too long.

"Everything will work out," she says. "Just—"

"—stay true and pay attention," I say along with her.

Her eyes look to the laptop, then back at me. She nods once and glides out of the house.

She's enigmatic like that. Father once called her "That Witch," but I would guess she'd heard worse.

I close the door and set Gizzi down, who bounces up and down like a jumping bean, wanting me to pick her up again.

I hope she has an OFF button.

* * *

The President of the United States sat across from me in a booth at some kind of diner. He was eating the tallest stack of pancakes I'd ever seen, pouring ketchup on them instead of syrup.

"You should have gone to college," he was telling me. "I could have made you Secretary of the Something-Or-Other."

"That's okay. I'm fine."

"You ever been to the Men's Club?"

I shook my head.

He took a bite of bloody pancakes and made a sound like it was the best thing he'd ever tasted.

"You'd like it," he said around a mouthful. I wasn't sure he was talking about the pancakes or the club. He took a big drink of

his martini. "Want some?" he said holding the glass out.

"No thank you."

"She's there sometimes. Oh . . . she looks so good . . . so good." His eyes got wistful. "It's better when they fight."

The waitress came up with a pitcher of water and filled my glass. I looked up to thank her and realized it was Sylvana. Her face was passive, but I noticed she wore a big red, white and blue button on the lapel of her white uniform.

JUST STAY TRUE AND PAY ATTENTION.

"I can get you a pass—maybe a membership," the President said, ketchup running out of the corner of his mouth. "Just be careful," he added as the waitress glided away. "Sometimes she kicks. Oh, and it hurts . . . It hurts."

Chapter 3

"Better three hours too soon than a minute too late." —*William Shakespeare*

January 12

I sit awkwardly on one of the benches in the lobby/waiting area of the Better Body Fitness Center. The workout—if it could be called that—was pretty laid-back, more minor chit-chat than anything. I hardly broke a sweat.

"Well, that's it for today," Jill said, heading off to the women's area. She smiled brightly and disappeared.

Now I wait. I had hit the locker room, stripped, showered, dressed, and came out not knowing if she was still in the building, or had already slipped out and was heading home. At least I smell good. I was hoping to see if she wanted to get some dinner, or maybe a coffee. Or a smoothie. Even thirty seconds of uncomfortable and inept conversation on my part to prolong this however I can.

Just about every female who walked out made me twitch, thinking it's her. It seemed like I waited two hours, but it was probably five minutes.

Jill comes walking out, all springy and happy-looking, casual clothes, hair tied back in a ponytail.

I practically leap up and try not to smile too hard.

"Hi!" she says. "Thanks for hanging out with me. Usually, I come with a friend, but she couldn't make it."

"No problem." *That was borderline lame*, I tell myself. "I was wondering if you wanted to get something to eat . . . or drink . . . ?"

She frowns slightly and checks her watch. "I can't. I have to be at the studio in half an hour to fill in for the weather guy at ten."

"Oh. Okay. Yeah. No problem." I smile. It feels ghoulish. I hope it looks better.

"Thanks again, Jake!"

And she hurries out the door while I try to not look as embarrassed as I feel.

* * *

Big dumb stupid, the voice says.

This time, I kind of agree with it. Though I wasn't quite sure what I did wrong, if anything.

I drive home, mentally doing an autopsy on what I have already determined is a dead relationship. I even know how bad that seems.

Relationship? What relationship?

Then I heard Patrick's voice: *Sounds like you sold a curio.*

I wasn't too pushy, I knew that. I wasn't pushy at all. Maybe that was the problem. Good girls liked bad boys, and I'm a nice guy. Odd man out. I should beat someone up and go to jail. Email her my mug shot.

I pull onto the grounds and around the side of my house.

I decide that it wasn't because I'd had my hopes up too high, but that I'd had any hopes at all.

I climb out of the truck and notice the back door is open. Not much, but enough.

I walk up the steps and push it open, looking in. Nothing.

Everything seems unnaturally quiet—but since this was in the far corner of the cemetery, that was normal.

I listen. A muted *thud* of a single step. From upstairs.

I don't own a gun, or even a baseball bat, so I grab a frying pan from the rack. I doubt it would make me dangerous or bad enough for good girls to re-consider, but I was more curious than frightened. Who would want to break into my house? I don't have much, not anything anyone would want—I'm not even sure I would want it—but it's the principle of the thing.

I start up the stairs, and just as I get to the top, Harold comes lumbering out of my bedroom. He stops, staring at me with something between annoyance and contempt.

"What are you doing here?" I ask.

He doesn't say anything for several seconds, looks at the frying pan, apparently trying to come up with something plausible. He might be the cemetery groundskeeper, but he had no need to be on this part of the grounds.

"I heard a dog."

"So why are you here?"

This confuses him, as if hearing a dog was a perfectly acceptable reason for breaking into someone's home.

"No dogs allowed."

"Except Gizzi." I say this as if talking to a third grader. "She's downstairs in the spare room. I'm watching her for Sylvana."

Harold hisses, like I had just uttered the name of something evil and unwelcome. Then he shambles past me and plods down the stairs.

I follow him, watch him exit through the back, then I lock the door behind him.

Only then did I shiver as if a ghost passed through me.

* * *

After taking care of Gizzi and Ginger, I lay in the hot water of the tub wondering what it means that Jill usually worked out with a friend who couldn't make it. Was I the replacement? The backup? That's it?

Maybe I'm over-thinking this. Of course I'm over-thinking it. I'm just trying to wrap my brain around that my first date—ever— was just working a treadmill for twenty minutes and helping her spot some light weight-training. I wasn't expecting wedding bells, but sheesh.

You got your hopes too high.

Yeah, yeah, whatever.

I let the tub drain, then shower quickly before getting out.

I can't say Jill misled me—I did that to myself, but was at a loss how I could do it differently.

I stand in front of the mirror and stare at myself. Maybe a little too pasty white. Jet black hair—too gothic? No tattoos, piercings, birthmarks. In decent shape. Better than most, not as good as some.

Maybe I should smile more and not skulk so much.

I go to the bedroom replaying every word she said. No clues there. Nothing at all, really. Should I call her?

No.

Email?

I wait for an answer, and receive none.

Gizzi lay on the bed, staring at me with doggie anticipation. Of what, neither of us knew.

I put on some jeans and go down to the kitchen, considering a bite to eat. Not really hungry. Gizzi follows me around, hoping I'd change my mind.

I look out the window, into the settling darkness.

The thing with Harold crosses my mind. He'd worked at the Rest Haven Funeral Home & Mortuary forever and was always a little creepy, but I'd never seen him in one of the buildings before, except the maintenance shed. I knew he hadn't been here because he heard a dog. He was looking for something, but what, I had no idea.

I open the laptop and consider sending an email to Jill.

Thanks for . . . what?

It was great seeing you today. Maybe we can work out again sometime?

Better. I type it out and stare at it.

Should I wait until tomorrow?

No answer.

I hear steps on the front porch, then a knock on the door.

Gizzi lets out a bark, then looks at me, and barks again.

"You wouldn't scare a baby." I stand.

She wags her tail and pants.

I open the door. Patrick is standing there, brown bag in one arm.

"Hey," I say.

He smirks, looking me up and down, taking in my jeans and lack of a shirt. "I hope I'm not interrupting anything."

"No, just got out of the shower."

"Cool. The game's on, and my TV is on the fritz." He walks in as Gizzi jumps up and down in joy as if Patrick is her best friend ever, even though they'd never met.

I close the door, a little puzzled. He'd never been here. I might have told him where I lived, but it's a big property. "How'd you find me?"

He sets the bag down. "This was the only building with lights on. Everything else was dark."

"What game is on?"

He looks at me like I'm joking. "Bulls. What else?"

"I don't know, the Bears, maybe?"

He shakes his head. "That game's over." He picks up the remote and turns on the TV. "It's too quiet here. How can you stand it?"

"I live on the grounds of a cemetery—if it weren't quiet, I'd be worried."

"You got a point."

Patrick comes from the part of town where if there wasn't

fighting and yelling, there was sirens and gunshots. He opens the bag and pulls out a couple of styrofoam containers.

"Hope you like Chinese."

"Sure. What happened to your TV?"

"No picture."

"Did you pay the cable bill?"

"I thought I did. They disagree."

I'll have to slip him a twenty before he leaves. I fetch a couple of sodas from the fridge and hand one to Patrick. He takes it with another smirk.

* * *

It wasn't until the 3rd quarter that I get up the nerve to bring up Jill.

"Oh yeah, how'd that go?"

"Nice . . . I guess."

He eyes me. "Did you say something dorky?"

I laugh. "No, nothing like that. At least no more than usual. I don't know, it was just kind of like . . ." I pause, trying to find the right word.

"A friend thing."

I snap my fingers. "Yeah. A friend thing."

He picks up the remote and hits the mute. "Did you take the leadership role?"

"The leadership role? We were just at the gym."

"Did you lead, or did you follow?"

I frown.

"Nevermind," he says. "Look, I've been . . . around, and one thing I think I know about women is that they like leaders, but not to be dominated. They want someone to follow, but not tell them what to do."

Sorry to say, this logic completely escapes me. I guess the look on my face communicates this.

"If you act like a lap dog," he says, pointing at the one on my lap, "that's how you'll be treated. If you take a little initiative, they'll respond."

"Okay."

"Would you rather hear 'Hey, let's go to the movies'? Or 'Would you like to go to the movies?'"

I pause, wondering if this was a trick question. "Um, the first?"

Patrick shakes his head. "Let me try this a different way— what would you want out of someone like . . . what's her name?"

"Jill. And what do you mean what do I want?"

"Do you want sex? Love? A friendship?"

"Yes."

He stares at me for several moments. "You're almost hopeless. But I get you. You want it all, but you got to pick one."

I blink a few times. "Why?"

"Because one leads to another. Now, if you pick sex first, it might lead to love, but probably not friendship. Sex and friendship don't really mix. If you pick friendship first, well, probably nothing will happen because that's all nice and stuff, but friends don't want to see other friends naked. That's why I made you put on your shirt. They might be your friend, then 'grow' to love you, but it could take forever 'cause they're waiting for the guy on the horse to gallop in and sweep them off their feet."

"I've got a horse."

He stares at me again, absently scratching his temple. "Okay, I might have found your problem. Maybe you should not talk— just nod. Don't talk about yourself. I mean, you sell furniture, live in a cemetery and have a little yappy dog. Not a lot of positives there."

"It's not my—"

"Will you just *shush*? I'm trying to give you a principle here." He sighs and finishes off his soda. "It would be a lot easier if you just wanted to get laid."

I hold out my hands and shrug. "Hey, I wouldn't be opposed—"

"*Please* stop talking." He looks in the general direction of the coffee table. "Okay, we'll do this one step at a time. What was your plan?"

I open the laptop and show him. He reads it and slides the computer back to me.

"That might work if all you wanted to do was work out with her again. No, tell her you had a nice time, blah blah blah, oh and hey, my friend Patrick is going to be playing at the Cannonball Friday night—you wanna go?"

I type out the message and send the email. We watch the rest of the game while I keep one eye on the inbox.

While I appreciate Patrick's input, I knew taking love advice from him was like me giving him pointers on sex.

Interlude

There are many things that are still troubling me. I find it difficult to rest, and foresee no peace. While everything appears to be moving ahead seamlessly, there are trifles that irritate.

The birth certificate is still missing. It must be found. The ogre said it is not in the boy's room. Either it is not, or HJ did not search as diligently as he suggested. The ogre is feeble. He has been here too long. I may need to request a replacement. The boy must not discover the truth, and with HJ bumbling around, he may.

After 15 years, I am finally rid of the witch. She had turned in her notice . . . but her timing is curious. Dymortis said she is not trustworthy, too true and not pliable. A soul of stone. I have found this to be correct, yet she is leaving. Why? I do not believe her reasoning, for it is both obvious and misguided. Although she is away from the property—albeit temporarily—her presence remains and is felt.

I must travel for several days as the powers beckon. The politicians will pretend to return to work, and I will need to be certain they are on track. But the time away should help alleviate the uneasy feeling I am having.

I will deal with my disconcerted and unsettled suspicions when I return.

Chapter 4

"I'm a troublemaker." —*Rivers Cuomo*

January 13

From my bedroom window, off in the distance, I see my father get into the sedan and be driven away. Another one of his trips. I feel some relief, which makes me also feel guilty.

A restless night of childish expectations—no reply from Jill—and surreal dreams. My hormones are running amok. It's the only explanation.

It wasn't the first time I'd had the dream, in someone's home, not sure whose, and trying to find my clothes. There were other people there, none of whom I knew, who didn't seem to notice or care that I was naked. But I cared, and kept searching. Jill was there, of course, but never seemed to see me, or say anything if she did.

That was the entire dream, just wandering around nude, people I don't know asking me questions or just saying random things while I looked for my pants. Never did find them.

After waking, and still somewhat disoriented, I take Gizzi on a brief walk and check on Ginger before heading into work. A drizzly, unimpressive day, not much to look forward to, and only a boring day of work to pay the bills.

You should find something better.

Yes, yes I should. But having forgone college and having only a high school diploma to show for it, I don't have a whole lot of choices.

Be inventive.

Shut up.

When I pull into the parking lot and stop the truck, I check my phone. Finally a message from Jill.

Have to go out of town for a few days for a family thing. Sorry I can't join you Friday night, but I'll call you when I get back.

Suddenly, my Monday brightened considerably.

* * *

January 17

As I drive to the Cannonball after work on Friday, it crosses my mind that it was a little strange that Sylvana, Jill and father all went out of town at the same time. Father was gone a lot, so that wasn't surprising—although why the owner of a mortuary/cemetery needed to travel at all was a mystery. He wouldn't be out trying to drum up business. I hope. At least he had enough staff to keep things running.

I had to go home and take care of the animals, so I arrived at the bar later than I would have liked. I park in the strip mall, walking past a closed donut shop, a storefront for a psychic with a large neon hand, a vacant unit with a big FOR LEASE sign in the window, and a smoke shop that might have been open, but it was hard to tell. Patrick's motorcycle is parked out front.

I walk into the bar, and Patrick is already on the stage, play-ing an acoustic guitar and singing Johnny Cash's "Ring of Fire." The place is busy, not packed, yet everyone—from the customers to waitresses and bartenders—are singing along at the top of their lungs to the chorus.

"I fell in to a burning ring of fire . . ."

I stand off to the side, taking in the scene. Patrick's voice is, well, amazing. He sings in this baritone that is full and deep and melodical with just a hint of raspiness to it. There are several young ladies on the dance floor in front of the stage swaying to the music and smiling at my friend.

He finishes and a female MC takes the microphone while rousing applause fills the air.

"Patrick Williams! Give him a lot of love 'cause he's one of our favorites. Now, we've got karaoke time—give it up for Stanford singing 'You've Lost That Lovin' Feeling.'"

I wave, Patrick sees me and makes his way over.

"Thanks for coming. You want a beer?"

"No, thanks."

"What? It's Friday night, you're in a bar, and there are a lot of ladies here."

"Well, I'm nineteen."

"So am I. I know people."

"Why am I not surprised?"

"Is that a yes?"

"Maybe later."

We suffer through three pretty bad singers ruining what used to be fairly decent songs. The bored crowd—mainly the group of ladies that had been on the dance floor—start chanting "We want Patrick! We want Patrick!"

It's all kind of silly. Here's my friend—half black, half Irish, a little imposing with his tank top showing off some ink, some butt-kicking boots, a shaved head, rides a motorcycle, and has a general attitude that comes across as *Don't mess with me*— getting cheered on by a bunch of wannabe groupies like he's a teenybopper.

The woman with the mic scans the crowd and yells: "Patrick, get your sexy ass up here!"

Patrick jogs up to the stage to the overwhelming cheers of the girls. He picks up his guitar, then tries his best to quiet the crowd down.

"Ssshhh," he says. "Calm yourselves down, we don't want to get all worked up."

More cheers.

"Now, I said *ssshhh* . . . We're going to do something a little calm and serene. Something that touches our soul and makes us reflect on ourselves and the human condition."

He plays softly on the acoustic guitar as the audience waits. Then he pauses.

"It was 1989, my thoughts were short, my hair was long . . ."

The crowd erupts. He picks up the pace and, once again, had a sing-along going.

"Sipping whiskey out the bottle, not thinking 'bout tomorrow
"Singing 'Sweet Home Alabama' all summer long
"Singing 'Sweet Home Alabama' all summer long . . ."

The crowd has thickened, and it's not easy to move around without bumping into somebody. Someone knocks into a guy passing by me, sending me sideways into the jerk on my left.

"Sorry," I say almost the second it happens, but his beer defies gravity for a few moments, with a lot of it ending up on his already stained t-shirt.

"Hey!" he yells, immediately shoving hard enough for me to completely lose my balance and go flying into three or four others.

Next thing I know, I'm on the floor being kicked and stomped, and then someone falls on top of me. At least I thought they had fallen until I realized it was Mr. Dirty Shirt and he began pummeling me on the head with his fists. Blow after blow lands on my face, with no way for me to defend myself since my arms are pinned.

Then, just as suddenly, a boot comes out of the crowd that was gathered around my thrashing, a boot that strikes Mr. Dirty Shirt square in the jaw, sending him backwards into an unconscious sprawl.

I try to get up, but the brawl had spread and it was impossible to stand without colliding into a fist or foot.

I can feel the blood running down my face as I literally crawl past legs to clear myself of the melee. A hand grabs my collar and lurches me up. I immediately spin and swing, trying to free myself—but a tattooed arm blocks my swipe and Patrick turns me around, pointing me at the exit.

Once outside he asks: "Where'd you park?"

My head is spinning and throbbing. My consciousness has shrunk to something like tunnel-vision as my body tries to disassociate itself from the pain. Then I realize it's just my eye swelling shut.

I wave my arm in the general direction of the pickup, and Patrick half-carries me. He props me up against the side and then stares deep into my eyes.

"How many fingers am I holding up?"

I try to focus. "None."

"Okay, so you're not brain damaged. I don't think you need stitches, but it wouldn't hurt to have it checked out. Don't move."

He lets go of me and opens the cab of the truck. I feel woozy, and decide to do my best to follow directions. He comes out with a pile of fast food napkins that I had been saving for a rainy day. He presses them to my left eyebrow where the blood had been coming from and holds it in place.

"There's a hospital around the corner."

"How convenient."

"It is. Gets a lot of foot traffic."

"No, I just wanna go home." My lips and tongue feel funny.

Patrick thinks about this for a minute, then nods. "I'll drive."

* * *

I wake up with my face feeling stiff. Even blinking hurt. I lay there wondering if I should just stay where I was, or get up, look in the mirror and scare myself. I guess it didn't matter since I have to pee.

I slowly rise, the pain not as bad as I feared but still more than I prefer. I shuffle to the bathroom and look in the mirror. The cut over my left eye is really just a scabby red line, my lip is less puffy than last night but still looked like botched plastic surgery, and the swelling around my right eye has deflated considerably, replaced by a colorful halo of red, blue and purple. I look exactly like someone who'd been in a bar fight.

After I leave the bathroom, I go downstairs to the living room, finding Patrick sprawled out on the couch wearing only boxer shorts, the blanket wadded up on the floor. Gizzi sits on the armrest over his head, wagging her tail. I make coffee, then turn on the TV before waking Patrick up.

"Wha . . . ?"

"Didn't want you to miss Dora the Explorer."

He props himself on his elbows and groggily looks around, finally landing on me.

"Good morning, Frankenstein."

I would have smiled, but I was afraid something would burst open and bleed all over.

"This is why I don't go to bars."

"How in the world did you start a brawl? You weren't even drinking."

"Long story."

He gets up, pointing himself at the bathroom. "Can't take you anywhere."

* * *

After we have coffee, something to eat, watch Dora, then the Doodlebops, we each take turns in the shower and I offer to show him around the grounds, Gizzi happily trailing us.

"You mean you really do have a horse?" he asks as we walk into the barn.

"Why would I make that up?"

"I thought you meant you *had* a horse, like when you were

nine."

"Nope. Ginger was originally a racehorse, but broke her leg. My father was going to put her down, but I begged him not to. Then . . ."

I pause, not sure how to tell the next part of the story.

Patrick pats Ginger's mane. "Then what?"

"It's hard to explain. Sometimes I think I imagined it."

He pets Ginger and waits. Ginger looks at me as if to say *"Well, go on . . ."*

"Sylvana said she'd be fine. Then she—"

"Who's 'Sylvana'?"

"My nanny."

"You had a horse *and* a nanny?"

"*Anyway,*" I say, "she knelt down and gently rubbed Ginger's leg. I noticed the ring on her hand kind of . . . well, glowed. Really weird."

Both Patrick and Ginger turn their heads to look at me.

"She had a magic ring?" Patrick asks. Ginger only stares.

"No, I didn't say that." I start to put the bridle on the horse. "I thought it was like a mood ring. I mean, she's worn it as long as I can remember. It always had this cool, eerie look to it, kind of emerald. I guess it just hit the light in a certain way that made it looked like it glowed."

"But Ginger's leg healed?"

"Yeah, she must have put something on it—you know, ointment or something."

Patrick did his little smirk, and nods. "Yeah. Broken leg ointment."

I lead Ginger out of the stall and put the saddle on her. "You want to ride?" I ask.

He seems to go a little pale. "Naw, that's okay. I might get horse-sick."

"Come on, sissy. If you can ride that two-wheeled pile of bolts, you can ride Ginger. We'll go slow. Here, put your foot through here . . ."

* * *

When we got back from our little tour of the grounds—keeping a good distance from a graveside service in the northern corner—Sylvana was waiting at the barn, looking, as usual, reservedly elegant and somewhat magisterial.

"Who's that?" Patrick whispers.

"Sylvana."

He thinks about this. "Of course it is."

Gizzi races up to her and jumps up and down.

"Good morning," she says as Ginger comes to a stop. "What happened to your face?"

"I . . . fell."

Sylvana considers this for several moments. "When you're finished taking care of Ginger, come inside and I'll take care of you." She looks at my friend. "You must be Patrick."

"Yes," he says. "How did you know that?"

"Collin has told me about you. You look quite dashing on a horse."

Patrick beams, then turns to me, whispering.

"Who's 'Collin'?"

* * *

When we get inside, I see Sylvana has laid out antiseptic, gauze, Q-Tips and a washcloth on the kitchen table. She pats a chair for me to sit, which I do.

"I'll see you later," Patrick says.

· "No, wait here," I tell him. "I'll drive you home."

"That's okay."

Sylvana gracefully turns to Patrick and smiles. "This will only take a few minutes." She points to another chair, and Patrick dutifully walks over and sits.

I look up at her, trying to count the number of times this

woman had sat me down to take care of bumps and bruises. She hooks a finger under my chin and tilts my head towards her just so, her thumb just barely touching the sore part of my lip. The fingers of her other hand gently lay on my eyebrow and just below my purple-ish and slightly puffy eye.

I turn my eyes towards Patrick who seems to be watching with some amusement. Then the smirk slides off his face and for the second time that morning, he goes a little pale.

He's staring at Sylvana's hands. In particular, her ring.

I know this, because out of the corner of my eye, I can see it glowing.

Chapter 5

"A watched child never learns." —*Robert Brault*

January 19

As promised, Jill calls. After some genial chit-chat, I work up the courage to say what I wanted to say. I was half-worried the anxious perspiration would run off my face, into the cell phone and short it out.

"Uh . . . I was wondering . . . if you're not busy . . . if you'd like to go out to dinner."

There's a pause. It seems to be a long pause, a pause great enough to read a book.

"Yes, I would like that."

"Are you . . . available tonight?"

This time, I stick my foot in my mouth before she has a chance to reply.

"I mean, if not, then maybe later in the week."

Another pause. Then a giggle.

"Tonight is good."

"Oh. Okay. Great. Then I'll pick you up at . . . seven?"

"Sure. Let me give you my address . . ."

* * *

My first date. Not counting the "workout." I'm both incredibly excited and a nervous wreck as I park in front of the address on Harding Street. I had gotten lost—twice—but still manage to pull up a couple of minutes early.

I check my hair in the rearview mirror. Good enough. I look at my eye. All cleared up. Scab over eyebrow, gone. Puffy lip, back to normal. I can't say Sylvana and her glowing ring did anything, but I woke up the next day looking completely normal. I've always healed quickly, and it wasn't until I told Patrick the story of Ginger's leg did I remotely make a connection.

Of course, I then promptly cut myself shaving, a stupid little cut on my right cheek that took forever to stop bleeding. When it finally did, I was left with a big, round scab that looked like a maroon mole. Might as well have a pimple in the middle of my forehead and a wart growing on the end of my nose.

I get out of the pickup and as I walk up to the door, I stop. A feeling that something was missing floods over me. But what? What?

I look down. I had my pants on, both shoes. Zipper up. Slacks clean and pressed. Shirt without any holes or stains.

Flowers. You forgot flowers.

Big stupid. I rub a palm against my forehead.

Okay, take a deep breath and continue on.

I did, and walk up the stairs.

I knock, and a few seconds later, the door opens. I smile.

* * *

A funny thing crosses my mind as we sit at Mastriano's . . . I'm completely at ease. All my tongue-tied, half-stuttering attempts at conversation are gone. I say what I want to say the way I want to say it. I've impressed myself.

"I know this may sound naïve, but aren't you a bit nervous or self-conscious being on TV? Talking to a camera?"

"It was weird at first, but I love telling people's stories, and the camera just becomes another friend," Jill says. "I got used to it pretty quickly."

She looks great—hair, clothes, make-up, jewelry. Her eyes twinkle and her face lights up when she talks.

"Do you like working there?"

"I love the job, but the people could use some improvement. It did get better a few weeks ago when Zorbo retired."

"Zorbo?"

"Russ Zorbo, the evening news anchor." She pauses, her nose wrinkling. "He wasn't a very nice man. So now there's a kind of battle going on as to who will take his place."

The waiter arrives to take our orders.

"This is a great place," she says after he leaves.

"Isn't it? I worried about where to take you since I don't know what you like."

"It's perfect."

And so the conversation goes. She tells me a little about her life, growing up in Chicago, being an only child, deciding to become a reporter. I notice she avoids talking about—or even mentioning—her parents. Maybe it's a sore subject. I can relate.

"So, what about you? Your childhood?"

I smile. How much do I tell her? Do I just give the highlights like she did? Or go a little deeper and draw her out?

Stay true and pay attention.

That doesn't help.

Just tell the story.

I take a deep breath, not sure where to start.

"Well . . . my life can be difficult to explain."

She cocks her head. "How is it difficult?"

I note she asked *how*, not *why*.

Go for it.

"Well, but from my earliest memories I remember always feeling alone, distant and estranged from any so-called 'normal' family life . . . because I didn't have one. Something inside me seemed very strange and empty—my father was always M.I.A. He was never home, always away entertaining at the Club, or traveling . . . or so he said. Playing in elite polo tournaments around the world, gone sometimes for months on end or even longer. He never really took any kind of interest in me or my schooling. To be totally honest, I really don't think my father ever really loved or even liked me at all."

"Oh, I'm sure he did."

"Maybe. But he never showed it, much less said it."

"Some men can't."

"I know. I guess I've never told him how I felt either, so maybe it's handed down."

"What about your mother?"

"I hardly remember her. She died when I was four from food poisoning. What little I remember, and from what Sylvana told me, my mother was very quiet with no sense of humor. I don't remember her showing any kind of affection. I guess she was a very lonely person . . . Isn't that funny? I really don't remember anything else about her at all, it's sad to say, but I got the feeling she was an impressionable and uninteresting woman. She had no hobbies or any kind of pastime from what I can tell. She would just be on stand-by and jump every time my father would bark orders at her. He really treated her like dirt too. Unlike most people, we never celebrated any holidays or birthdays either—my father always said holidays and birthdays are a meaningless waste of time."

"Wow, and I thought I had it bad."

I give a small smile. I found talking about this kind of freeing, as if locking this up inside was, in fact, holding me back. And while something deep inside my mind said to go slow, go careful . . . another part just wanted to barrel ahead.

"My father is a very egocentric man who suffers from narcissism and supported separating people his whole life."

"You sound like a psychologist."

I shrug. "I studied a little about what was going on with me, and it turned into revealing something about others." I pause. "While growing up, he always made me feel insignificant, and that my life had no purpose or meaning. I now realize growing up over a funeral parlor was especially weird just knowing all these dead people were downstairs, friends and relatives shuffling in and out. Seeing all the endless crying and suffering from these people made me begin to think constant pain and suffering was normal."

"You mentioned . . . Sylvana—who's that?"

"My nanny—she was the only one who really took the time to nurture and guide me, make me see that there was more to life than death and pain."

"She sounds like the balancing force."

"She kept me grounded. My father would sometimes take me along in the hearse to pick up the dead bodies once the local coroner was done with them. A tag was always securely attached with wire to the toe. I didn't know any better then, but my father would play this silly game of finders-keepers. He would show me how to pillage through the clothing, and sometimes even the houses of the dead, looking for jewelry, money, collectables—anything of value. When I was really young, I just did it, but as I grew older I knew it was wrong. He treated the dead so . . . rudely. He was careless and disrespectful. I remember watching my father and the groundskeeper secretly switch the dead bodies from their casket to a cheap pine coffin before lowering them back down into the vault just before dusk—unbeknownst to the families. The groundkeeper is a lazy, unfriendly asshole too!"

Jill's face frowns. A finger goes to her lips as if she were thinking. "A wise woman once told me—pity the person who has to swear to express themselves."

It's my turn to frown. I'd heard the same thing—almost word-for-word—from Sylvana. Maybe it was one of those sayings like *If you don't have anything nice to say, don't say anything at all.*

I could feel myself blush. "I'm sorry . . . I just get carried away sometimes. I must have picked up this bad habit from my friend."

"That's no excuse. Don't ever blame your actions on someone else—especially your friend. You are and must be the only one responsible for your own words!"

I put up my hands. "You're right, that was wrong of me."

As if on cue, our meals arrive. I pause, knowing I should say something.

Jill looks at me. "Is something wrong?"

Say it.

I clear my throat. I don't know if she will think I'm silly or old-fashioned or what, but I also thought that I'd been pouring my heart out to her—a virtual stranger—and if she wasn't uncomfortable with that, then . . .

Just say it.

I, for one, know I need it.

"Would you mind if I said Grace?"

She beams. "I'd love it."

I did, and then we started in on our meals.

"Tell me more about your father," she says after a couple of bites.

"I know I sound like I'm ragging on him. I think of one of the Ten Commandments—honor thy mother and father. That bothers me."

She nods. "That's true. I should apologize for making you uncomfortable."

"No, not uncomfortable—just conflicted. My father did many things that I now see as wrong, and honoring him doesn't mean hiding the truth."

The truth is, and what I didn't say out loud, was that my father is a callous, evil man. I've never liked him, and find it hard to be respectful to someone who has so little respect for anyone else—including his own flesh and blood.

I grow quiet, not sure what to say, my feelings churning. I wish I hadn't gone down that path, dredging all this up—but now that it was flailing around inside of me, it's like I couldn't keep it capped off.

Stay true and pay attention.

"Are you okay?" Jill asks softly. "I shouldn't have asked you to open up about such painful things."

"No, I needed to, I guess. Never told anybody." I pause. "There's one thing maybe you can help me figure out."

"What is it?"

"I don't know if it was real or a dream—I have some pretty wild dreams."

She doesn't say anything, just waits.

"This is really hard to talk about." I pause again. "The night before Sylvana moved in, he came into my bedroom, swept me up from a deep sleep, and carried me downstairs. He scurried through the dark funeral parlor that was normally off-limits to me, and took me through a hidden passageway in what seemed to be an embalming room located somewhere within the basement of the funeral home. Everything rushed by so fast. I was disoriented, trying to open my eyes but I'll never ever forget the frightful naked lady lying dead on the steel table. Her bruised body wasn't displaying a toe tag and . . . I wasn't sure, but . . . she had an eerie resemblance to my mother."

It had been a long time since I thought about this, though there had been a few nightmares to remind me.

"But you're not sure?" Jill asks.

I shake my head. "It was kind of hard to see. Her head was lower than her feet and she had hoses hooked up to each side of her neck. One of the hoses led from a machine, the other hose led down to the floor where the blood was draining out. My father hurried me along."

"To where?"

"Down a hall. Then he grabbed me by my hair, forcing me to look through this small window in a door. On the other side were weakened, sickly children strapped to hospital beds, crying. I'll never forget what he said to me."

I pause and look down briefly.

"What?" Jill whispers.

I look up at her, trying not to cry. "'Jake, if you're not a good boy—and I mean a really good boy—you will find yourself in there along with them too! This is our little secret. If you tell anyone, and I mean *anyone*, you will regret it. Do you understand me, you worthless little bastard? And I will know!'"

"Oh my gosh."

"I was so terrified, consumed with fear, all I could do was nod my head up and down in agreement."

"What about the children? What happened to them?"

"I have no idea. Like I said, I don't even know if they're real. I never heard or saw anything of them again." I pause. "You know, I wonder if . . ."

"If what?"

"Well, there was this thing the day before where I wanted to play hide-and-seek with my mother. I yelled 'Find me if you can!' I made the mistake of going into the basement."

"Where the mortuary is?"

I nod. "I even hid in a coffin."

"Yuck."

I smile. "I didn't find it that odd. I lived there, so it was almost . . . I don't know. I wanted to say 'normal,' but I was just used to it."

"Did she find you?"

"Oh yeah. She wasn't pleased since she didn't want to run all over the house to find me in the first place, and then she finds me not only in the mortuary that was off-limits, but playing dead in a coffin."

"You were only four?"

"Yes, but what haunts me the most is the fear I heard in her voice as she crept down the stairs whispering for me. After finding me and taking me up out of the basement, she paddled me with a wooden spoon as if she was scared for her own life."

"Sounds like she had good reason."

"You know what else is weird? My mother did not have any kind of formal funeral service. I've seen services for strangers, but if there was one for her, I wasn't invited."

"That is very odd."

"What really bothers me is that I went downstairs—something I knew I wasn't supposed to do—and the next day my mother is dead. The day after that, my father drags me down there to see the screaming children."

Her hand reaches out and touches mine. "It wasn't your fault."

"I know that in here," I say, tapping my temple, "but not here." I touch my chest.

"Well, the thing with the children, you're not even sure it was real."

"Yeah, but if you put the three things together, it seems a little more real."

"Did you have a lot of those kinds of dreams?"

"Yes, but I usually knew they were dreams. That one . . . not so sure."

"What did he do after he showed you the children?"

I can only shake my head. I can't tell her the next part which was so normal, yet so terrifying to a child, that a normal person might just say *"Grow up, get over it."* But I'd spent a good part of our dinner telling her little horror stories, I didn't want to top it off with a very ordinary kids-wets-his-pajamas tale. Him spanking me and calling me a fucking little bastard, then making me walk back and sleep in them.

But that is what makes the story real. That is why you know it really happened.

I shake my head as Jill waits for a reply. "That's enough."

There's a long pause as she just looks at me.

"Do you know what *Laus Deo* means?"

"Wow," I say, smiling. "Yes, I do. After my nightly prayers, just before I would go to sleep, Sylvana would kiss me on my forehead and say *Laus Deo*. Then we both would say together 'Praise be to God!' That was our way of saying good night."

Jill smiles back. "Sylvana . . . sounds very special."

"She was."

"Was?"

"She's leaving. I guess I don't need a nanny anymore."

Jill giggles. "Hopefully you two will stay in touch."

"Yeah, I think we will."

* * *

I get out of the pickup and go around to the passenger side, opening the door for her.

"Thank you, kind sir," she says as she steps out. As I close the door, she softly takes my hand.

My heart feels light as air. My head too.

I escort her up to her condo, trying to think of something to say.

"I had a lovely time, Jake."

"Me too. Sorry I went on and on about my father."

She shakes her head and smiles, her eyes twinkling in the porch light. "I asked for it. It helps me to understand you." Her hand comes up to my cheek, feeling warm. One of her fingers is on my little shaving cut, the maroon mole.

I lean in and give her a brief kiss. Then I look into her eyes, and I know it sounds childish and immature, but the feelings . . . they are incredible. I can only hope I wasn't imagining it.

"Thank you for a wonderful evening," she says.

"Thank you for making it wonderful," I reply, knowing I sound like a bad greeting card, but not really caring. I mean it.

She gets out her key, unlocks the door, smiles shyly, steps inside, gives a little wave, and then pauses.

"I want you to know," she says. "I think you're perfect."

Then the door closes, and she disappears.

I can still feel the warmth of her touch on my face.

I go back to the pickup wondering what she meant. How was I perfect?

I get behind the wheel and look in the rearview mirror. Hair still flawless. I stare at my own eyes and think, regardless what she meant, at that specific moment, yes, I am perfect. I feel perfect. I don't ever want to be different than I am right now.

My hand moves up to my cheek where her fingers had been, as I start the truck.

It's not until I'm halfway home that I realize the cut from shaving was gone.

I reach up again and touch the spot, feeling nothing there.

Hhmm. The scab must have fallen off.

Chapter 6

"I should have killed the Witch when I had the chance." —*Lord Dunraven*

I lay in bed, things rolling around and around in my head. First, I wonder if I had scared her off. Maybe she thought I was damaged goods and had just too much baggage to deal with. She didn't act like it bothered her, but I had to wonder if the reporter part of her just covered it up.

I couldn't help but feel I had doomed the relationship before it even started.

Then I start thinking about the things that I had inadvertently pieced together—my mother, my father, the screaming children, and my mother's sudden death.

Food poisoning, my father had said. *She had eaten some bad chicken. It made her sick, and she died.*

Being 4 years old at the time meant my memories would not be exactly clear, but the last time I saw my mother, she didn't seem sick at all.

I felt a little nauseous as I lay in the darkness, wondering what happened to my mother, and if my father had anything to do with it.

Of course he did.

I close my eyes and tried to shove these thoughts out of my mind, trying to find a way into sleep.

But that didn't prove to be any better.

* * *

There's someone in the middle of a room. A photographer, standing behind one of those ancient cameras on a wooden tripod. Bent over, huddled under the black cloth as the camera clicks, and photograph after photograph slides out, onto the floor.

The black and white photos were all of the same man, a distinguished older gentleman who looked to be in his 80's. I pick up one of the photos scattered around the floor.

It is inscribed "All the best, Edwin Graybill."

I look to where the photographer was aiming the camera and I see the old man in the pictures lying on an antique couch, apparently napping.

I approach the couch and look down at the gentleman. Suddenly, a voice screams "Now it's your turn!" and a hammer appears over his head as the man's eyes open. The weapon slams down into the man's skull. Blood erupts, splattering the couch, the wall, floor.

The hammer comes down again, and again. Soon, the man's head is decimated, lolling to one side, nearly decapitated.

I look down at the floor and see a river of blood has reached my feet—and I notice flecks and chunks of both brain matter and skull fragments on my shoes.

I turn my head and stare at the hammer, following up to the hand, the arm, and the body of the assailant.

Jill smiles at me, her face streaked with blood.

"He should have known better," she says. "But you know, Collin—you're perfect!"

Then she bends down and picks up a tooth that had fallen out of the dead man's mouth. She straightens up, looks the tooth over as if it is a jewel, then slips it into her pocket and walks away.

I turn to leave and see a newspaper on the table.
"Historic Mogul Edwin Graybill Dies From Congestive Heart
Failure" reads the headline.

* * *

Despite the horrific dream, I awake refreshed. After all, the woman I'm falling for thinks I'm perfect. If she ever talks to me again.

It's just after 8 o'clock. I need to get going.

I get up and look out the window to check the weather. This time of year, Chicago can change on practically a whim—warm and sunny one moment, cold and rainy ten minutes later. It is currently partly cloudy with a chance of sun.

I see Harold off in the distance at a fresh gravesite. The casket is in place, ready for the service. He's puttering around. Then he stops, looks about, and unzips his pants. He begins urinating on the coffin.

Really? I know he's barely a human being, but I feel queasy. Even a dog has better manners.

I head for the bathroom, and the shower. Maybe that will help me feel clean.

* * *

Heading out to the truck, I glance to the left, out towards where I saw Harold earlier by the gravesite.

I stop, thinking.

I look around. No one I can see.

I check my watch. I'll have to hurry.

I jog out to site of the upcoming service, still looking about to make sure no one is watching.

I carefully lift the lid of the coffin.

This particular model was known as the Madrid, made out of premium solid mahogany with a high-gloss finish and a velvet interior. It sells for a couple grand. And everything looks exactly as the people who paid for it would have expected. Except inside, instead of their dearly beloved, there are sand bags.

I close it carefully and hurry to my truck, wondering what new scam they were up to that involved burying an empty casket.

And what in the world did they do with the body?

* * *

The day goes pretty smoothly. I sent a text to Jill, thanking her again. To both my surprise and relief, she sent one back almost immediately, saying she had a great time and we should do it again.

I suggest Friday.

She replies *OK!*

Needless to say, I'm on Cloud Nine.

* * *

Patrick asks if he can come over since his TV is still "on the fritz," and I say sure. He shows up with a pizza for my trouble.

At halftime, with the Bulls down 21 points, he stands and looks out the window.

"You live here with your father?"

"He lives in the big house."

"Looks dark."

"He's out of town."

Patrick turns and looks at me. "You should show me where you grew up."

I check his expression to see if he's serious. He seems to be.

"Why would you want to do that?"

"I don't know. Bored. Something to do. Find out how the mysterious Jacob Davis came to be the weirdo that he is."

"That's not making a very good case."

He moves to the door. "Come on. Let's go."

I sigh and get up, following him out the door, grabbing the

flashlight on the way out.

We walk the grounds, the beam of light helping us from tripping over headstones. It's probably half a mile through the cemetery. Sometimes not far enough away from my only surviving parent.

"This isn't very spooky," Patrick says.

"Ssshhh. Not so loud. Harold might be around."

"Harold?" he whispers. "The groundskeeper guy you told me about?"

I nod.

My father's house is gigantic, an old gothic-style mansion dating from the 1800's. To me, it's not that ominous . . . though it does have its secrets.

We step up on the porch.

"Crud. I forgot the key."

"'Crud?' That's the best swearing you can do?"

"I'll go back and get it."

"I think I can handle it. Point that light over here." He reaches into his pocket and pulls out a couple of wires.

"What are those?"

"They used to be paperclips. See this one? It's got these waves in one end. It's called the rake. The other just has a hook."

"Is it called the hook?"

"As a matter of fact . . . Now you stick the rake in like this . . ." He slides it in and wiggles it a bit. ". . . then slide the hook in . . . like this . . . you'll feel a click . . . then turn carefully."

The knob turns, and the door opens.

"Ta-da."

We walk in and I shine the light around.

"At least this is a little spookier. Where are the lights?" Patrick asks.

"We should leave them off. Don't want to attract attention."

I aim the flashlight and show off the living room, full of ancient uncomfortable furniture. Only the couch was good for naps, but it smelled old.

There was a noise as Patrick crashed into something. "Fuckin'
A," he says.

"I think you mean 'crud.' Don't break anything. It would be
hard to explain."

"What's this way?"

I point the light deeper into the house, and we enter the gigantic formal dining room. The chairs were big and ugly and sitting in
them was more unpleasant than they looked. The beam caught the
glass of the crystal chandelier and Patrick gasps.

"Damn, that thing's enormous. Must be worth six figures."

"Yeah, if this place were an antique store, it would need
armed guards twenty-four/seven."

"I didn't know your family was loaded."

I pause. "I didn't either. But now that I think about it, we are.
Not that I ever see any of it."

"Maybe it's not yours."

I laugh. "That's true. It was like living in a stranger's home."

I show him around the kitchen, which was better than most
restaurants.

"So where is it?" Patrick asks.

"Where's what?"

"You know . . . the place where all the fun happens."

"I'm not supposed to go down there."

"You're not supposed to be *here*."

"True, but—"

"Oh, come on. He ain't gonna know, and I ain't gonna tell."

I consider this. I was curious, but it was mixed with dread.

"Please." He sounds almost giddy.

I take a deep breath.

"Okay. This way."

I lead him out and down a hallway to the staircase. Somewhere
upstairs, the house creaks.

I point the light down the stairs.

"If this were a bad movie," Patrick whispers, "this is where
Freddie jumps out."

I step down and take each stair carefully.

When I reach the bottom and stand in front of the door, I wonder if it would be locked. My mouth is dry, my heart beating a little faster than it should. I kind of hope the knob wouldn't turn, but I knew Patrick would take care of that. I reach out and put my hand on it, turning slowly. The door pops open.

"*Opa!*" Patrick says from behind me.

"Shush."

"Why? Afraid I might wake someone?"

I give him a dirty look, but I doubt he saw it.

We enter, and I point the beam around. Suddenly, the overhead fluorescents flicker on.

"What the—" I say as I turn around. "I told you, no lights."

"Hey, I didn't do it. Must be on a sensor."

I will my heart to slow down. At least there are no windows down here.

The room is different than I remember. Of course, it had been years since I was here, so a lot could have changed. The lighting gives it a clinical appearance, which fits as it appears to be laid out like a doctor's examination room. A table with a paper cover, white gleaming counters, cabinets with glass doors showing off bottles and containers.

"Your dad's a doctor?"

"I think this is where they pretty up the bodies."

Patrick points to a pair of steel side-by-side doors. "Elevator?"

"Yep. There's another where they bring them down, this one they use to take them up. It goes into the viewing area."

He walks to the far doorway. "I bet this is the way to where the magic happens."

I follow him and walk into where my nightmare had started.

Again, the lights come on by themselves.

In the middle of the room is the stainless steel embalming table. Nearby is the machine that pumps the blood out and pumps the embalming fluid in. Tubes are attached to jugs of formaldehyde and methanol, along with other mystery chemicals. Patrick begins opening drawers and looking in. He pulls out a rather grue-some looking instrument.

"What the hell is this?"

"No idea." It looks like a tooth extractor, only bigger.

To the left is a pair of swinging doors. Patrick heads towards it.

"I'm not going in there," I say.

"Okay. Why?"

"I'm just not."

He shrugs, then walks back towards me. He points behind me. "What's that door?"

"I think it's his office."

Patrick goes over and tries the knob. "Locked." Then he smiles. "Come here. Let me show you how to do this." He pulls the wires out of his pocket.

"I don't know."

"It's easy. I promise."

I take a deep breath and sigh. *In for a penny,* I think. I step up and he hands me the re-purposed paperclips.

"Okay, put the rake in first, towards the bottom."

I slide it in, wiggling it a bit to get it as far back as possible.

"Now slip in the hook, jiggle it. You should feel a click."

I didn't, and try again, jiggling.

Then, very faintly, I feel it. I turn the knob. The door opens.

"Excellent," Patrick says as we walk in.

The lights in this room did not turn on automatically, but I find the switch. Moody, dim bulbs flicker on, giving the room a gothic appearance.

The office is large but so full of stuff that it seems cramped. The antique wooden desk is big—big enough to make me wonder how they got it in here. Leather-bound books and journals are stacked neatly on top, and I pull the chain on the desk lamp to get a better look.

Patrick is looking in a glass case. "Flags, plaques, medals. It's like a trophy case without the trophies."

"Maybe those are the trophies. Smell that?"

Patrick inhales. "Old burnt firewood, stale cigar smoke, and aged scotch whiskey."

I pick up a skull sitting on the desk. "Hey, it's your old girlfriend, still waiting for you to call."

Patrick doesn't look amused. "I treat my ladies better than that. Look at the back."

I turn it around, and see a hole. Most likely a bullet hole. I put it down quickly.

In another glass trophy case, I see more human skulls, plus hand bones, revolvers, swords, and what looks like personal effects—a stove-pipe hat, jewelry, bow ties, ascot, pocket watches, an assortment of quill pens, spyglasses, medals of honor, military jackets, hand-drawn battle maps, folded flags. Almost all the items have a small brass plate on or near them with numbers, as if for identification.

On one wall facing the desk is a beautiful stone fireplace with a large canvas oil portrait. I stare at it for a long time. Patrick follows my gaze.

"Who's that?"

"Looks like my father."

He walks up and reads the brass plate on the hand-carved wooden frame. "Lord Harod Dunraven, 1875."

"What?"

"That's what it says."

"But that's . . . impossible. That's my father, not Lord Whatever."

"Is his name Harod?"

"Henry. Henry Davis."

"Dunraven is kinda cool." Patrick deepens his voice. "I am Lord Dunraven, King of the Manor."

I walk up and double-check the brass plate to see it for myself. How weird.

To the left, I see a map on the wall, dated April 9, 1870 and titled *The Redevelopment of the Business District.* It looks like

Chicago. Beneath the mounted one, there's a wooden bin with rows of other rolled maps neatly laid in place.

"What?" Patrick asks stepping up beside me and looking up at the map on the wall.

"Do you know about the Chicago fire?"

"Not really. Something about a woman's cow. History ain't really my thang."

"The cow 'thang', as you put it, is a myth. In reality, no one knows how the fire started. But if you look at this map, and the part outlined, that's basically the parts that were devastated."

"Yeah. So?"

"According to the inscription, this map was made a year and a half before the fire."

Patrick thinks this over. "Someone planned the fire before it happened?"

"I don't know, but it kind of looks that way."

"Your dad?"

"No, it couldn't be. That was a hundred fifty years ago. Great granddad, maybe."

He's silent a minute.

"So we have a skull with a bullet through it, portrait of your father, but not your father, maybe a great grandfather with a different name, and a map of a fire before it happened."

"Something like that."

"No wonder you're scared of him."

"Who said I'm scared of him?"

"Okay, apprehensive." He walks over to another display. "Sure is a lot of money here. I mean literally—bills. Why do they have big black X's on them?"

"I have no idea."

"It's all really old. Kinda funny looking."

I go to the desk and open one of the journals. It starts from just over a year ago. *"I am worried about what Collin knows. I am sure the Witch has spoken to him of matters past. I will need to keep a closer eye on him so he does not act, or over-react, to what he thinks he knows. I should have killed the Witch when I had the chance."*

I can't believe what I'm seeing.

"Wow, look at all these knives," Patrick says. "These are amazing."

I close the journal and try to think fast. I want to read more—I *have* to read more. But I can't stay here to read it.

Should it stay or should it go?

Take it.

I slip it under my arm.

I turn and see the file cabinets, and open one. Burial records, hundreds, maybe thousands. I see a section labeled *"MAPS"* and pull one out. It is a layout of one section of the cemetery, graves marked and detailed. I pull out a couple more. Same thing, different sections. I remove more and slip them all inside the journal.

"What's that?"

I shake my head. "I'll show you when we get back. Come on, let's go."

Chapter 7

"Since love grows within you, so beauty grows. For love is the beauty of the soul." —Saint Augustine

"That was very interesting," Patrick says as we walk into my living room. "You must have led a remarkable life."

I smirk, taking the leather-bound journal to the other room. "You could say that. You want something to drink?"

"Sure." He turns on the TV. "That place is like a museum. Too bad you can't sell tickets and give tours."

I go to the kitchen and return with a soda. "I do have an idea. But I need you to promise me something."

He looks at me suspiciously. "Depends."

"You cannot tell anybody what I'm about to say, ever. If you don't want to do it, that's fine. Just keep it to yourself once you leave here. Okay?"

His expression doesn't change. "Okay."

I pause, choosing my words. "It's kind of illegal."

"Kind of?"

"Is that a problem?" I already feel defensive. I know some of Patrick's rough life—drug addicted/dealer dad, mother who lived elsewhere and didn't give a crap. In that respect, he and I were not that much different. Messed-up parents and figuring things out on our own. I didn't want him to go all moral on me.

"Again, it depends," he says. "There's illegal, and then there's twenty-five to life without possibility of parole."

I shake my head. "We're not going to hurt anybody."

"Good, 'cause you're really bad at fights. So, what's this grand plan?"

"Well, this morning, before I left for work, there was this coffin ready for the morning's graveside service . . ."

* * *

I'm lying in bed, reading the journal. Much of it is not really understandable, with mentions of people I've never heard of and ramblings about his *noitu lover.* I have no idea what a *noitu* is, but thinking of my father having a *lover* kind of creeps me out.

My cellphone vibrates, and I check the screen.

Jill.

I smile and press *answer,* thinking that even though we've only kissed, this is the kind of lover I should be thinking about.

* * *

I really need to get more sleep.

I spent way too much time on the phone with Jill, and woke up feeling less than alive. At least there were no nightmares.

By the time I get off work and head over to the gym to meet Jill, I'm somewhat better off, but still feeling out of sorts. Of course, between the workout and being with her, I'm rejuvenated and suggest we get something over at Juice King.

She orders some kind of thick green glop that looks so unappealing, it's hard not to make a disgusting face as she takes a drink. Or bite. It looked like it was chewy.

I ordered a strawberry/banana smoothie that is probably only slightly healthier than an ice cream sundae, but just as good.

"You know, I told you about growing up with my father,"

I say as she has some more liquid goo. "Well, I found one of his journals, and it's—"

"Found?"

"Yes, found."

"You probably should put it back before he returns from his trip."

"I will," I say frowning. "How did you know he was out of town?"

She pokes the back of my hand with her finger. "You mentioned it at dinner, silly. I hope you're not losing your memory before you even turn twenty."

"Maybe I'm old before my time."

"You just need to be careful. From what you told me, he's not a good guy. He's . . . well, sounds dangerous."

"Yeah, I know, but—"

"He probably killed your mother, abused you, and is probably keeping a very close eye on what you do. He's going to know you took the journal, and it won't turn out well."

I pause, perplexed. On one hand, I'm appreciative that she's concerned about me. On the other, she seems quite paranoid. More than me.

Yet I couldn't say she was wrong.

* * *

March 4

Over the next several weeks, Jill and I see each other a lot. I feel myself being so comfortable with her, drawing closer both as a friend, and as a . . .

Well, in my mind we were lovers. Physically, nothing more than kissing. And I'm not exactly complaining. Holding her, kissing her was like magic. It really was the most special, intense feeling my heart has ever had. I was so relaxed with her, confident. My moods had shifted dramatically to the point that the dark somberness that often sunk into me had disappeared altogether. What had no doubt been intense infatuation had transitioned into what I only could call love.

Maybe that sounds trite. Maybe it is. But it's what I imagined love to be—and then some. Having not really experienced closeness with another human being, I sort of imagined being this emotionally intimate with someone, this vulnerable, this exposed, would have scared me to death. Instead, it all felt quite natural, and I was totally at ease every moment we were together.

Even when she said: "We need to talk."

Maybe I was caught off guard. Or had a momentary mental block. But instead of thinking something was wrong, that she was going to drop a bomb on me that I didn't see coming . . . I simply said: "Sure."

We're at her place. She had made an amazing lasagna that I couldn't get enough of. Our mutual love for Italian food was what helped me put up with her occasional glass of green goo. I'm totally relaxed and quite light-hearted, sitting on the couch as she sat next to me.

She takes my hand.

"I need to tell you something. You need to know."

It's funny what runs through my mind. She's an escaped convict who needs to flee the country. She's really a transvestite named Jason. She has terminal brain cancer and only has a month to live. *The nightmares are all real.*

That made my breath catch slightly, but I push it away. My heart has gone from 0 to 60 in 1.3 seconds. My mouth is dry. My palms are clammy. Is it hot in here? It's hot in here.

"Collin . . ."

Oh dear. I had told her I preferred my middle name, and now she's using it. My blood pressure is now so high, I'm surprised my hands weren't throbbing. It's way too hot in here. *What is happening?*

". . . I know what's on your heart, and how you feel . . ."

No, I don't think so, because my heart just stopped and I

think I'm having a stroke. I'm not sure what a stroke feels like, but I'd bet my right leg this is it.

". . . I know you might be frustrated, and that's okay . . ."

Frustrated isn't quite the word I'd use. Panicked. Terrified. Freaked out. All perfectly good words.

". . . It's keeping you from saying what's really on your heart, but let me tell you . . ."

Oh, here it . . .

Wait. What?

". . . You are more than special to me. I guess I knew it the moment I saw you. In my head I don't really believe in love at first sight, but over this last month, I realized it is true. It is love. There are times when I'm alone and I try to talk myself out of it, to find some fault with you that would give me a reason to . . . to walk away. But I can't. The more I'm with you, the more I realize I can't be without you."

She smiles, and her eyes twinkle.

"I've known this for a while now, but I wasn't sure you felt the same. And then I realized how frustrated you may be. Here you are, a man, all your emotions probably very confused, probably wanting to . . . you know . . . and there I am keeping you at arm's length."

Now I'm totally confused. I don't know that I was feeling frustrated—except I did, sort of. I think. Maybe it's the stroke.

". . . Anyway, I want you to know that I am deeply, madly in love with you, and I think you're perfect."

To say my mind went blank at this point would imply that I was cognizant of it being blank.

". . . I just feel I should be completely honest with you so you can decide what it is you want to do. But . . . there is one other thing I think you should know . . ."

Okay, here comes the transvestite part.

". . . There are certain things that I think should wait until after marriage, things that should be very special and not compromised. I suddenly realized the other day that you may be hoping, or wondering . . . but it's really just my principles and high standards I have for myself—and for you. I don't want to lose what I so deeply believe . . . even if it means losing you."

Alright. I know at this point I'm supposed to say something, but what it should be is a complete mystery. Stupid stroke.

The gears in my brain start to grind. I begin to understand.

No sex until after marriage. Okay.

I can live with that.

Marriage?

Wow. I hadn't really gone there yet. I suppose . . . Is she saying she wants to marry me? Or that she's not going to sleep with me so I can leave if I wanted to?

Yes.

She's waiting for me to say something.

Hhmm.

I consider several approaches, then just go the direct route.

"I . . . I love you, Jill. And if I have to wait a hundred years, I will."

Apparently, those were the correct words because her face lights up and she throws her arms around my neck and squeeze so hard I was in danger of another stroke.

But I return the hug, and feel myself melt a little more—in a good way.

Then she pulls her head away and plants her hands on either side of my face and her lips on my mouth, giving me a kiss unlike any before. It seems to last an eternity.

And that's okay with me.

* * *

I stand in the doorway, smiling.

She kisses me again, briefly.

"I know we've only known each other a few weeks," she says.

"Six weeks, one day and twelve hours."

"And we still have a lot to learn about each other, so it's too soon to think of what might be the next step. But I also know," she adds, standing on her tippy toes and bringing her face very close to mine, whispering, "that it won't be a hundred years."

I slip my hands around her waist and gently kiss her once more, not wanting the night to end. After what seems like a gentle eternity, she pulls back and looks deeply into my eyes.

"I will always love you, Collin."

"And I will always love you, Jill."

Her finger touches my chest, pointing. "I want to always be in here, and never leave. To be one with you in a way that no one ever has before."

I kiss her quickly. "I think it's already happened."

She smiles, almost sadly. "We still have time."

I caress her hair, and smile back. "I should probably leave so I can spend the rest of the night dreaming of you."

Regretfully, I let her go and step back, then turn and head for the stairs, down to the street.

Halfway down, I pause and turn. "Don't forget to lock it."

"Goodnight, Collin."

I smile and wave, watching her close the door. I go down to my truck, not able to lose the smile from my face.

Interlude 2

January 6

The wind is blowing and my limbs are aching. I need some relief. My age is reaching its limits. I will depart next week and seek solace. He will give it to me and I will once again be rejuvenated. It cannot come too soon.

The boy is less of a worry to me this hard, cold winter. He does not seem a threat, with no ambition I can sense. Dymortis warns me otherwise, saying he will become wise and understand his place, but I do not see how. The Witch is not informed enough to empower him, though I have no doubt she has her suspicions. Her voice and manner are kind and soft, but the eyes burn when they look into me. And that ring—that wretched ring. I wish I could use a hatchet and remove it from her hand permanently. Its dull black glow taunts me.

But for now, I must take Dymortis at his word. He sees Jacob as a threat, so a threat he shall be. The boy is weak for I have kept him as such, but he is away from me now, and it is more difficult to gauge his status. I must consider various methods at my disposal that will allow me to keep a distant thumb on his comings and goings.

There will be a hunt this weekend out in the country, and although I cannot say I am looking forward to it—for it is too cold and my ancient bones are already complaining—the members of The Club will be satiated for a while. Their bloodlust and desires need an outlet, and I am only too glad to provide it . . . for a price.

Now to bed I must go. A brief respite, but welcome. Perhaps more shall be revealed, although I expect nothing. Dymortis is quite clear in his guidance, yet frustratingly vague in his reasoning. However, he has yet to steer me wrong, save for his miscalculations at El Alamein, for which he bore as much—or more—pain than I. At least I was able to retreat home while he forged ahead. I had much more respect for him after that, and have resisted the doubt . . . as I am sure he had done of me.

There is much to do. I will be ready.

Chapter 8

"Let the fear of a danger be a spur to prevent it: He that fears otherwise, gives advantage to the danger." —Francis Quarles

May 5

I close the journal with more questions than answers. It was the most disturbing entry yet, even though I don't know what much of it means.

Over the weeks, I have snuck into my father's office and taken one journal, replacing it with the previous one I "borrowed." I started with the oldest ones, which were undated, but I don't think they were his. They looked ancient and were written in some language that I didn't recognize. Probably just part of his collection of mysterious old things.

I did come across one hand-written journal—there are dozens filed in a trunk tucked away in a corner—that was somewhat water-damaged, but appeared to be dated 1809 and written by someone named Sebastian McCollum. I've kept that one at home, spending time trying to decipher some of the smeared writing because the parts I can make out are quite interesting. Reads like a novel. It is about a man (unnamed) stalking another man named Lewis who is carrying some journals that must be confiscated before he reaches Washington DC.

But my father's journal bothers me for obvious reasons. I mean, why does he need to keep an eye on me and what doesn't he want me to know? Why does he think Sylvana is a witch? Who is Dymortis? Why would this Dymortis be interested in me?

Part of me wants to think that perhaps my father has some sort of dementia, paranoia, something to make him worry about me in such a distrustful way. Another part thinks that this may be some sort of fiction. The language is stilted and he doesn't talk like that at all—although it wouldn't be difficult to imagine him saying "Now to bed I must go." I've just never heard him say it. And the thing about hunting didn't make sense. He's never gone before, and, as far as I know, doesn't even own a gun. And that's what makes me think it might be a kind of story, weaving tall tales and fantasies with other stuff that really happened. Or might have happened.

But, still, I can't help but think what Jill said about him being dangerous.

I climb into bed and turn off the light. It's almost 11:30. Jill would be home soon, off her shift on the 10 PM news doing a new segment called "Health Matters." Tonight's report was on a new drug that may help Alzheimer's patients. She looked great.

I lay in the darkness, staring at the little red light on the smoke detector, waiting for her text letting me know she got home safe and sound.

I am sleepy, yet words from the journal still wander around my mind.

The boy is less of a worry to me. How do I worry him?

The Witch is not informed enough to empower him. Empower me with what?

Dymortis . . . sees Jacob as a threat. What? Why? How?

It could all be gibberish. Maybe my father is a candidate for the Alzheimer's drug.

The red light stares at me.

It is more difficult to gauge his status.

The men came in March to install the smoke detectors—three in all. One between the living room and kitchen, one in the spare bedroom, and one here.

Then, a couple of weeks later, some other improvements arranged by my father—new bathroom fixtures and cabinets. New kitchen lighting. Cleaning out of the furnace ducts.

I must consider various methods at my disposal that will allow me to keep a distant thumb on his comings and goings.

My phone vibrated.

I reach over and pick it up, seeing *I'm home, and I love you!* on the screen. *Sleep tight!*

I text her back quickly that I loved her too and couldn't wait to see her tomorrow.

Then I set the phone down and lay back, looking up at that light.

The red glowing light.

* * *

I wake up with an idea.

I check the clock—10:05 AM. Good thing it was a Tuesday.

I get in the shower, shave, get dressed, grab a bite and head out. I park on the street and go inside. The place is empty, but a chime alerted whoever was in the back that I was here. A few moments later, he appears.

"Hello, can I help you?"

It's been a while since I'd seen him, and he looks older than I remember—and he was old then.

"Mr. Burkfelt, it's good to see you!"

He pauses, staring at me with watery eyes. Then recognition comes across his face. "Jacob? My, how you have grown! Are you a senior now?"

"I graduated last year. A lot has changed. How are you doing?"

"Well, Jeannie passed away three years ago, but other than

that . . ."

"Yes, I was there for the funeral. It was over at the Churchill Cemetery. Very beautiful."

I didn't want to ask why he didn't choose Rest Haven, my father's funeral home, but I suppose he had his reasons.

"Thank you. You must have been five feet tall last time I saw you. What are you now? Six foot?"

"Six-one." I tower over him. His slumped posture doesn't help. "I came to look at rings."

"Ah, for a young lady? You must be seeing someone quite special. Come over here, and I'll show you what I have available." He shuffles over to a display case that is old, but sparkling clean. "If you don't see something that you like, I can make it up for you. I have equipment in the back for custom jewelry."

I step in front of the counter and lean in to look. There is quite an array, from some that look incredibly cheap to unbelievably expensive.

"What kind of ring are you interested in?"

"Engagement."

He slides open the back and pulls out a tray. "Here are some of my better ones. Don't worry, they're not as expensive as they appear."

I look carefully at several, and find them all quite nice. "Did you make these?"

"All but the bottom row. I enjoy doing it, and I have a lot of time on my hands."

One in particular catches my eye—a gold band with a pair of roses on either side of a clear stone.

"Is this a diamond?"

"Yes, a higher grade one. From Germany, not Africa."

"Is there a difference?"

"Besides the moral dilemma? There are fewer of these German cuts, and the African are more plentiful, and therefore, cheaper."

"Moral dilemma?"

"Blood diamonds, mined with slaves. I choose to avoid those."

"Slaves?"

He nods slowly. "You should read up on it. Not pleasant."

"How much is this?" I ask, just as I see the tag. *$4000.*

"Two thousand for you, Jacob."

That's still more than I anticipated to spend.

But this is for Jill.

"I don't want you to lose money," I say.

"I won't."

The ring sparkles at me. He shows me others, but none seem quite the same.

"I have a few new ones in the back," he says, hobbling away.

I wander around while he is gone. The store has a certain charm, despite being old and a bit gloomy. I see a FOR SALE sign in the window—but instead of facing the street, it's pointed inside.

"Time for me to retire," he says from behind the counter, setting down a tray of rings. "If you know anyone who would be interested, please let me know."

I turn back. "I'd buy Burkfelt Jewelers in a heartbeat if I had the opportunity. I'm looking to start my own business, but start-up financing is hard to come by."

"Yes, I'm sure it's more difficult for a young man like yourself. What type of business are you considering?"

I pause, wondering how much I should say. "A casket refurbishing company."

His face sours slightly before he catches himself. "Staying in the family business, I see."

"Not really. My father doesn't know about it. I haven't really started yet. But I do have a partner—he'll do the refurbishing and I'll handle sales."

Mr. Burkfelt nods slowly. "Refurbished caskets don't sound very appealing. You may want to reconsider that."

I feel embarrassed. "Yes, that does sound . . . bad."

His eyes stare at me carefully, thinking. "It might be possible that I could arrange an investor. And if the business takes off, we can discuss perhaps you taking over this place."

I'm surprised. I came in looking for an engagement ring and end up with a possible offer to have an investor and maybe take over a jewelry store.

"I would like to . . . explore that," I say.

"Well, I know you're probably busy today," he says, eyes twinkling. "Maybe you could come by tomorrow and we can talk some more."

"Yes, I'd like that."

"Now, why don't you tell me about this special lady."

* * *

I call Jill when I get back to the truck. But her voicemail comes on.

"Hey, it's me. I think you're off tonight, and if you'd like, why don't we meet at Senor Mazatlán's for dinner. Seven o'clock. It's our four-month anniversary—well, almost—and we should celebrate! I love you!"

I get home, finding Patrick sitting on my front porch, smoking.

"Hey."

"Hey," he says. "Am I early, or are you late?"

"Sorry. Lost track of time."

He stomps the butt out, picks it up and follows me inside.

"We might have an investor."

"Really? Who?"

I give him some of the details, fibbing a bit. I don't want to tell him about the engagement ring in my pocket since I think Jill should know before Patrick, so I tell him I drove by the jewelry store, saw the FOR SALE sign in the window, and went in to talk with Mr. Burkfelt.

"And he'll give you money?"

"Well, we're going to talk some more tomorrow, but it could work out."

"Nice."

"Now, let's talk about what we do next. I was trying to think of a name. What do you think of 'EZ Rest Casket Company'?"

He goes to the fridge, grabs a soda and pops it open. "Rest EZ, not EZ Rest. That way it's similar but different from 'Rest Haven.'"

I nod. "Good point. Rest EZ. Sounds better too. Okay, so let's look over the maps. Here's what I'm thinking . . ."

I lay out my plans. I show the point where we should start, and how it leads to the next several areas.

"What if we get caught?" Patrick asks.

I've thought about this. I don't have an answer.

"We just need to make sure we're not."

"Yeah, well, I don't plan on it, but what if?"

"We won't."

He just looks at me with a smirk. "Okay, Batman, if you say so. What are we going to do for workers?"

"How many do you think we'll need?"

He frowns. "Four. To start. With it being so physical, you can probably expect a pretty good turnover."

I do the math. "Can we get away with two to start?"

"If you and I pitch in, sure."

"Then let's do it." I point at the map. "If this is correct, these tunnels will save us a ton of time."

"*If* they're tunnels."

I tap my finger on the table. I glance at the clock. "Let's go check and see what we can see."

We go out to the barn, maps in hand. I've been in here hundreds of times and thought I knew it inside and out. But according to the piece of paper in my hand, I don't.

Patrick goes to one corner, and I go to the other while Ginger eyes us.

"Found it," Patrick says, almost immediately.

I walk over to see a wooden part of the flooring beneath the old garden wagon that I figure was made in the 1800's and hasn't moved since I've been on the planet. We get on either side, and try to move it. It complains loudly at first, but through sheer muscle we get it going.

Patrick scrapes away a layer of dirt, revealing an iron handle inset into the wood. He yanks it up, creating a loud screech from the old rusty hinges. He opens it completely, then we stare down into the hole. I can see a ladder leaning against the side.

"Need flashlights," he says.

"I'll go get them and change real quick. Looks like we're gonna get dirty."

I come back a few minutes later in old jeans, t-shirt and holding a pair of Maglites.

"Ready?"

"Let's go."

He starts first, taking a tentative step on the first rung. Then he carefully tests the next. I hold the beam of the light towards the bottom as he goes down. It takes a couple of minutes, but he finally calls up that he had reached the bottom. I fold the map and stuff it in my back pocket before starting down next. The rungs gave a little, but seem sturdy enough. I take less time, feeling confident the ladder wouldn't fall apart when I was halfway down.

The tunnel was a lot taller than I expected—I didn't even have to stoop, though I'd still have to be careful not to bump my head on a beam or something.

"Hey, check this out," Patrick says. There's a *click* and a line of dim, yet working light bulbs came on. The flashlights would still help fill in the shadows.

I start coughing—probably sucking in too much dust.

"You okay?"

"Yeah." I choke out, realizing it's just a hack, as if I smoked too much or was on the wrong side of a barbecue.

We make our way carefully down the tunnel, which is reinforced with cement pillars and cross-beams on the ceiling. It looks very sturdy, well-constructed. The smell of dirt and stale air is pretty heavy. About fifty feet down, we come to a cut in the side that goes back about ten feet, but up at least fifteen feet high. I shine the light and see, sitting on a ledge, a casket. I pull out the map.

"This must be plot twenty-one."

"That's what the plaque says."

I step out to look and sure enough, on one of the pillars is a brass plate with the number 21 engraved on it.

"They didn't spare much expense," Patrick says.

"Well, the casket is accessed through here. We need to figure a way to slide it out and get it down."

"I just don't understand why they would do this."

"I'm not a hundred percent sure," I say, "but this is the older section of the cemetery. I would guess the body would be in the casket when they lowered it into the ground, then they came in here and took the body out."

"But why?" Patrick asks.

"That, I do not know." I begin coughing again, my mouth and throat feeling dry. I should have brought some water.

I look up into the cut-out, at the side of the wooden casket. "I'll bet you dinner that's empty."

"You said that when you checked that one casket before the memorial service, and it was already empty."

"Yeah, it was a closed-coffin service. Bad car accident. The body wasn't viewable. So they probably never put the body in since they knew no one would see it."

"So if it was an open-coffin service, they then do the switch down here?"

"That's my theory."

Patrick starts looking around. "We're going to need a lift of some kind. Lift up, slide out, bring down. Then we're going to need to wheel it out and somehow get it into the barn."

I stick the flashlight under my arm and put the map up against the wall, pointing. "See this? That looks like some kind of chamber. When I was a kid, I remember coming across an entrance to an underground garage. I snuck in, but it was just full of tools and stuff. This chamber is roughly in the same place where I found that garage, or whatever it was."

Patrick frowns. "It's just this big opening in the ground?"

"Basically, but it was all covered up by overgrown bushes. Looked like it hadn't been used in years then. Bet it still hasn't."

"So if that chamber is there, and is connected to the garage, that's how we get these caskets out of here."

"Yep."

He smiles. "Then let's go."

Chapter 9

"We must embrace pain and burn it as fuel for our journey."
—Kenji Miyazawa

I sit at the corner table of Senor Mazatlán's, waiting for Jill. I should have picked her up, but for our last several dates, she wanted to meet, so I didn't even think about it.

She hadn't called back, but I hadn't asked her to. I still expected a text message or something.

I check the time. 7:14. The waiter checks on me. I tell him I'm fine. I sip my water as the place gets noisier. I call her. Voicemail.

By 7:30, I know I have to go check on her. I give my apologies to the waiter and leave, trying to figure out which route she most likely would have taken in the event she was in an accident on the way.

Despite my worry, I drive carefully. My hands grip the wheel a little too tightly, and my eyes try to take in everything, particularly looking ahead—as well as down each side street I pass—for any signs of spinning lights, ambulances, or fire trucks. Other than a tow truck assisting someone with a flat tire, there is nothing.

Maybe she was called away on an assignment for the station? Covering a plane crash or a triple homicide on the South Side?

She would have texted.

I worry that the last I had heard from her was last night before sleep—and that was a text message. I actually hadn't heard her voice, other than the recording on her voicemail, in two days.

It's just some mix-up. She never got my voicemail. That's all. I'm blowing this out of proportion.

No you're not.

It takes forever to get to her neighborhood, and I practically squeal to a stop, bolting from the pickup and launching myself up the stairs.

I hold back from pounding on the door and instead politely knock. I count to five. Ring the doorbell. *Eight, nine, ten* . . . knock harder, then ring the bell again. Wait, listening. The dog next door barks. I ball up my fist and pound, yelling her name.

"Jill! Jill! Open up!"

The dog goes nuts.

I pound some more.

"Jill!" I scream.

The whole neighborhood seems to not just go quiet, but silent. Even the dog shuts up.

I stand there, wondering what to do. Break down the door? Call 9-1-1? Try to—

Hands in your pockets.

I pause, breathing too heavily.

Hands . . . what?

The paperclips.

Paperclips?

I slide my hands in my pockets, and there they are. I had been carrying them since Patrick gave them to me . . . no idea why . . . until now.

I close my eyes to recall what Patrick had told me. The rake first, then the hook.

My hands shake.

I start to slip it in, and it quickly gets stuck. I can tell this was a different type of lock than my father's fairly old ones.

I wiggle the wire, and it finally slips in. I stick the other in and began twisting, finally feeling the click. I turn the knob, and—success! It's unlocked. But the door won't open.

Deadbolt.

I want to scream again. Frustration mixed with fear fills me. I'd have liked nothing better than to kick something.

Instead, I walk back to the truck, get in, slam the door, then slam the wheel with my fists. I can feel myself going crazy. If that little bit of sanity didn't hold me back, I'd race back up the stairs and kick the door in.

I pull out my cell phone and call Patrick.

"Hey, what's up?"

"How do you pick a deadbolt?"

"How do I pick a deadbolt?"

"Don't mess with me, I'm beyond mad."

"Okay, okay, calm down. What's going on?"

"I need to pick a deadbolt. *Right now.*"

A long pause.

"You need a screwdriver and a sliding glass door."

"A . . . what? I said don't mess with me!"

"I'm not. Skip the deadbolt. Find a window or sliding glass door and pop the lock with a flathead screwdriver."

"I just want to pick the deadbolt!"

"I know, but it doesn't sound like you have the right tools or the patience to do that. Find another way."

I take several deep breaths, clearing my head. He's right.

"Okay, thanks." And I hang up.

I get out and open the small metal toolbox in the bed of the truck. I find a flathead and head back across the street and up the stairs. I go around the side, open the little gate to the patio and approach the sliding glass door. No point of trying to look in—the blinds are closed.

I stick the screwdriver in the jamb and it immediately slides open slightly. Either I'm really, really good at this, or it was already unlocked.

I glide the door open, slip between the vertical blinds and shut the door behind me.

The condo is dark and completely silent. Only the sound of my breathing and heartbeat. No clock, no refrigerator, nothing. Everything seems normal in the gloom.

"Jill?" I whisper. *"Jill? Are you here?"*

No reply. None really expected, but it would have been nice.

"Jill?" I say a little louder as I carefully make my way towards the back.

It suddenly occurs to me she could have gone out of town again. Away, like she had before.

And she forgot to say anything?

Yeah, no.

"Jill? It's me." I enter the short hallway. The bathroom on the right is dark, as is the doorway to the bedroom ahead.

"Are you okay?"

I step in, seeing the bed and a vague lump underneath the covers.

Thank God.

I step up and gently touch the bump that would have been her foot, then shake gently.

"Jill, are you okay?"

Nothing. I shake again, a little harder.

"Jill?"

She must be a very heavy sleeper.

I pause, considering just slipping out and going home. She's obviously sick and probably just needs her rest.

She needs you to take care of her.

Yes, that's what a boyfriend-soon-to-be-fiancé should do.

So, at the risk of waking her up and freaking her out, I go over to the nightstand and switch on the light.

And there she lay. All I can see is her hair and the top of her forehead, the covers pulled up quite high.

I reach out and touch her shoulder, gently squeezing and shaking.

"Jill . . ."

Nothing. She's really out of it.

I pull the covers down slightly to reveal her face and—

I lurch back in horror.

Her eyes are open, her skin a slight blue tint to it.

"Oh my God, oh no oh no oh no oh no . . ."

I just stand there staring, not quite believing what I'm seeing.

She's not sleeping, she's . . .

There must be something, some explanation.

I pull down the covers, preparing myself for some kind of gruesome discovery, like stab wounds or a gunshot . . .

Instead, her body lay on its side, as if she had just rolled over to get comfortable. She was naked, skin pristine and flawless, no wounds, no blood, no apparent injuries.

I cautiously reach out and touch her shoulder as if she would suddenly jump up and yell *Boo!* Instead, all I feel is coldness.

Oh my precious Jill. Oh my dear love. How . . . ? Why . . . ?

I should call 9-1-1.

No.

But—

No.

All I do is stand there and stare, falling into shock. How could . . . what . . .

I have no idea how much time passes. Minutes, hours, days. I'm numb, worse than numb. All my joy, all my love, was lying in front of me, no longer able to smile, to laugh, to hold my hand. I lived my whole life without love, without joy, and now what little that had been given to me was no longer here.

Finally, I reach down and gently close her eyes.

Sleep . . . now you can sleep.

Then, I walk around and lay on the bed, on top of the covers, trying to think. Just staring at the ceiling, wondering what to do.

And the only thing that crossed my mind was: *Laus Deo.*

Praise be to God.

Chapter 10

"I fell in to a burning ring of fire." —*Johnny Cash*

I seem to be floating in a forest or jungle. Below me is an unused fire ring with tree stumps surrounding it like stools. I count twelve stumps. The night air is humid, thick and heavy, but it doesn't explain my hovering at least a hundred feet above the ground.

A line of ten people in dark hooded robes file in from the forest, each taking a spot in front of a stump. One of the figures leans in and lights wood in the fire ring, quickly illuminating the area—but even if I were close enough, I couldn't see their faces.

An eleventh figure walks in from the jungle, robed and hooded. The others raise their hands as the figure walks around the ring. Then the person climbs up on the edge of the concrete surrounding the fire and removes the robe, tossing it into the flames.

Even from this high up, I can tell it is Jill. She is naked, and her skin glows in the radiance of the blaze.

I yell, screaming, but there is no sound. Nevertheless, she looks up at me. Is she smiling?

She raises her hands and, suddenly, she is floating too, just over the fire. Her face turns up to me.

Yes, she is smiling.

And that is when I begin to fall. Plummeting. No control.

Straight towards Jill and the fire below.

In an instant, I collide with her, feeling her piercing not just my body, but my soul.

All goes black.

* * *

I begin to come around, lying on the ground. Like Jill, I too am naked, with stones and sticks poking my skin. I hear music. Violins, a double-bass, a piano and a pair of bandoneóns. Then this orquesta tipica *begins playing in 2/4 time, a romantic dance melody that originated amongst the rioplatense in South America.*

I don't know how or why I know these things. I'm not even sure I can spell rioplatense.

I open my eyes to only darkness. I carefully stand, wondering what happened to the ten hooded people, to the fire, to Jill.

Then small flames emerge from the ground, small at first, then growing all around me, blocking me in.

Through the flames walks an old short man wearing a white jacket, white pants and black dancing shoes. He walks up to me, arms out, and embraces me.

The music returns, some kind of tango.

"Molinetes!" the elegant man says, who starts leading me in a dance.

I'm trying to pull away, feeling worse than awkward, dancing naked with this stranger.

Before I can step back, he reaches out, grabs both sides of my head with his hands and kisses me on the forehead.

The music stops.

He smiles at me, showing hideous crooked brown/yellow teeth.

"You may be the Chosen One, but you are not going to escape from me this time!"

He lets go of my head, and—poof—is gone. The fire grows more intense, the smoke choking me, making me cough. I am looking for a way out of this burning hell when an even more intense scorching pain sears my chest, and I pass out from the pain.

* * *

I wake staring at the ceiling, still lying on the bed.

I raise my head to look around the room. I am startled to see I am naked. My skin from my feet up is red, like a sunburn. There is dirt and debris stuck to my flesh as if I had been lying on the ground. But what truly shocks me, making me scramble out of bed in terror, is the angry red welts emblazoned across my chest, like some sort of branding.

I stand next to the bed, looking down at the marks, feeling heat emanating from them. I can tell it's some sort of pattern, but can't see what.

I put my hand through my hair, trying to think. I look over at—

She's not there.

Jill's body is gone.

Oh no, no. You must still be dreaming. Wake up, wake up, wake up.

I slowly go around the bed, eyes wide, half-expecting to see her corpse lying on the floor, having fallen off the mattress. But there's only carpet.

What is going on?

Wake up. You have got to wake up, now!

I feel pain. I feel the carpet under my feet. I walk out of the bedroom, to the bathroom, and turn on the light.

My hair is disheveled, face dirty, there's some kind of twig stuck to my left ear.

And I stare at the throbbing, swollen design on my chest. I think of a steer being branded, and now know what they go through.

How did that get there?

The dream—surrounded by the wall of flame, then the searing pain . . .

But . . . that was a *dream*.

It looks to be some kind of emblem—a geometric shape. What did they call those? Parallelogram? Quadrilateral?

Trapezoid.

Yes, a trapezoid, and then some kind of ziggy-zaggy S shaped thing—maybe a lightning bolt?

Leave.

Yes, I've got to get out of here.

I walk back to the bedroom and find my clothes folded neatly on Jill's vanity. I put them on quickly and head to sliding glass door. I exit the way I came in and hurry to the truck. I get behind the wheel and start it up—just in time to see a Channel 6 news van coming around the corner and down the street.

I put the pickup in gear and calmly drive away so as not to attract any attention.

* * *

I arrive home and go directly to the shower. The water is painful, no matter the temperature, stinging my skin—particularly the brand on my chest. It even hurts when I cough. I had started coughing on the drive home, like you do when you get too close to a fire's smoke. I even realize I smell like burnt wood.

Still I carefully manage to get clean, and then pat myself dry.

I wrap the towel around my waist when I hear a knock at the door. I debate whether to answer it. I'm really not in the mood for company.

More knocking.

I go to the door and look through the peephole. It's Patrick.

I sigh and open the door.

"Hey," he says, then his eyes go wide as he looks at my chest. "Geez, what the hell is that?"

I just shake my head, turn, and walk into the living room.

"Did you go out and get drunk? Lose a bet?"

I reserve my right to remain silent, mainly because I have no idea what to say.

"You're all pink. You look like a lobster. I hope you didn't—"

"She's dead, Patrick."

He goes quiet. I imagine he was staring at me in disbelief—but I could only guess because I couldn't look at him.

"Jill?"

I nod.

"How? What happened?"

"I don't know. She was just . . . dead."

A long silence as he absorbs this, perhaps gauging if I'm serious, deranged, or both.

"Man, I am so sorry."

I'm afraid to speak. I can feel the tears coming and didn't want that. I walk to the hallway and up the stairs to my bedroom.

I throw the towel on the bed and start to get dressed.

"But how did you get all sunburnt?" Patrick asks from the doorway. "Even your ass is bright red."

I shake my head. "I don't know. I don't know. It was a . . . rough night."

"Jeez, I guess so."

I realize how this might sound, how it looks. I'm bright red, some kind of tattoo thing on my chest, talking about a rough night and that Jill's dead.

"I didn't kill her."

"Okay."

"She was just dead. No wounds, no bullet holes, nothing. Just like she was sleeping."

A long pause as I pull on my pants.

"Were you attacked? That thing on your chest . . ."

"Yeah, I don't know."

He waits for me to add something. I don't.

I begin coughing, a hard, hacking cough that takes me a minute to get under control.

"You okay?" Patrick asks. "On top of everything else, it sounds like you caught something."

"I'm fine," I rasp, not convinced I was.

I pull on a t-shirt and slip by him, going back downstairs. When I reach the bottom, another knock at the door.

Why now? Why did I have to become so fricking popular?

I throw open the door, ready to yell at whoever was annoying me.

Tama jumps back as if I was going to hit her. I suddenly feel bad for scaring her.

"I'm sorry," I tell her, meaning it.

Tama worked in the mortuary—a Goth girl with jet-black dyed hair, pasty white skin, and multiple piercings in her ears, nose, lips, and probably a few other places. She had gone to Beautician College and ended up making cadavers look nice for their viewing. She was my age or slightly older, quiet and seemed sweet.

"Are you okay?" she asks, looking a little alarmed, making me wonder for a moment if I forgot a crucial piece of clothing.

Shirt, check. Pants, check.

"Yeah, just tired." I try to smile. It feels ghoulish.

"Um, a . . . client came in, and it had instructions to contact you for arrangements."

Client was the polite term for a body.

"Me?"

Tama nods. "I thought I should check with you before I begin."

I look over at Patrick and the moment I did, I realize who Tama is referring to.

"Okay, let me get my shoes."

I hurry, and a minute later we were walking to the mortuary. None of us say anything.

Inside, Tama leads us into where she works—the same place Patrick and I had gone through a few weeks ago when sneaking around while my father was out.

On the table is a body wrapped in a white sheet. Tama unveils the feet, showing the toe-tag. She holds it out for me to see.

Stone, Jill, W, F, COD Undetermined

Hold for arrangements, Contact: Jacob Davis

I sigh, feeling the finality of it sink deeply into me.

Then I feel Patrick's hand on my shoulder.

And we just stand there.

Finally, after a couple of minutes of silence, Tama covers up the foot.

"Um," I say. "No embalming. No cosmetics or dressing. If she could be put in the lock up, I'll make the graveside arrangements."

"Okay," Tama says, then adds: "I'm sorry for your loss."

My eyes fill up with tears, and I try to blink them away. After a pause I say: "Me too." Another pause. "Can I have a few minutes alone?"

* * *

I can't sleep. What was there to sleep for?

All I can do is wait, laying in the darkness.

It seems to take forever.

Finally, at midnight, I get up and go outside. I fetch the shovel from the barn. I wouldn't be able to use the equipment I usually used. I have to handle it the old-fashioned way.

Tama had told me plot 1259 had been arranged, and that all was paid in full. But by whom?

I headed out to 1259 and stand there, just staring.

36 inches wide, 48 inches deep, and 96 inches long . . . 36 inches wide, 48 inches deep, and 96 inches long . . . 36 inches wide, 48 inches deep, and 96 inches long . . .

I start digging.

Chapter 11

"If you are going through Hell, keep going." —*Winston Churchill*

After falling into the grave, hitting my head on the shovel, cutting my forehead, knocking myself out, coming to, seeing Harold, and then watching him spit on me, I make it out of the hole and stumble back to the house, coughing most of the way. I go upstairs and look in the mirror. My face is a horror show.

There's a gash from my hairline to my left eyebrow. A mixture of blood and dirt cake the rest. I could be in a production of *Frankenstein* as the lead.

So tired. So confused. Too much, too many weird things. Jill dead, the strange dreams, her body disappearing, then showing up at the mortuary, the mark on my chest, the gash on my forehead.

The coughing starts again. I bend over, trying to get it under control, until it subsides. I strip, then start the shower. I stare in the mirror as I wait for the water to get hot. I stare at the emblem.

No blood.

There wasn't. Jill had no injuries. Nothing obvious that could have caused her death.

She was healthy.

Maybe it was something congenital—a heart problem. A brain aneurism. Something no one would have known.

Steam starts to fog my view, so I turn around and step in the shower.

An autopsy might have helped, but that wasn't going to happen. To get an official cause of death, I would have to make a police report and then try to explain what I did and didn't do. How I found the body. Why I didn't report it. There were things I could explain, making me sound suspicious, and things I couldn't explain that would make it sound worse. The body had disappeared, then showed up—and I never called the police. How could I explain all that?

I allow the water to flow over me, trying to make me clean.

So tired.

I need to finish the grave preparation, give her a proper burial.

I don't think I have the energy.

I rinse and turn off the shower, dry off and wipe the steam from the mirror. The gash looks less ghastly, but still pretty bad.

I go to the bedroom and climb beneath the sheets, feeling the comfort and peace start to wash over me.

* * *

Sleep didn't last long when there was knocking on the door.

I almost decide to ignore it, but get up and put on my jeans before going to answer it.

Patrick stands there, looking a bit surprised.

"You're falling apart, man. What happened this time?"

"I fell."

"I can see that."

"I need to get some sleep—what's up?"

"Chauncey asked where you were, why you weren't at work. I told him a little what happened, and he asked me to come check on you."

I pause. Didn't sound like Chauncey at all. Maybe he did have a heart in there somewhere. "Tell him I'll be okay."

"Can I get you anything?"

"No, I just need some sleep."

"Okay." He looks uncomfortable. "I'll check on you later."

"Thanks." I close the door and go back to bed. It took only moments before I was asleep again.

*　*　*

She appears in the doorway, almost glowing in a long white flowing gown. She looks like an angel, smiling and so beautiful.

She goes to the foot of the bed. Her hand comes out, reaching towards me.

I pull off the sheets and climb out of bed, hesitant.

Her smile is so warm and loving.

I draw close to her, and reach out to touch her arms. They are unbelievably soft.

Her hand comes up and touches the tattoo on my chest, her finger tracing the lines.

"You are one of us," she whispers.

I frown. "One of what?"

Her finger moves to my lips, and her eyes twinkle. Then her gaze goes to the cut on my forehead. Her finger follows.

From the edge of my hairline, it slowly moves down to my eyebrow. I can feel a tingling heat as her finger moves—warm, yet gentle.

Then the finger slides down my cheek, down my neck, onto my shoulder.

Part of me is aware of being unclothed, standing naked in front of her, inches away.

"Do not be afraid," she says, her voice soothing. "You are not alone. I am with you always."

Her hand is again on the branding, touching so lightly.

"I miss you, Jill."

"I'm right here," she says, her fingertip on my chest, over my heart, pointing. "Always."

"I don't know if I can live without you."

Her eyes lock onto mine. "Your time has yet to come. There is still much to do."

"Do? Do what?"

"Soon." *She steps back, and turns toward the doorway.*

I stand there feeling helpless, wanting so badly to follow.

She stops and turns towards me.

"You're perfect, Collin. Always remember that."

Then she turns back again and disappears down the hallway.

I wipe the tears from my cheeks, feeling both an overwhelming sadness, and a strong undercurrent of peace.

* * *

I slowly come awake, and all is dark.

I get up and use the bathroom. After flushing, I stop to look in the mirror. All I can do is stare blankly.

The gash on my forehead was now only a slim pink line, a faint scar.

I gently touch it, and feel nothing—no bump, no pain, only flat, smooth skin.

In some weird way, I'm not surprised. So many odd things have happened, to have a three-inch cut magically healed just seems to be another part of my day.

While standing there, I start coughing again—not a sick cough, like I had a couple of lungs trying to clear themselves—but a wheezing/hacking cough from deep inside my chest, a nagging uncomfortable pain. I can't help but wonder what's going on with me.

Finally, I shake it off. I brush my teeth, then go to the bedroom and get dressed. I have more work to do.

* * *

11:45, almost midnight. I get in the pickup and go to the mortuary, annoyed that when I reach to the side door, I realize I had forgotten the lock-pick wires. I try the handle anyway, and it's unlocked.

Thank you, Tama.

I open the door and step in, closing it just before the lights come on.

I go to the walk-in cooler where the bodies are kept, open the metal door, step inside and see the casket, the only one in here. A couple of bodies are wrapped in sheets, laying on stretchers, waiting for Tama to come in and fix them up.

I open the lid to the casket and see Jill's pristine face, looking so peaceful.

I touch her cheek and feel the soft coolness.

The plan is to get the casket to the grave and lower it into her final resting place. I would need help. But even with that, looking at her now, I don't have the will. I could not hide her away like that.

I stand there for a long time.

"I love you, and I always will. But I don't know what to do."

No, you do know.

"I don't. I really don't."

Silence.

I begin coughing again, and for the first time, wondered if something is wrong, if I should see a doctor.

No, Collin, you're perfect!

I take her hand. So soft, so cool.

I want to be with you forever.

I frown. I'm not sure at this point what is real and what isn't, what I may be imagining and what might be stuff my imagination is creating.

But I did know I couldn't bury her.

I knew where she should be instead.

The problem was how to do it.

I think for a couple of minutes, then pull out my cell phone.

* * *

"You want to what?"

"I know it sounds weird, but it's not. I have to . . . well, it's just important to me."

Patrick watches me carefully, unconvinced. "And what about Jill?"

I shrug. "I don't want her buried."

"So . . . cremation?"

"I kinda hate to do it because I also want to find out what happened to her. Twenty-one year olds don't just die in their sleep."

"And how are you going to find out?"

"I don't know yet. I need some time to think it through."

He stares some more, looks over to the casket, then back at me.

"That cut on your head is gone."

"Yeah, I woke up and it was like this."

He pauses, thinking. "Some really weird stuff is going on. Really weird. And it all started when you met Jill."

"I know, and it means something, but I don't know what."

Patrick is quiet a long time, frowning, thinking. He's not convinced, yet couldn't find an argument against it, other than it's weird.

He takes a deep breath, then lets it out slowly. "Okay, I guess. How are we going to do this?"

* * *

We sit in the living room, scarfing breakfast. I can't remember the last time I ate and even after the second breakfast sandwich, I'm still hungry.

Patrick points at the small cardboard box that holds Jill's remains. "Are you gonna get a vase? Or a—what's it called?" he asks around a mouthful of food.

"An urn."

"Yeah."

"Something like that."

He stops chewing for a minute and looks at me. "You mean you're thinking something else weird? Let me guess—you want to put Jill's casket in the upstairs bedroom."

"It would only be weird if it were in *my* bedroom."

"Oh, so you can start sleeping in it?"

"No—now that would be weird . . . wouldn't it?"

"So why do it?"

"I don't know yet. But I sense there is a reason."

He grins his devious grin. "No, dude, a casket in the house is weird. No way to explain it away."

I take a bite of the third sandwich. "I have an idea."

"Oh, Lord, here it comes."

"No, no, I think you'll like it. What if you moved in here? I got that downstairs spare room just over there you can crash in. Bathroom, kitchen, rent-free. Since we'll be spending so much time working underground on our project, it would be easier for you."

Patrick looks at me with some surprise. "Okay, now you're starting to make some sense. Especially with the words 'rent-free.'"

"Good, I'll even help you move."

"But we can't quit our day jobs yet."

"No, but soon. We've got three caskets out that you can refurbish, and then I can sell them. And based on the records, there are a lot more." I pause. "There is one more favor I need to ask of you."

"Uh oh."

"Well, it's not too bad."

He sighs. "What is it this time?"

"Tomorrow night, after dark . . ."

Chapter 12

"There's nothing like a trail of blood...to find your way back home." —Sixx A.M.: "Life is Beautiful"

May 9

We walk to the small gathering by Jill's grave—about a dozen people, all dressed in black. I don't recognize anyone—not that I had met any of her family or friends. I wonder if that's who they are. I want to talk to them after the service. We quietly take seats in the front row, just in front of the coffin.

Patrick and I had snuck back to the mortuary and wheeled an empty casket out to the gravesite—more shame dinging my conscience at doing another duplicitous act. While I knew in my head there are things I had to do that weren't exactly right, in my heart, I knew I had to do them.

The Pastor reads scripture, offering Jill to eternal life. I have no idea who he is, or who asked him to be here, but his voice is soothing.

"Good people pass away; the godly often die before their time. But no one seems to care or wonder why. No one seems to understand that God is protecting them from the evil to come. Isaiah Fifty-seven, Verse One.

"All praise to God, the Father of our Lord Jesus Christ. God is our merciful Father and the source of all comfort. He comforts us in all our troubles so that we can comfort others. When they are troubled, we will be able to give them the same comfort God has given us. Second Corinthians One, Verses Three and Four.

"Now may our Lord Jesus Christ himself and God our Father, who loved us and by his grace gave us eternal comfort and a wonderful hope, comfort you and strengthen you in every good thing you do and say. First Thessalonians Two, Verses Sixteen and Seventeen."

And then he read Ecclesiastes 3:1-8:

There is a time for everything, and a season for every activity under heaven:

> *a time to be born and a time to die,*
> *a time to plant and a time to uproot,*
> *a time to kill and a time to heal,*
> *a time to tear down and a time to build,*
> *a time to weep and a time to laugh,*
> *a time to mourn and a time to dance,*
> *a time to scatter stones and a time to gather them,*
> *a time to embrace and a time to refrain,*
> *a time to search and a time to give up,*
> *a time to keep and a time to throw away,*
> *a time to tear and a time to mend,*
> *a time to be silent and a time to speak,*
> *a time to love and a time to hate,*
> *a time for war and a time for peace.*

The words pierce me like an arrow. I feel a little dizzy and slightly nauseous. The world around me spins. I look over at Patrick, who is staring somberly at the Pastor. Everything is lop-sided and woozy—as though I am drunk or on drugs. I don't know if I can talk, or if I want to. I certainly wouldn't be able to walk.

Then a burning begins, first on my chest, where the myste-rious tattoo is—then deeper, inside my chest. It almost feels like there's something inside, growing. I feel not only my heart beating, but can hear it—and it sounds like two. It's not racing or beating faster, it just sounds like it has split and become two.

I become faint and the last remaining conscious thought I have is *Am I going to pass out?*

Then a veiled woman on my left reaches out and touches my knee. Suddenly, I feel calmer.

I look down at the hand and see a familiar ring—it is glowing a soft blue.

I raise my head to look at the face, but it is not Sylvana as I expected. Best as I can tell under the large-brimmed hat and through the veil, she is ancient—well into her nineties, or beyond.

Her head turns and she leans towards me.

"Jill was right . . . Collin, you're perfect!"

With that, all becomes silent, and everyone is staring at me. I notice for the first time they are all veiled, male and female, and it reminds me of the dream, where I floated over the fire and the dozen people there were all in dark hooded robes.

Only myself, Patrick and the Pastor are showing their faces.

"Laus Deo," the Pastor says.

"Laus Deo," the others say in unison.

Then they all stand, and turn to leave.

"Wait!" I bark out, trying to stand and still feeling a little light-headed.

They ignore me and continue departing, all of them getting into several long, black limousines. The vehicles all smoothly drive away.

I turn to ask the Pastor what was going on, but he is gone as well.

As I wonder what just happened, I look at Patrick and notice he is still staring blindly towards where the Pastor had been standing. In his hand is a bundle of pink roses.

"Where did you get these?" I ask, but he doesn't reply—he only continues to stare as if in far-off thought.

I take the roses and step up to the casket. I lay them gently over the top.

"Jill," I say, even though I know the coffin is empty, "I will always love you. And I will never say goodbye."

I close my eyes and say a prayer. *"Give me strength for whatever is happening to me. Please protect Jill and let her know I am always with her."*

She knows.

The voice sounds like it came from right next to me, but when I open my eyes, no one is there.

I turn to look at Patrick, and he is blinking, looking around.

"Is it over?" he asks.

"Yes everyone's gone."

"Wow, that was weird. The last thing I remember is a veiled person handing me those roses, then—poof—it was like I was put into some kind of spell." He looks stunned. "I'm glad that is over."

I nod. But little did I know, it had just begun.

* * *

A short while later, I'm in my bedroom, looking out the window where Jill's empty coffin waits.

Harold, the groundskeeper, is preparing it for burial, and after removing the draping and flowers, he begins to lower it into the earth. Once it reaches its final resting place, I notice he momentarily stands at the edge and peers in, shaking his head in disgust.

Before he turns and walks towards the backhoe to lower the concrete vault lid over her casket and finish filling in the dirt, he spits on the casket.

What is wrong with that guy?

* * *

Shortly after nightfall, Patrick and I head out with shovels to Jill's gravesite. It takes us two hours. And it was about as tough as getting the casket in the house could be.

We are both exhausted. But, finally, we set it in place, and

Patrick steps back and rubs his head. "There you go."

"Thanks for your help. It's really nice, isn't it?"

"Yes, it's lovely." He rolls his eyes.

"Well, I like it," I say.

He nods, acknowledging how important it is to me. "Well, I'm in need of a shower. Do you have a spare towel?"

"Sure, in the hall cabinet."

He salutes and leaves.

I stand and admire the curio. Before Jill, I didn't really think about them, other than a sales item at the furniture store. Now, I have a special memento that I would cherish forever.

There's a bit of guilt. My moral choices lately had not been what I would normally have considered, much less carried through, but yet I had done them. Stealing empty caskets from plots to resell for personal gain. Sneaking Jill's body into the retort—the oven chamber—to cremate her remains. Breaking into her condo not once, but twice—the first to discover her body, the second to steal the curio she had purchased from me weeks earlier.

I could pretend to justify all of it by telling myself they are victimless crimes. No other person harmed or cheated by what I've done, but I also knew it didn't mitigate my culpability. I don't know what Jill would think, but it made me feel more uncomfortable just considering it.

And somehow I knew it wasn't going to get easier.

* * *

If I thought I had weird dreams before, then I don't know how describe the other things that happened. I would like to pretend I had been asleep when some of them occurred, but I cannot say for sure I was.

As I mentioned, I've heard voices for years—at least since puberty, maybe longer. I kept them to myself, not daring to tell anyone, even Sylvana. Lately they seem to have increased. Not just the voice that sounds like me in my own head, but now other voices. Sometimes female. They happen at random times and in various places. On the way to work, while making a sandwich, riding Ginger, watching TV.

But mostly they come at night.

"Help me."

It's a child's voice. I can't tell if it's boy or girl, four years old or nine, but it's young.

"Me too."

"Help us get out of here."

I lay in bed, kind of hoping I've imagined them. They were rather faint.

"He's coming!"

That made me sit up, not because it scares me, not to wake myself up from whatever dream/nightmare I imagine it to be . . . but because it sounded like it came from down the hall. There's an echo, with a resonance to it that made it sound like it had not occurred inside my head, but was real.

I carefully climb out of bed, listening, almost willing the voice to come again, to repeat what I heard.

Nothing.

I step towards the door, head cocked.

Silence.

Into the hallway, eyes wide, trying to take in as much light as possible, to see if someone was there.

No one.

I go to the top of the stairs and look down.

Could it have been Patrick?

No, that didn't make any sense. He wouldn't be sneaking around making little kid voices.

I step carefully down the stairs, one at a time, listening, watching.

Slowly, I reach the bottom. Thin light from outside dimly illuminates the living room, but nothing unusual there.

A slight sound of a light footfall behind me, and I turn.

A man with a club held over his head loomed, and I jump

back.

"*No!*" I said.

"Jesus, Collin, what the hell are you doing?"

It's Patrick, his voice sounding almost as frightened as mine.

"I thought I heard something. What the hell are you doing?"

"I heard something too."

In the gloom of the night, I can't see his face.

"You heard the voices?" I ask.

"Voices? No, I heard you sneaking down the frickin' stairs. And why the hell are you naked?"

I had no reply for that, other than I slept naked, which I didn't think I should try to explain at this point.

Just as I open my mouth to say something like *I'm sorry, let's just go back to sleep,* Patrick suddenly yells "Hey!" and bolts for the front door, still wielding the baseball bat. He throws the door open and races outside, and I quickly follow, helping me understand why people wore pajamas and why, maybe, I should as well.

Once I get outside, Patrick has already disappeared around the side of the house, so I race after him. When I come around the corner, I see him standing in the middle of the area between the house and the barn, bat in his right hand, head swiveling around, looking about a little wildly.

"What is it?" I ask as I come up next to him.

"I thought I saw that creepy guy."

"Harold? Where?"

"Peeking in the window. I didn't think he could move that fast."

I look around, gazing carefully into the shadows of the cemetery.

"I don't see him."

"I don't either. But it was him."

"I believe you."

Patrick turns and looks at me, checking to see if I'm sincere.

"What voices did you hear?" he asks.

"A child. Well, children, actually."

He thinks about this. "You think Harold made those sounds?"
I shake my head. "I doubt it. I don't think he's that imaginative."
Patrick smirks. "We also didn't think he was that fast."

"True," I say, nodding. "Between me hearing things and you seeing things, we could both be committed for a seventy-two hour psychiatric watch."

"Especially with me standing in my boxers with a baseball bat, and you stark naked. We better get inside before the ghosts start asking you for a date."

* * *

Needless to say, I didn't sleep after that. Just laid there, staring at the smoke detector with its steady red light, listening intently for children's voices that didn't come. It was for the better. I would be content never hearing them again.

I turn on the bedside light and Jill's curio caught my eye. Inside, I had set the box containing her ashes. I stare at it, wishing there was some way I could . . . I don't know. Memorialize her. Not for the world to see, just for me. Something better than, say, a picture in a locket, or an urn sitting on a mantle.

I grab my laptop and fire it up, searching for ideas. It doesn't take long for something to catch my eye. I do a little more research and know it was exactly what I'm looking for.

I get the container of Jill's remains out of the curio and check the box, to make sure it was strong enough to ship out to the company I found on the Internet. It's more than sturdy.

The price made me pause. But only for a second. There was really nothing that would stop me. I'd just have to sell a few caskets from our little project.

Okay, more than a few, but it would be worth it for Jill to be with me always. Literally.

Interlude 3

March 18, 1912

J.P. estimates the boom in iron prices is at its peak and it is the time to cash in. He doesn't know how correct he is yet, but within a few weeks it will be obvious. The "accident" will put a hold on construction of current vessels and stifle those that are planned. Iron will tumble, as will precious metals. The Executive Officer on the ship is agreeable—I paid him $5000 in advance to make our plans happen. Once the ship goes down, it will be a few weeks as the markets react, and then we buy again. But first I must sell before the slump.

If this works as it should, the sinking will also take down the Executive Officer and J.P., who has yet to know of the arrangement. I can then take over J.P.'s shares and effectively double my holdings.

* * *

April 4, 1912

J.P. has backed out of the planned trip. His nemesis, John Jacob Astor IV, will be on the ship, and Pinepoint will not consider being on the same vessel as Astor, even one as large as the RMS

Titanic.

But this could work even better in my favor. Astor has vast more wealth. His death will put his fortune into disarray, and further destabilize the markets. I may not get my hands on J.P.'s fortune as quickly as I wished, but it will just be a matter of time.

* * *

I close the journal. Something tickles my memory.

I get up, and get online. I look up rich men of the early 20th Century. One was John Pinepoint—J.P. The richest man in America at the time. July 1, 1837—May 3, 1913.

And the richest man in the world? John Jacob Astor IV. Born July 13, 1864, died April 15, 1912.

He was one of the casualties on the *Titanic*.

I get dressed and sneak over to my father's house, slipping into the dark and eerie office.

I flip on the light and go to the trophy case against the far wall. And there it is. A blue handkerchief, labeled No. 07131864-04151912. Stitched into the cloth: The initials *J.J.A.*

The numbers catch my attention. And the answer jumps out at me.

07131864 was July 13, 1864—the date of Astor's birth. 04151912, the date of his death.

Everything has labels, many with similar numbers.

I begin writing some down. The skull with a hole in the back, sitting on the desk: No. 02121809-04151865. A brown tie with a blood stain in another trophy case: No. 04201889-04301945. A very old dagger, caked with dirt lying on a shelf below: No. 12150037-06090068.

I hear a noise from above—a footfall?

I move to the door and turn off the light, opening the door slowly. I creep out, listening. I'm not sure if my father is home or not. I should have waited.

I move to the doorway leading to the preparation room where

Tama worked.

From somewhere behind me, the house creaks.

I hurry across to the exit, and slowly turn the handle, then just as slowly, I open the door. It seems to take minutes.

A light comes on in the hallway in back of me, and I scurry out the door, pulling it quickly yet quietly closed behind me. I then run off to the left, around the back of the house, then straight out towards the garage, racing around the corner before stopping.

I ease back to the corner and ever so slowly peek my head around to see. Nothing for a minute. Then the outline of a figure appears, stopping. I hold my breath.

The figure turns and goes back the way it came.

No doubt, my father, in his pajamas under a deep maroon smoking jacket.

I wait several minutes before slipping around the rear of the garage and taking the long way around back to my house.

I get on the computer and type in the first number—02121809, or February 12, 1809.

What came up shocks me.

Abraham Lincoln.

The skull on my father's desk was the assassinated President's? That explained the hole in it, anyway. I check the second half of the date, April 15, 1865, and sure enough, that was the day of his death.

Of course, there's no way I can prove it's really Lincoln's skull.

04201889—April 20, 1889—was the date of the birth of Adolph Hitler. The bloodstained tie. 04301945, the date of his death.

The 12150037-06090068 was a little more difficult. December 15, 0037 - June 9, 0068? It took a little searching, but it came up as the lifespan of the Roman Emperor Nero. The dagger was the one that took his life?

Why does my father have these things?

More intriguing: *How* did he get these things?

Chapter 13

"Do you remember me? / And the kid I used to be? / Not the same as I used to be! / Oh, Do you, remember me?" —Apolcaypica: *"I'm Not Jesus"*

June 19

Selling the empty caskets turned out to be easier than getting them out of the subterranean gravesites, cleaning and refurbishing them, and shipping them. But after hiring four men to help with getting the coffins out of their resting places and Patrick working his trade on restoring them, we got the process down to a pretty smooth system. It went so well, Patrick and I were able to quit our jobs at Phillip's Furniture Store. I would like to think they missed us more than we missed them, but probably not for long.

Though I offered the hired men—who may or may not have been legal residents of the state of Illinois, and who barely spoke English—minimum wage, I also spotted them a $20 bonus for each casket brought safely to the staging area where Patrick worked. Once he was done reconditioning them, he would arrange for shipping.

I, meanwhile, spent most of my time on the phone or the road—or both—contacting every mortuary and funeral home in the area I could find. They were delighted with not only the price, but the quality. I quickly had more orders than we could ship.

One of the caskets the guys brought up was quite ornate—stunningly beautiful. I could have fetched a handsome price for it, but it would have taken a lot of re-work in order to re-sell.

Engraved in the side—and it looked like it was hand-carved—were the words *David W. Parnell, Loving Father & Husband, 1938-2004.* I could not sell it with that name on it, but it also made me wonder all the more why the caskets were buried empty . . . and where the bodies went. I doubt they were cremated as that would only create an added expense for my father's business. It would be cheaper to bury the bodies in the coffins since it would have all been paid for.

Even after paying the four hired hands and covering expenses, we had quite a profit left over. So much so that I had to figure out a way to stow the money away. I wasn't really interested in using banks—part of it was distrust, part of it knowing they were obligated to report large deposits. I wasn't interested in the government wondering where I was getting all this money.

Yet, in some fashion, I had to use banks since checks were coming in, and that's where you cash them. For the time being, I stored the cash and checks in Mr. Parnell's empty casket. It made a nice piggy bank.

And then I wondered if Mr. Burkfelt would be able to help.

Yes, add money laundering to your résumé.

I ignored the voice and made an appointment. I never had the chance to meet with him as we had previously scheduled weeks—months?—ago, as events had taken me on a new course. But he was not only open to the idea, he made some suggestions that made the arrangement even better—like using some of the money as a down-payment to buy his business. I even talked to him about what I found on the Internet about a way to convert Jill's ashes into something I could keep with me at all times.

"Cremation jewelry, sure," he said. "It requires a special machine. I ran across an ad a few months back, someone selling a Quintus Diamond-View. It creates synthetic diamonds. Is that what you're thinking?"

I asked him to look into it, and he said he would. I was very excited. Everything was starting to come together.

If only the voices and the nightmares would go away.

* * *

I'm in someone's house, although I have no idea whose. It's quite nice, very expensive. I wander through, seeing awards and commendations amongst the nice furnishings. On the walls are photos of a somewhat familiar face posing with celebrities and politicians.

Out the plate glass window looking into the backyard, I see a man sitting in a chair, reading a newspaper. He seems to be older, with a head of perfectly styled gray hair. There's a TV on, and his attention shifts between the paper and the screen.

I walk through the sliding door, onto the patio and see Jill on the screen, holding a microphone with the Channel 6 logo. My heart leaps. It seems like it has been so long since I've seen her.

I look at the man—who doesn't seem to notice me—and it's the same guy as in the photos inside the house. He's wearing white tennis shorts and a pale green polo shirt. His attention is glued to Jill's report on the screen, and I realize it's Russ Zorbo, the recently retired anchor from Channel 6.

I look back at the TV, and see that it's no longer there—instead, Jill is standing in its place, continuing her report in front of us.

"The prosecutor says it will take several weeks for DNA results to come in from the forensic lab as there is a backlog of cases that need to be processed, but he is confident the semen collected from the victim will be proven to have come from Russ Zorbo, former TV anchor of WCBC . . ."

I look at Zorbo, and see he is watching Jill with a kind of dreamy smile on his face. I also notice his hand is slowly rubbing a large bulge in his crotch.

I look back at Jill and see the microphone that had been gripped in her hand had turned into the handle of a baseball bat.

"In the meantime, the grand jury will convene, and the prosecutor believes an indictment is imminent. We'll keep you updated as developments warrant. This is Jill Stone, Channel 6 News— now step back, Collin. This is going to get messy."

She raised the bat, hitching it over her shoulder as if she were standing at home plate, waiting for the pitch to come right down the middle, then swung as smoothly as the best pro, connecting solidly with the side of Zorbo's head, creating a loud hollow sound like hitting a piece of wood—BONK! Blood erupted from his scalp as his hairpiece and what I am pretty sure was his ear went flying past me.

He slumped over to the side, eyes wide yet lifeless.

She swung again, and again, his skull soon cratering and becoming nothing more than soft tissue. When she finally stopped, the head was barely attached to the neck.

"Film at Eleven you son of a bitch!" Jill said, dropping the bat and walking into the house.

* * *

I stand in the kitchen, barely awake, waiting for my coffee to cool off, but get impatient. I pull a couple of ice cubes out of the freezer and plop them in as the TV jabbers on in the background. It was coming up on 5 p.m.—after working through the previous night, this was our morning.

"If you order carpet for two rooms, you get a third room free—but order soon! The sale ends Friday!"

Patrick comes out of the bathroom, fresh from the shower, towel wrapped around his waist.

"You look like death warmed over," he says, grabbing a mug from the dishwasher.

Having been up nearly 30 hours, he wasn't far off from what

I felt. "At least if I'm dead, I'm in the right place," I said.

"Are these clean?" he asked, checking the ceramic cup in the light for any stains.

"I ran it yesterday."

"*Coming up on Channel 6 News at 7, the passing of Russ Zorbo . . .*"

"What?"

I hurry into the living room, suddenly wide awake.

"*Stephanie Kramer is in Highland Park with our report on the death of a local icon. Stephanie.*"

"*Paula, it was just two months ago that Russ Zorbo, Channel 6's main anchor for twelve years, retired on the heels of us losing another member of our family, reporter Jill Stone, who passed away from an attack during a home invasion robbery. Zorbo was sixty-five, and found dead on his patio, with a newspaper in his hand in front of a TV set tuned to Channel 6. Responders to the scene say Russ passed away from an apparent stroke. Attempts to resuscitate him were unsuccessful, and he was pronounced dead at the scene. Russ Zorbo began his career forty-five years ago at KCOP in Los Angeles . . .*"

"They're lying," I say.

"Huh?"

"He didn't die from a stroke, the first responders didn't try to resuscitate him—his brains were smashed in."

Patrick stands there in his towel, holding his mug now filled with steaming coffee, staring at me. "And you know this how?"

I open my mouth to reply, then snap it shut. I couldn't exactly say I had a dream and saw the whole thing happen. Because I didn't "see" it.

"Jill did not die from a home invasion attack," I say. "That, I know."

He just looks at me, almost wisely, but he doesn't say anything. I knew what he was thinking.

Then how did she die? What killed her?

That, I did not know—no one did since there was no

117

autopsy—but it wasn't from an attack. Her body had no wounds or trauma.

I shake my head. "There's something going on."

He nods, smirking, but still doesn't say anything.

*　*　*

The men show up at the staging area for their usual 9 p.m. shift. Patrick begins work on the latest casket to make its way up while the rest of us go down to pull more out. Three of us are working on a very nice cherry wood unit when I hear shouting. It sounds like *"Hey—stop—help! Help!"*

I race back to the staging area, and find Patrick pinning a man down, hand around his throat, other hand balled up in a fist, ready to pummel the guy.

"I said what are you doing here?" Patrick is more menacing than I'd ever seen or heard him before.

The man can only gasp with the pressure to his throat.

"What's going on?" I ask.

"He was pouring gasoline around outside," Patrick says. "Trying to burn us out." Patrick gets up, pulling the middle-aged man up by the collar. "I'm going to ask you one more time, what are you doing here?"

The man looks like a truck driver or construction worker, someone with muscle that had gone soft over a decent paunch. His hair is greasy and he has a full beard.

"I was hired to get this business closed," the man says hoarsely.

I pull over one of the plastic chairs the guys used on their breaks. "What's your name?"

Patrick pushes the guy into the chair while I pick up a crow bar we used to pry open the coffins with stuck lids.

The man doesn't answer, only huffs and puffs, watching me warily.

"You tried to kill us," I say. "You know what happens to people who try to kill us but don't succeed?"

Fear crosses his face, followed by terror as I raise the crow bar and slam it down on his left knee. The man blats a yell of pain as his leg goes askew.

"We make sure it can't happen again!" I scream, swinging again, connecting with the right knee.

Fury rages through me. I could have easily done what I saw Jill do in the dream and swing at the guy's head. And I would have enjoyed it.

"What is your name?" I ask as the man holds his shattered knee, half-crying, half-screeching.

"Spencer," he says between maniacal sobs. "Spencer Crais."

"And who hired you, Spencer Crais?"

"A man . . . a man I met in a bar . . ."

"And his name?"

"Horace . . . or Harold . . . *I don't remember!*"

"How much did he pay you?"

"Five thousand . . . I still have it . . . It's in my truck . . . You can take it . . ."

"Oh, I will," I say, raising the crow bar and smashing it down on top of the man's skull, splitting it open and embedding the metal halfway down his head.

We stand, staring, me breathing hard, feeling a sickening rush of adrenaline mixed with horror and disgust.

"He was trying to kill us," I say softly, blinking at the corpse I just created, wondering what I had become.

The voices come back, the children.

Help us. Collin, help.

Then more, all crying and weeping and screaming together. They are so loud, I can only close my eyes and hold my palms against my ears.

After several seconds, the voices subside.

Patrick stays silent. I can't look at him, afraid of what I might see.

I'm going crazy, and he's watching me as it happens.

Then he walks over to one of the discarded caskets that is

too deteriorated to refurbish and wheels it near the chair. He steps around behind and grabs the man under the arms, and I take the legs that feel like a bunch of broken sticks encased in blue jeans. We pick the body up and place it in the coffin. Patrick calmly takes the end of the crow bar, and jiggles it until it is dislodged from the skull.

"What do we do now?" he asks, setting the bar against the wall.

I wipe my forehead with the back of my hand, and feeling what I thought was sweat. But it is blood. I look down and see splatters of red all over my shirt and arms.

I look at Patrick and see he is dotted with it too—though not as much.

I try to think. It would be easy to get rid of a body here—plenty of empty plots.

But . . . I have another idea.

* * *

We drive the utility cart around the cemetery grounds with the dilapidated casket on the back until we get to the tiny house that isn't much more than a large shed. The lights are out. Either he is asleep, or out.

We slide the box off the back and onto the ground, then push it right up to the door. Whether Harold the groundskeeper was inside or out on the town, he wouldn't be able to miss the present that I've left him.

Chapter 14

"The truth about forever is that it is happening right now."
—Sarah Dessen

July 8

I walk outside to get some air, and my cell phone rings. I check the screen. Unbelievably, it says *Jill*.

"Hello?" I say, wondering who—or what—I was going to hear.

A female voice, sounding like an older woman, said: *"Jill was right—you're perfect!"*

"Who is this?"

"You did a good job with the gasoline man. The next phase of the conspiracy against you is well under way. Be diligent!"

I ask: "Who is this?"

"A friend of Jill's. She spoke so warmly of you. And now I know why."

"What's your name? What do you want?"

"Not just me. We would all like to meet you. You must come, and you will receive the answers. I also have something of Jill's that you will want—something very, very special."

"Okay . . . where do you want to meet?"

"You must take an airplane to Matagalpa—you may need to take several connecting flights. Once you're there, some men will meet you to take you on the rest of the journey."

"Wait—how do you spell that?"

"Like it sounds—Matagalpa."

"Where is that?"

"You'll see. You must prepare to leave now. The next flight leaves in four hours. You must be on it."

"But—"

"Go now, Collin. There is no time to talk—only to do!"

And the line goes dead.

I go back inside and tell Patrick I have to leave on a quick trip, and ask that he take care of things.

"Okay. Anything I need to know?"

"I'll fill you in when I get back. I have to hurry to catch my flight."

Before driving back to the house, I pull out my cell phone and tap into maps to look up the location of "Matagalpa."

Matagalpa, Nicaragua.

I shower, change, pack quickly, and hurry to the airport.

As I drive, I can't help but feel I was either heading for my destiny, or my doom.

* * *

It takes nine hours to get to Nicaragua, after three connecting flights, the last being a small prop plane that might have been built fifty years ago. The landing on a dirt runway outside of Matagalpa is a bit bone-rattling, but of the four passengers, I was the only one that was sweating.

Sometime after dark, I stand outside the plane as the others wander off towards a rickety building that hadn't been painted in a couple of decades. I wonder where my ride is that the lady on the phone mentioned. Twenty minutes later, something that looks part Jeep and part truck rumbles up—a stout 6 wheel off-road vehicle with several gas cans mounted on the sides. One of the two men inside waves at me to climb in.

I get in the back, and try to get comfortable, sitting in the bed while the other two rode on the bench seat up front. First, we head down a rutty asphalt road that soon turns to a more rutty dirt path that goes deep into the jungle.

I bounce around in the back, my hopes for a nap not met, the occasional branch of a tree brushing or slapping the top of my head. The roar of the engine drowns out everything else.

I have no idea how long it takes. Hours and hours and hours. A couple of times, they stop to add gasoline and pee off in the bush.

Just as the sun starts to faintly glow through the brief glimpses of sky, we come to a stop. One of the men says something in Spanish and waves me down. I jump off the back, and he points into the jungle, saying something while gesturing with his hand. Up, down, around, up, down. Then he gives me a piece of paper with a series of hand-drawn lines—a crude map. It's impossible to tell how far I have to go, but it's clear I have to walk it.

I thank them, shake their hands, grab my backpack—glad I hadn't taken a suitcase—and head into the dense foliage.

As the light grows better, I find a path—more like a line where the plants had been tramped down—and just stay on it the best I can. Bugs attack me. I can hear animals chattering and scurrying away if I get too close. Branches snap at my legs, and I stop a couple of times to rest, finding small cuts up and down my shins. I slap at the insects that try chewing on me.

I walk and walk, unsure where I'm going or if I'm even going the right way. I want nothing more than to stop, lie down, and sleep. But I'm sure either the bugs or creatures I hear would eat me alive if I do that.

* * *

Eventually—it seems to be around noon based on the position

of the sun—I hear a sound that makes me stop and cock my head.

Rushing water. More specifically, a waterfall.

I turn to my left and come upon a beautiful clearing, with bright green grass. Off to the right is the waterfall, about thirty feet high, cascading into a large clear pond. Towards the left are a series of stumps surrounding a fire pit. I stop and stare at it, knowing it looks just like the one in my dreams, the one I floated above while twelve hooded figures chanted and raised their hands. But I'm so tired, hot and thirsty, I don't care.

At the edge of the pond, I take off my clothes and step into the clear, cool water. I make my way over to the waterfall, allowing the stream of water to pour over me, cleansing both my body and my soul. The water massages my flesh, relaxing me. I drink, and after quite a while, I make my way out and lay down on the soft ground underneath a stone out-cropping, providing cool shade.

It doesn't take long for my aching, tired body to drift off to sleep.

* * *

"Collin," a voice whispers.

I try to ignore it. The peace of a dreamless sleep was too appealing.

"Collin, wake up. It is time."

Regretfully, I open my eyes. I'm laying on my side, arm curled under my head, a cool breeze washing over my skin. I see a pair of feet beneath what looked like the hem of a brown robe.

I turn my eyes up to see a middle-aged, smiling woman.

"Come," she says. "We need to begin."

She holds out her hand, and I force my way into a sitting position, looking around at my surroundings. Night has fallen again. Other than the smiling woman, there are eight, nine . . . ten others, men and women, all in brown robes, some hooded, all watching me.

I become aware of my lack of clothing. I sit awkwardly for a moment, but the woman only continues to smile, holding out her hand.

"Please," she says. "It's okay."

I take her hand and stand as a man approaches, holding open a brown robe. I slide my arms in before he wraps it around me, tying the rope-like belt around my waist.

They lead me towards the fire pit, which is already lit, and the man guides me to stand in front of a stump. The others take their places in front of their stumps, and the ones that do not have their hoods up now pull them over their heads.

While it is obvious this was some kind of cult, I wonder if it is Satanic. Hoods, fire . . . what next? Human sacrifice?

I look past the fire, at the woman directly across from me. I can only see her face from the nose down, but she seems familiar . . . like . . .

"Sylvana?" I say.

"*Laus Deo*," the other hooded figures say in unison.

I suppose if they're saying "Praise be to God", then this probably isn't a satanic gathering. Unless it's a different God than I'm used to.

I keep staring at the woman across from me, hoping she'll reveal her face.

The woman who had woken me spoke.

"Collin, we are Soulmadds and now, so are you! I know this doesn't mean anything to you yet, and only in time will you comprehend this. We want to offer you a gift to be opened only when you return to your common home. It will aid you in mastering a secret ability that resides deep inside your soul. Jill has chosen you, Collin, to enter our ancient Royal Soulmadic Council."

"I'm sorry. Royal what?"

"You will understand soon. We are here to help you pass into the new realm. There will be no pain, though it may seem frightening. Do not be afraid. For God so loved the world that He gave His one and only Son, that whoever believes in Him shall not perish but have everlasting life."

"Laus Deo," the others say.

"We are not here to force you into anything, Collin. We are here to assist you, that if you choose to believe, that you will be commissioned into a new life, one that you have already begun to experience, but now one that is much more full of joy and mystery, delight and pain. You have been chosen, not by us, but by the One who foresees all, and know you are worthy of the commission."

"Laus Deo."

"Jill Stone is your key. She may have only been with you a short time on this Earth, but she will be with you forever, in your heart, mind and soul. She said you were perfect, and you are. If you choose to be so blessed, and so cursed, just raise your arms, and you will be taken up into the heavenly embrace."

They all pause to wait for my response.

I'm not sure what to say.

I take some time to think.

"Look, if this is some way of you . . . I don't know, baptizing me, or trying to get me to say I accept Jesus Christ as my Lord and Savior, then didn't have to have fly all the way down here and walk through half the jungle. I do believe—though I can't say I act like it very much. I mean, I don't think about it a lot, and go to church even less, but I do believe. I'm not sure how waving my hands in the air is going to prove it."

"While it is true you may not have led a clean and spotless life," the smiling woman says, "none of us have, but we know you are a believer. This is not about that. It is not about what you have done or what you haven't done. It is about what you will do."

"Laus Deo."

I frown. "I guess I don't know what this 'commission' is, and why I should commit to it. I mean, is this some kind of test of my faith? If I don't do it, does it mean I am not a believer? I just don't understand."

"You are pure, Collin," the woman says. "Your flesh has stayed pure even with great temptation. You have chosen the correct and moral route when faced with both terror and trials. When the man attempted to kill you, you may have felt you over-reacted by killing him. That is expected, and shows your heart. But the man was bought and became the most simple form of evil. What you do not know is he had killed before, and if you hadn't put him to death, he would have killed again. Life is not about running away from death, but understanding there is no death. Only transitions. In the meantime, you have a lot to do. The evil will not rest. Even now it is plotting against you. Have you heard of Dymortis?"

My head jerks slightly at the name. "Yes. I have." It was written in some of my father's journals.

"He is the orchestrator, and he will not stop until one of you is vanquished. As a Soulmadd, you are commissioned to defeat him and his followers, some of whom you know, some you have yet to meet. It is this challenge we ask you to step into."

I think about this. It's all pretty heady stuff.

"What if I say 'no'?"

"We are not given that knowledge yet, but I can guess that the evil will only grow worse, and slowly, the world will succumb more than it already has."

"You're making it sound like I am some sort of . . . savior."

"There is only one Savior, and, no, it is not you. But as a follower, you can assist Him in the quest."

"Why doesn't He just take care of it? I mean, He could if He wanted to, right?"

"It is not His time. That is all we know."

"You're saying this like I am the only one who can save humanity. Trust me, I am not some Superman who can battle evil and make the world a happy place. I'm not that guy."

"You are right to say you are not the only one. There are others, but at this time, it is about you and your choice. If you choose not to accept this commission, I can assure you that you may return to your life without any consequence . . . though the special blessings that have been bestowed upon you may disappear."

"Special blessings? Like what?"

Her hand reaches out and a finger touched my chest. "Some you know, some you fear, some have yet to be revealed. Some are visions, some are voices, all are instructive. And each is a blessing, even if they bring pain and misery."

She pulls her hand away and go silent. All stare at me. The fire crackles.

"So, I can just turn around and leave if I want?"

"Yes, if you wish."

"And nothing bad will happen to me?"

"'Bad' will always happen, but we will not stop you, nor harm you."

"I am free to go?"

"You have always been free."

"Okay, well, I think I'll just go home. It's kind of hard to make a decision when it's not very clear what, exactly, the decision means."

"We understand." The man next to her holds out something, some kind of box wrapped in what looks like leather. "This must, then, go into the fire."

"What is it?"

"We do not know, we were only told that it is one of the blessings, a gift from Jill that she thought was important enough for you to have if you decided to move forward. It was told to us that it contains puzzles, leading to answers . . . and something very special to Jill that she thought you should have."

I stare at the box, licking my lips. I'm curious—no, more than that. I'm drawn to it. I start blinking and thinking. If it really was from Jill . . . it was very difficult to say no to that.

Puzzles. Answers. Something special.

I have already encountered puzzles, their meaning unknown. And the promise of answers was alluring. But it meant committing to something that was . . . so . . . so much bigger than me. Whatever it was.

We stand for several minutes in silence while these thoughts run through my head. I have to commit—to what, I'm still not sure, but it sounded horribly difficult and terrifying—or walk away and . . . well, that wasn't clear either.

I close my eyes and try to pray. I was hoping for a reply, an answer . . . but nothing comes.

I open my eyes and look at the box again.

I hold my hands out.

She takes the box from the man, and turns towards me.

"Once you take possession, you will be lifted up, your soul dedicated to the commission. Your beloved Jill has been with you, is with you now, and will always be with you. The two have become one, and your love will never die."

She pauses, holding the box in front of her.

"Do you, Collin Jacob Graves, take Jillian Samantha Stone, to have and to hold, for better or for worse, for richer, for poorer, in sickness and in health, to love and to cherish, from this day forward?"

I blink several times, a little confused.

"I . . . I do."

"Collin Jacob Graves, do you accept this commission and all it entails?"

"Yes, and why do you keep calling me that?"

She smiles and hands the box for me to take. "All will be revealed. Take hold, and do not let go. May God's blessings and love forever protect you and hold you."

"*Laus Deo.*"

I take the box. I'm immediately surrounded by a translucent white light, like a foggy cocoon. I can see through it, see the fire, the hooded figures. Then I'm lifted off the ground, some kind of levitation, slowly at first, then turning, then spinning, higher, up into the great darkness as I hold the precious box against my chest.

The fire and the people around it became smaller and smaller as I rise higher and higher into the sky, spinning faster and faster, until I close my eyes and lose consciousness.

Chapter 15

"Things alter for the worse spontaneously, if they be not altered for the better designedly." —Francis Bacon

I wake up on my bed thinking I might need to visit a doctor about these strange dreams. A psychiatrist. It might be the onset of mental illness—or, considering the voices I've heard for most of my life, it has intensified. I feel like I'm going crazy, but kind of sideways. Most of the time, I feel fine.

It wasn't just that the dreams were bizarre, but that they were so real, as if they had really happened. And some had. I wonder if, from this point, I will be able to discern the difference between the dream and reality.

I sit up and realize I wasn't naked nor in my clothes. I stand, looking down at the long brown robe.

"Hey, you're back," Patrick says from the doorway. Then he looks me up and down. "A little early for Halloween. What are you? A monk?"

I open my mouth to reply, but can't explain. I look around the room and see the leather-covered box sitting on the bed.

"I . . . uh . . . I don't know." I scratch my head. "Something really weird happened."

"I hope so. Must have been a great party. Next time, invite

me." He smirks.

"No, I mean it's really weird." I undo the belt and take off the robe.

"Okay," he said, realizing I was serious. "Any weirder than that?" He points.

I look down at my chest. The tattoo/branding mark that had been like a scar in a type of squarish pattern with criss-crossing lines and a circle in the middle was no longer pink. It was a light blue.

I touch it and feel an unusual warmth.

I look up at Patrick. "Yes, weirder."

"Well, if you want to fill me in, there's coffee." He heads downstairs.

I look around the room for my clothes, and didn't see them. Probably still in Nicaragua, along with my backpack.

I get dressed, and notice all the minor cuts and bug bites I encountered while trekking through the jungle were gone. Okay, so the dreams had become reality, or the reality had become a dream—not sure which.

I go downstairs, bringing the box with me. Patrick is draped over the couch, watching TV.

"We were able to extract three more while you were gone. I want to take a day off, and I'll get to refurbing them tomorrow."

"Good." I pause. "How long was I gone?"

He blinks at me, then looks over at the clock. "You left yesterday morning, so about twenty-four hours, maybe a little more."

Nine hours of plane flights, four or five hours of a bumpy ride in an off-road vehicle, endless hours hiking through the jungle . . . that's at least 18, if not more. Taking the nap, standing in the fire pit circle, taking hold of the box . . . and there had to be a trek back: Hours and hours of walking, truck ride, airplane. So how did I return home in less than six hours?

Of course, I knew what I experienced, without knowing what happened.

I set the box down on the table.

"What's that?"

"We're going to find out." I stare at it. "I was told it's a gift from Jill."

"So it *was* a party."

"No. It was . . ." I pause again, choosing my words. "It was like a group, these people who call themselves 'Soulmadds' and are working on the side of good, and God."

"Soul what?"

"Madds. Soulmadds."

"What does it mean?"

I shrug. "They basically said that all these weird things that have been happening to me are part of a plan to . . ." I shake my head. "Trying to say it out loud, it sounds too bizarre."

"Like a magical color-changing tattoo isn't bizarre enough?"

I get some coffee, then sit in the chair. And I tell him everything. As I start, even I don't believe some of the stuff I'm saying. But I go through it all, as best I can.

"So . . . you're now specially chosen to . . . what?"

"I guess I'll find out."

"And your Nanny is part of it?"

"Well, I think so, but I don't know for sure."

"It explains her magic ring and super healing powers."

"And, what's interesting to me, is that I've known her since I was four."

Patrick thinks this over for a few moments. "So, you think you were 'chosen' since then?"

"I don't know, but I can't really say it's a coincidence."

His gaze falls on the box, and mine follows.

I pick it up and carefully undo the small straps, then unfold the soft leather covering. Inside is a dark wood box with an emblem carved in the top.

"Nice," Patrick says. "Looks like a western red cedar."

My fingers run over the emblem. It's the same design that is on my chest.

Patrick notices this, and his eyes grow wide. "Wow. Okay . . .

wow."

"Yeah, I think it's the symbol of the Soulmadds. I'm sure the other people who were standing around the fire ring had this on their skin too."

There's a small brass latch that I lift up, then open the lid. Inside is a couple of small black pouches. I pick up the first, open it, and dump the contents into my palm. It's a ring—not unlike Sylvana's, only pink.

"That's pretty," Patrick said, winking at me. "Should help you get picked up in bars."

I smirk and try to slide the ring on—the only finger it fit was the pinky, so there it went. I look at it on my hand. While the stone is small and nice, the metal is quite ornate and seems very old.

I pick up the other pouch and empty it into my hand—a key.

"The key to her heart?"

"Maybe." I read the wording stamped into it. "Five Star."

"Let me take a look."

I hand it over, and Patrick inspects it.

"It's not a standard, not like you'd find in doors. It's thicker than most—it won't even fit in most locks. Not a vehicle key. I would guess it's a special security key, not rare, but not something you'd buy off the shelf."

"I think your former Bad Boy life can come in quite useful."

"Who said anything about 'former.' Once a player, always a player."

"Alright Romeo, whatever you say. So how do we find out what this key goes to?"

"Five Star. Not a brand I heard of. So it's probably the name of the thing it goes to."

"A Five Star lock? Like a MasterLock?"

"No, like a business. Five Star Bank or something."

"A safety deposit box?"

"Maybe. Why don't you look it up on the Internet?"

I get my laptop and type in *Five Star key*. The third listing was something local—Five Star Private Storage.

"There you go," Patrick says.

I click the link. *High Security Private Storage—Not Your Average Lock-Up.*

"Wanna go on an adventure?"

"The game is afoot, Sherlock."

"I gotta make a stop on the way."

* * *

Five Star was fairly close to where Jill had lived, and the moment we pull into the parking lot, I realize they were right in their advertising—it's not the average storage facility. Solid brick walls, no windows, and only one way in—through the office.

We walk up to the counter and a rotund surly man looks at me over his iPad.

"Hello," I say. "Do you have a unit under the name of Jacob Collin Davis?"

"You don't remember?"

"Of course I do. But you have five locations, and I don't remember if it's this one or Arlington Heights."

The man harrumphs, puts down his tablet and types on the computer. "ID?"

I pull out my wallet and hand him my driver's license.

A few moments of keyboard-clicking and staring. "Nope. Sorry." He hands my ID back, not sounding the least bit sorry.

I think for a few moments. "How about Collin Jacob Graves?"

The man looks at me with a *you've gotta be kidding* expression. "How many names do you have?"

"Just the two."

"Well, if you don't have proper ID and password, I can't let you in, no matter who you say you are."

I look at Patrick. He shrugs. We leave.

"Where did you get the name Collin Jacob Graves?"

"I don't know, it was used when I was in Nicaragua."

"Is it you?"

"I guess. Maybe some kind of Soulmadd code name."

"Well, I can get you an ID that says that, if you want."

"That would be great."

"It would be about fifty bucks."

"No problem. How long will it take?"

"Let's find out." He pulls out his cell phone. "Louie. I need a card . . . ASAP, a rush job . . . Sure . . . Yeah, we can be there in fifteen . . . Thanks."

"Where do I go?"

"He's on the South Side. Turn right up here."

* * *

An hour later, we're headed back to Five Star.

"Won't he think it's weird that we come back with a new ID?"

"Maybe. But worth a try."

We walk into the office, and no one is behind the desk. I stand there, waiting, while Patrick wanders over to the door labeled *Locker Entrance*. He tugs on it, but it's locked. I notice the three cameras mounted on walls. It's like a minimum security prison without the personality.

A woman comes out from the back. She could be the sulky guy's wife, being roughly the same size.

"Howdy," she says. "How can I help you boys?"

"I need to visit my unit."

"ID please."

I hand her my newly-minted driver's license, and she types it into the computer.

"Four-twelve. You boys have a great day."

The *Locker Entrance* door buzzes, and Patrick opens it. We walk through a series of hallways until we find 412. There's a roll-up door, a lock on the left, and a keypad on the right.

I put the key in and turn. The door doesn't move, but the keypad beeps.

"It says *Enter password*," Patrick says, staring at it.

"I don't have a password."

"Looks like there's a fingerprint scanner here."

I step over and look at it. I put my thumb on it, a faint light comes on, then the door starts rolling up.

"*Voila*," Patrick says.

"How did they get my thumbprint?"

"This is your dream, not mine."

The unit is a ten-by-ten and pretty clean. A spider web up in the corner, but otherwise almost pristine. And practically empty. The only thing in there was a small package about a foot square, wrapped in brown paper sitting square in the middle of the concrete.

I pick it up, finding it incredibly light. If there's anything inside, it doesn't weigh much.

We lock up, go back to the front desk, and I tell the lady I'd like to close the account.

"Could I see your ID again?"

I hand it to her, and she types. "Okay, well, you're paid up until the end of the year if you change your mind."

"Okay, thanks."

* * *

Just as we get home, my cell phone rings. It shows a number I don't recognize.

"Hello?"

"May I speak to Collin Graves, please?"

That name again. Not that I mind, but it's so odd it keeps coming up. "Speaking."

"Hi, this is Elaina Krupps. I'm an attorney at Krupps, Daniel and Associates, and I wanted to see if we could schedule an appointment with you regarding an insurance policy."

"Uh, other than my car insurance, I don't have any policies."

"I understand, but this is regarding your status as sole

beneficiary of a life insurance policy."

"Life insurance?"

"Yes, a policy taken out by a Jill Stone."

"Oh. Yes. Jill. Of course."

"I understand she recently passed away, and I'm sorry for your loss."

"Yes, thank you."

"Would you be available to sign some paperwork so we can transfer the benefits over to you? Would sometime this week be good?"

"I can come by tomorrow morning, if that would be okay."

"That will work fine. Say ten?"

"Sure."

She gives me the address, and hangs up.

"What now?" Patrick asks.

"I guess Jill had a life insurance policy."

Patrick offers his patented smirk. "Score," he says.

Chapter 16

"The supernatural is the natural not yet understood." —Elbert Hubbard

When we get home, I notice something by the front door.

"What's that?" Patrick asks.

"Looks like my backpack."

I put down Jill's package and pick up the new delivery, unzipping it. Yep, my stuff.

"How'd it get here?" Patrick is looking around.

"Same way I got home, I guess."

"Ah, the magic carpet."

I take the backpack and package into my bedroom. For some reason, I feel it should be opened in private. Patrick had gone off to check on the workers anyway.

Faintly, I hear the sound of . . . flutes? Not just one, but many, like a symphony.

I go to the door and listen, wondering if maybe Patrick had turned on the TV and was watching PBS—not something he would do unless WTTW had started airing the Bears.

But, no, the sound wasn't coming from downstairs. Despite it being faint, it seems to be coming from inside the room. I return to the bed and realize it's coming from the package.

A music box?

I carefully open one end and begin to unwrap the brown paper. It reveals a plain cardboard box. I open the top, and immediately, the music stops.

Then, a whisper: *You're perfect.*

I look inside the box. What I see catches my breath for a moment.

A framed photo of Jill. Black-and-white. A very artistic pose— possibly a head shot or promotional picture from the TV station. She is strikingly beautiful.

I put it on the nightstand and stare at it for a while, until my eyes tear up and I have trouble seeing.

I wipe my face with the back of my hand and try to focus again, looking in the box. Laying on the bottom is some kind of book. It's pink with yellow flowers. I pull it out.

Diary, it says in fancy white script.

I have found him. He is perfect, and I think he will do well. I so look forward to being with him during his journey, to be by his side.

I could go on and on about his heart, or his looks, his strength of character, his love, but words do not apply.

It went on from there. I can feel myself blush as I read it, but also feel the sweetness and tenderness that makes me miss her more.

The final entries, however, make me pause.

I arrived home late, having an assignment for the late news, and saw him. He's been there three nights in a row, just sitting in the beat-up old orange truck. I have to keep an eye on him. I tried to go to bed, but I couldn't sleep, and any small sound made me sit up. So then I sat at the window, watching, until he started the truck and drove away after 3:30 AM.

* * *

I cannot move. He has gotten out of the truck and walked

to the bottom of the stairs, looking up, as if he were thinking of coming.

Okay, he turned around and went back to his truck. My heart is beating so fast. I should call the police, but he is driving away.

* * *

The truck is back, but I see two people inside. The big, slow-moving man and someone else. Can't quite make him out.

Should I call the police? Collin?

Again, the truck starts, and drives away. I hope I can go to sleep, but I doubt it.

Orange beat-up truck.

Sounds like the one Harold drove around the cemetery.

* * *

The next morning, I head to the lawyers, wondering what to expect. Beneficiary to Jill's life insurance policy couldn't be much. Being a reporter sounds glamorous, but Jill had confided the pay wasn't dazzling, despite being on a channel in the third largest TV market. It was a small independent station where new reporters cut their teeth or went to play out the end of their career.

Of course, it wasn't about the money. I was honoring Jill's wishes since she had honored me to receive them. Whatever they were.

I find the building downtown, on Michigan Avenue, the ritzy part of the city. Patrick called it the Midwest Beverly Hills. I feel a bit self-conscious using the valet parking for my dumpy white pick-up truck, but apparently, that is all they have.

I get on the elevator and go up to the 17th floor, where the doors opened onto a mostly glass and chrome reception area. Everything glistens, even the people. The receptionist at the desk has very shiny teeth.

"Hello," she says brightly, as if glad to see me. "How may I help you?"

"I have an appointment to see Elaina Krupps."

She clicks on her computer. "Mr. Graves? Javier will show you to a meeting room." She perkily smiles again as a dapper man in a suit appears at my side.

"Right this way," he says, heading off through a doorway.

He leads me to a large conference room with a glass wall on one side overlooking the hallway where busy people go back and forth, and a wall of glass on the other overlooking the Magnificent Mile. He opens the glass door and invites me to take a seat, asking if I would like anything to drink.

"Uh, no, I'm okay."

"Very well. Ms. Krupps will be with you momentarily." And then he leaves.

I'm glad I at least dressed in khakis and a button-down shirt so as not to totally embarrass myself.

The instant I sit at one of the 12 chairs around the table, the door opens and a thin, middle-aged woman in a dark brown business suit walks in smiling.

"Mr. Graves, I'm Elaina Krupps. It's a pleasure to meet you."

I stand and shake her hand. "My pleasure as well."

"Okay, I have some things to go over with you. I wish it was under better circumstances," she says, taking the seat next to me. She sets a folder down on the table. "Ms. Stone had taken out a policy with the Trojan State Insurance Company over some possessions she had, and it was her instructions that in the event of her untimely demise, these items were to be transferred to you."

"What kind of items?"

"I'll go over those in just a moment. First, I do need to see some identification—a state-issued driver's license, passport, validated birth certificate."

I paused, thinking. I left the fake ID at home, not thinking I'd need it.

"Well, there's a little problem," I say, shifting uncomfortably in my seat. "You have my name as Collin Jacob Graves, but that's not my name."

To my surprise, she shows no reaction.

"I know," she says. "Legally, it is Jacob Collin Davis. When this matter came to our attention, we had to do a background check since the . . . items are of a particular value. We needed to be assured they were being transferred to the proper person."

"Particular value?"

"Yes, I'll get to that in a minute. But before I do, I'm in the position of giving you some news that you potentially are not aware of."

"Okay."

And then she opens the folder and slips a sheet of paper in front of me.

ST. ANTHONY HOSPITAL

CERTIFICATE OF BIRTH

I scan it, not quite understanding.

LAST NAME: GRAVES

FIRST NAME: COLLIN

MIDDLE NAME: JACOB

I look up, confused. "What is this?"

Her face is passive, and she only points at the sheet.

MOTHER: CATHERINE MAMIE CLARK GRAVES

FATHER: RANDOLPH SIMON GRAVES

"This is your mother, and this is your father."

"But . . . but . . . my mother's name was Linda, and my father is Henry Davis."

She slides out another sheet of paper.

CERTIFICATE OF ADOPTION

I sit back, stunned and shocked.

"I'm adopted?"

She pulls out yet another piece of paper—a copy of a newspaper article.

Chicago Couple Killed in Plane Crash

I scan the first couple of paragraphs, telling of a Randolph and Catherine Graves who were killed in a tragic flight over the Atlantic.

I look at the date. I would have been three months old.

"Wow," is all I can say.

I look out the window at the skyscrapers across the street.

My father is not my father.

Actually, that explains a lot.

While part of me feels awkward and guilty over discovering the man who claimed he was my father barely had anything to do with me, another part is very comfortable with the thought.

He provided for you.

Yes, that is true. I should give him props for that, even if he did avoid me most of the time. I did have food, clothes and a place to sleep. He didn't beat me or belittle me. Except that one time when he dragged me into the basement to show me the screaming children. If that was real, which now seems more likely than not. But he also didn't hug me or show any love. So, there's that.

I get out my wallet and show her my driver's license. She looks it over and nods.

"I'm sorry if this was a shock to you," she says, sounding sorry. "We weren't sure if you had been told or . . . figured it out."

"No, it's okay. I'm glad to know," I say. Then I take a deep breath.

"As far as the bequeathment, I have some other news that might be equally shocking. And life-changing."

She slips another piece of paper out of the folder and sets it in front of me. It is very simple: *I, Jill Samantha Stone, in the event of my death, hereby leave all my worldly possessions, as listed on the following page, to Collin Jacob Graves, a.k.a. Jacob Collin Davis.*

Then it's signed and dated.

I turn to the next page.

7 BARS, BULLION, GOLD

I'm blinking at this, trying to understand, trying to grasp it.

"She left me gold bars?"

"Yes. Based on today's market, they're worth about three and a half million dollars."

"What . . . How . . ." I pause. "Where did she get seven gold bars?"

The attorney shakes her head. "I don't know, but we did verify and validate them. They're currently in Denver, and once the documents are signed and transferred, we can begin the process of having them shipped to you."

My mouth is suddenly bone dry, my tongue like sandpaper.

She passes me another piece of paper, and a pen.

"Initial here, here, and here, and then sign and date at the bottom."

* * *

I see her form in the darkness, can smell her perfume.

She moves from the foot of the bed to the window, her outline perfect in the light of the moon. "I have waited so long," she says.

I can only watch her, mesmerized.

She turns to look at me. I cannot see her face, but I know she is smiling.

She approaches the bed, pulls back the covers and slips in next to me. Her soft skin is so warm against mine, her left leg slipping over my thigh, nestling between my legs. Her head lay on my shoulder, her hand gently moving over my chest.

I tilt her head up and begin to kiss her, feeling both the warmth and softness of her wash over me, into me. My hand strokes her hair as her hand slides down my body.

Many times I have dreamt of something like this, but never have I experienced these sensations while dreaming, felt the fingers on my skin, her breast against my chest, her hair through my fingers. It all seems so real, feels so real.

I kiss her lips, her neck, her shoulder as her hand touches me where I have never been touched before.

The sensation is unlike anything I had imagined to this point, so light, so gentle, so loving.

"I love you, Collin," she whispers, sliding on top of me, her fingers guiding me into a warmth and ecstasy I had never experienced. She kisses me deeply and my entire soul seems filled with nothing but the most profound love for this woman. I don't move, just lay there accepting her kisses and allowing us to just be as one.

Then she rolls to her left, and I roll with her, now over her.

She looks up at me with the most beautiful eyes and smile.

"I have no idea what I'm doing," I whisper.

"Neither do I," she says, "but I think we'll figure it out."

Slowly, I begin to make love to her, as her hands glide over my back, and she breathes softly into my ear.

Chapter 17

"The saddest thing is when you are feeling real down, you look around and realize that there is no shoulder for you." —Unknown

July 14

I received a delivery—but not the one I was expecting.

It's a padded envelope. I sign for it and take it inside.

To: Mr. Collin Graves

The return address says *Burkfelt Jewelers*.

Inside the envelope is a box. Inside the box is a ring.

I had dropped off the ring that was in Jill's storage unit along with her ashes to Mr. Burkfelt, and he had already completed the job.

I am stunned to see an immaculate two carat princess cut diamond with an odd pink hue to it—not bad, just unlike anything I'd ever seen. It is remarkable.

I call Mr. Burkfelt to thank him, and he tells me the ring itself is quite special—hundreds, perhaps thousands of years old.

"I wouldn't call it priceless," he says, *"but it's pretty close."*

* * *

With the things I've seen in my father's—adoptive father's—office, the entries in the journals, and the thought that he could have been the other person mentioned in Jill's diary sitting in the orange pick-up truck, has made me wonder if he had something to do with her death.

I've figured that he is a collector of morbid items, death trophies, but how he came to have them in his possession is beyond me. I mean, Lincoln's *skull*? That's insane—if, of course, it's really Lincoln's. There's no way for me to verify that.

The journal entries are just as puzzling. Some of the books are ancient. The print in those is faded and difficult to read, and many of the pages are fragile and sometimes stuck together. And the dates are outrageous, some going back hundreds of years, all the same handwriting as the more recent journals. I'm thinking they're some kind of imitation, like a history book written in the perspective as if he were there. That is, assuming again, he wrote them.

It's bad enough that he is so obsessed with the dark and morbid sides of events, but considering he owns a funeral home and cemetery, I guess I shouldn't be surprised.

I'm riding Ginger around the property, thinking about what I should do, if anything. We stop at the wall that separates the cemetery from the Meadows Polo Club and Resort, hearing the laughter of what seems to be a raucous party. I don't know a whole lot about the Meadows, other than seeing some of the members come and go, and they're all older—60+—and drive exceptionally expensive cars. I know my father—*Henry*—goes there frequently, but I haven't been on the property. I've peeked, I've watched, but not actually stepped foot on it.

I look off toward my father's—*Henry's* house, and see the town car has pulled up. I watch, wondering if he's just going out to dinner, or out of town. It's quite a distance, and with dusk settling in, it's not easy, but I wait. A minute later, Henry steps out of the house, and the driver follows carrying suitcases.

Ginger and I wait until the car pulls away, and I realize I'm already working on plans to break into his office again.

* * *

I lay on the bed, waiting. I may have dozed off. At one point, I stare at the smoke detector's red light, wondering.

He's gone. I can check.

I turn on the nightstand lamp and pull a chair over, placing it under the plastic white disc mounted on the ceiling. I can just reach it. I tug on the cover and in a moment it snaps off, a pair of wires connecting it. The red light comes from what looks like a small LED. Right next to it is what looks like another LED, except it is not lit. I notice one of the wires goes to the red LED, the other wire to the unlit one.

I look a little more closely—or as close as I can standing on a chair with the smoke detector cover still 18" away from my face. I can see the unlit one is different from the red one—round and flat, like a little, tiny camera lens. It stares blankly back at me.

Okay, so if he is watching, I . . . well, I don't know what. It's creepy, yes, but at this point, not unexpected. I'm just glad I put most of Jill's things in the other bedroom where no "smoke detector" was installed.

I reach for the wire, ready to pluck it out and disconnect it . . . then think twice. He'll know I know. I have to consider the consequences.

But maybe he already thinks I'm onto him. Has he watched me lying in bed, reading his journals—or whatever they are? I'll have to assume so. I'll just have to do my reading elsewhere from now on. Plus, there was the Gasoline Man I killed and dumped on Harold's porch. If that didn't tip him off, nothing will.

Play the game.

Yes, that is probably best. Keep him thinking I don't know.

I put the thing back together, leaving the wire intact. For now.

I check the clock. Just after midnight. Time to go.

I head downstairs, and Patrick is laid out on the couch

watching TV.

"Hey."

"I'm going over to his office."

He looks at me with passive interest. "You think that's a good idea?"

"He's out of town."

"Doesn't answer the question."

"Of course it's not a good idea, but I have to find out what's going on, who he is, what he's up to."

The look on his face is easy to read. *Why?* it says.

I feel defensive. I *am* defensive. But I'm still going to do it.

"Let me get my shoes on," he says.

* * *

There is so much stuff to go through, I felt a bit overwhelmed. I wonder if the stuff that looks interesting is meaningless, and the stuff that looks meaningless is useful.

Then, I get an idea and pull out my cell phone.

"You get reception down here?" Patrick asks, standing by the door as if he's on lookout.

"I don't know. I was going to take pictures instead of taking notes."

"Ah, good idea."

He retrieves his from his pocket, and we methodically begin to shoot photos of the objects and their tags.

I take shots of the items in one of the display cases—mainly a lot of what looks like knickknacks to me: Cuff links, a comb that looks like it's made of metal, salt-and-pepper shakers, scissors, a metronome, the handset to an old telephone. One of the item's tags is hanging off to the side, so I have to take the shot on the right side of the display case. And I notice a latch that seems to be holding the case to the wood siding of the wall.

I haven't heard of a display case being latched to a wall, and can't think of a reason why it would need to be.

I undo the latch, and the case moves away from the wall slightly. I slip my fingers into the space, and the entire display case begins to swivel away from the wall. Behind it is, basically, a hole in the wall big enough to walk through.

"Hey, look at this," I say as I fetch my flashlight from my back pocket.

"Whoa, a secret passage," Patrick says, sounding impressed.

I point the beam of light into the hole and quickly see it's another room with a lot of bottles and jars on shelves. I step through and look for a light switch, finding it just to the right. The fluorescents flicker on, a lot of dust and cobwebs highlighted by a slightly dank, musty smell.

I step into the middle of the roughly 10 x 10 room and Patrick follows.

"What is that?" he asks pointing at a large jar with some kind of organ inside.

"No idea," I say, taking a few pictures, making sure I get the label.

09301888

"Do you think these are from the bodies brought to the funeral home?" Patrick asks staring at another jar containing a full human head. "Like he takes out their organs and saves them?"

I slowly shake my head. "No, I don't think so. See these numbers? They're dates. This one is from September 30, 1888."

He double-checks the head he was looking at. "09, 03, 16, 58," he says. "Doesn't sound like a date to me."

"September 3, 1658."

"1658?" he says, looking at it again. "It's four hundred years old?"

"Well, three-fifty, give or take, but, yeah."

"Whose is it?"

"Take a picture and we'll find out."

I move on to the next jar, which also has a brain, or more specifically, a pair of sections. *04181955.*

"This is freaking me out!" Patrick says. "Look! Eye balls!"

I step over to see. "Um, if I remember my biology class correctly, not eye balls. But you got it half right."

He looks at me, going pale. "You mean . . . ?"

"Yeah." I go back to the first jar we looked at, *09301888*. "I'm still trying to figure out what body part this is."

"Well, if he's got testicles in this one, maybe that's . . . you know . . . "

I turned the jar around, and considered it from a different angle. "I guess it could be a uterus."

"Oh, geez. I've seen some stuff, nasty stuff, but this is over-the-top creepy. What would he be doing with a freaking *uterus* in a jar?"

I point to the shelf above it. "What do you think that is?"

He just stares at it for several moments, then shakes his head and turns away.

"Dude is sick in the head. Just sick in the head."

* * *

We're going back to the house when Patrick suddenly yells *"Hey!"* and takes off running.

I chase after him, though he's moving like the wind. He reaches the barn and turns the corner around the back before I have a chance to get halfway there.

I come around and see Patrick rolling around on the ground with some man, a middle-aged guy with a bad comb-over. Unfortunately, Patrick wasn't winning, being pinned on the ground, and a fist trying to bludgeon him.

I race up and swing my foot, connecting squarely in the middle of the guy's face, and he topples over like a wet bag of sand.

"Son of a bitch," I scream. *"I think I broke my foot!"*

I hop around for a moment until I notice Patrick isn't moving. His eyes stare like glass into the night sky, blood running from his nose, down his cheek.

I kneel down and put my hand on the side of his face, turning his head towards me, looking into his eyes. The ring on my hand—Jill's ring—begins to glow. I feel my hand warm, and a few seconds later, Patrick starts to blink, trying to focus.

"Hey, are you alright?"

"No." His hand comes up and wipes at his nose. "Ow! I think he broke it."

"Lucky he didn't do more."

I look over at the man, who is moaning and trying to get up.

I get up and hobble over to the barn, go inside, and come out with a shovel.

"What are you doing here?" I yell at the intruder.

"*Gar yupel sank.*"

I raise the shovel over my head and slam the flat part down on his skull. It makes a kind of metallic thud/twang sound.

I stare at his body, breathing hard. He's not moving.

Patrick is trying to get up, eventually standing on wobbly legs. "Who is he?"

I shove my good foot under the man's shoulder, then lift and push, rolling him over. He looks kind of familiar, but I can't quite place him.

"Can you help me get him into the barn?"

Patrick nods and takes a leg. I take the other and we drag him inside. As we go over the threshold, something catches at his butt. We tug and get him unhooked, pulling him inside.

* * *

He's not dead, and finally comes around.

"Jer-ry," I say in a sing-song voice. "Wakey up. Time to answer some questions."

His head lolls around on his shoulders from the chair he's tied to.

Patrick wanders in, a bag of ice in his hands. "You know who he is?"

"It took me a while, but this is Jerome Galway, owner of

the prestigious Galway Casket Company, and also the county coroner."

"Really. The coroner. How do you know him?"

"He supplies my—he supplies *Henry* caskets."

"Yesh," Jerome says thickly. "You're hurring my bushnesh."

"His what?"

"Business. I'm guessing Jerry has been feeling the competitive pressure of the Rest EZ Casket Company, and came to snoop around."

"Yesh . . . shnoop."

"That doesn't explain this," I say, holding up a gun.

"Wha?"

"This fell out of your pants while we were dragging you in here."

His eyes go soft, like an admission of guilt.

I turn to my friend. "How you feeling?"

Patrick shrugs. "I've had worse."

"I need to ask a favor of you." I reach in my pocket and pull out the keys to the truck. "I need you to go somewhere while I reminisce with my friend Jerry."

* * *

My phone rings.

"Okay, I'm here. Looks like there's an alarm keypad."

"Alright, hold on a moment." I squat down in front of Jerome Galway. "I need the alarm code."

"Jake, please, I'm begging you." His speech has come back, unfortunately. Dude won't stop talking.

"What is the security code to your warehouse?"

"Same as the address—3790."

"You understand that if the alarm goes off, or the police show up, things will get worse for you."

"Your father will be very upset."

I smile. "I don't have a father, Jerry. That man who says he is . . . lies."

"I don't know what you mean." But his eyes says he did.

I stand, and with one hand, take the shovel by the handle and wedge the blade firmly against his crotch. "Now, what happens when he enters the code?"

"He . . . he has to hit the pound sign after entering the code."

"Patrick," I say into the phone, "the code is 3790, then hit the pound sign."

I hear beeps, then what sounds like a motor.

"The large door is opening, and I'm inside."

"Call me when you're done."

I hang up and consider my prisoner. He watches me warily, blood caked over half his face from the head wound.

"What are you going to do to me?"

I pretend to think. "I don't know yet. If I let you go, you'll only tell him."

"No, no I won't. I promise." He looks for a moment like he's going to cry, but then blinks as if he just had an idea. "If you let me go, I'll tell you."

"Tell me what?"

"You have to let me go."

I shove the blade of the shovel hard into his crotch, and he screams in a wail as if he were dying.

I wait until he gains some control of himself, though he's still moaning.

"Tell me what?"

He pants harshly for several seconds, then takes a deep breath. "Your father sent me to spy on you."

"I know that. Tell me something I don't know, or I'll turn you into a eunuch." I wiggle the shovel a little to get my point across.

"Oh God, no. I'm—*I'm bleeding!*" he squeals.

I look down and see the crotch of his pants is starting to stain with blood. Quite a lot of it.

The phone rings.

"Okay," Patrick says, *"the place is an inferno. I'm driving*

155

away before the fire department shows up."

"See you soon." I hang up. "Jerry. Tell me about him," I say, waiting. I see the blood is running out of the leg of his pants, over his shoe, onto the floor.

He rolls his eyes up at me, and there's a small smile. Kind of ghoulish. "He is a very powerful man. More powerful than you can imagine."

"Powerful enough to make you coroner?"

He sneers at me. "Coroner . . . is nothing. I'm just a speck on his wallpaper. He has . . . he can . . ."

I see he has gone completely pale.

His eyes roll back and his head falls forward.

Interlude 4

I walk into a reception area. It is quite elegant. A brass sign on the wall says WELCOME TO THE MEADOWS. The polo club and resort next door to the cemetery? Must be.

A man in a tuxedo is standing behind a counter, smiling. Everything about him is immaculate.

"Good evening, sir, welcome to the Meadows. Do you have a reservation?"

"I think so."

"Last name, please?"

"Graves," I tell him.

He checks a leather-bound book. "Coffin?" he asks.

"Collin."

He smirks and pulls out a towel and a lock with a key in it, and hands it out to me. "Mr. Henderson will escort you to the Gentleman's Area. Enjoy!"

A young man appears, dressed not unlike an old-time bell boy. He leads me to a finely polished wood door where we wait a moment until there's a buzz and the door is unlocked. He opens it and we step through.

"The lockers are at the end of the hallway," he says, then steps back out into the reception area and pulls the door closed behind him.

I look down the dimly lit hallway. There is a doorway without a door on the left, and I pause, looking in. The room is lit with dull red lights and I see a few mattresses on the floor. There's a bench and a heavyset naked man is sitting on a towel, stroking himself and smiling at me.

I turn and continue down the hall, seeing a glass door with a chrome handle. I open it, and steam billows out. I step inside, enveloped by the thick, hot, humid air. The walls are tiled and there are several men inside only wearing towels, all staring at me. I leave.

Across the hall is another glass door, and I peek in. It looks to be a sauna with wood wall and benches, and two naked men sitting on towels stare back at me. One is older with perfectly coiffed white hair, and I recognize him—Greg Hawthorne, the famous movie actor. The other man is black, muscled, and vaguely looks like rapper I've seen on TV.

What the hell is this place?

I continue past a hot tub with half a dozen men lounging in it, then find the locker room. It is empty, but I am not interested in disrobing. I'm not sure if this is just a place where men hang out, or if it's a sex club. I haven't seen any women. I'm not really interested in staying any longer, and begin to head back toward the front.

An unmarked door opens and a man comes out, smiling at me. He is forty-ish and impeccably dressed in a designer suit and shiny black shoes.

"Mr. Graves, the show is about to begin. You don't want to miss it."

He takes my elbow and leads me through the door, down a corridor to a room like a small movie theater, with rows of seats facing a curtain. He guides me to a seat in the front row, and I noticed most all the other seats are taken by males of all types wearing only towels. There's large hairy men, and old flabby men, and young muscle men with tattoos. I see the actor and the rapper sitting next to each other. There's a man I recognize as Daryl Baumer, quarterback for the Chicago Bears, and Ralphie Gibbons, a reality TV star. Jason Serrano, the teen heartthrob is a few seats away from me, and square in the middle of the front row is a man who it would be difficult not to recognize, even though he wore nothing but a towel.

The lights dim, and I take my seat. The curtains begin to part, showing a stage encased in glass. Spotlights illuminate an empty stage with a plain gray backdrop and a door in the center.

The men in the theater all hush.

The door opens, and a 50-ish woman with red hair enters. I recognize her—it's the woman with the large breasts and the reddest red hair I've ever seen. The one Jill killed in the bathtub in one of my dreams . . .

This time she's dressed in a kind of leather dominatrix outfit, with a cut out for her breasts and crotch—which shows pubic hair matching her head. She holds a whip, which she cracks dramatically a few times, only there's no sound because of the glass.

She turns and goes back through the door, returning a moment later, holding a leash. She tugs on it, and what enters surprises me.

A naked girl, 7 or 8 years old, shuffles onto the middle of the stage, hooded. The "Madame"—for lack of a better term—kneels and places a shackle around one of the girl's ankles, the other end chained to the floor.

The men in the room all gasp and I'm relieved they're as horrified as me . . . until I look around and see the smiles. Several men have their hands under their towels.

The hooded child is obviously crying, and I stand up, scanning the room for a stage door, looking for a way to get to her.

"Mr. Graves, you need to have a seat," the man in the suit says.

"I need to get up there—I need to get to her!"

"No, sir. The lottery has already been chosen and the lucky guest will appear momentarily. Please, take your seat."

I look around the room for an ally, for someone as horrified as I am - but all the men are starring at the stage.

The man in the suit pushes me down, and a handcuff is placed around my wrist secured to the chair.

"Please sit back and enjoy the show," the man says before leaving.

The Madame exits through the door on the stage, and a moment later a man steps out—naked. I recognize him as Russ Zorbo, the news anchor on Channel 6, only younger and less gray.

He approaches the young girl - whose arms are now crossed in front of her as if she's cold - takes her wrist and pulls her hand towards him. She tries to jerk away, but he holds her firmly, smiling out to the audience.

Then he removes her hood, and I see the terrified face of a child, wide, big blue eyes and lips quivering with fear.

I know immediately.

It's Jill.

Zorbo lays her down on the floor, feet towards the audience, and kneels down.

I look away, feeling horribly nauseous. I look to the man in the middle of the front row, the most powerful man in the world, who seems to be in a sexual trance, eyes locked on the perversion happening.

Even through the glass, I can hear the screams of the child, and I tug, yank and wrench at the handcuff on my wrist, hoping to somehow break free.

Then I see my father, Henry Davis, dressed in his usual tweed suit and maroon tie, walking in the second row, stopping in the middle, leaning down and whispering into the ear of the newly elected President of the United States.

The President nods, but his eyes never leave the rape taking place before him.

Chapter 18

"Sometimes I love being a teenager; sometimes I hate it. I love being carefree, yet I hate being so confused." —Unknown

July 24

I wake up shaking.

Patrick is standing over me, looking a bit horrified. He lets go of my shoulder and steps back.

"Are you okay, man?"

I'm breathing hard, sweating, eyes wide, but the images from the dream still so very real.

"I . . . I'm okay," I manage.

He looks at me, not sure.

"Worst dream ever," I tell him.

"Okay, well, you were screaming loud enough that a couple of the dead people were complaining." He offers his little smile, but his eyes are still worried.

"I'm fine." I give him a thumbs-up.

He nods, and leaves.

It's late afternoon. Time to get going anyway.

* * *

We had deposited the remains of Jerome Galway on the doorstep of Harold the Groundskeeper, just like we did the Gasoline Man. Apparently, Harold can't take a hint. No word yet from him on our first housewarming gift.

In the spare room next to my bedroom, I work on decorating. I put the curio in the corner, arranging the items meticulously. The photo, her diary, the note, other items that remind me of her. I had her coffin brought up and set on the floor—even though it never contained her remains, it is a symbol, a reminder. I cleaned it thoroughly, inside and out. The pink silk interior was beautiful, and I stare at it, thinking what she would have looked like, lying inside so calm and peaceful.

"Draw closer."

I blink and look around. No one but me. Yet I heard it like it was a voice in the room. Jill's voice.

"Collin, draw near to me . . . I have things to tell you . . ."

I'm not sure what it means. Draw near to . . . what?

"Close the door."

I consider this. No one is in the house as Patrick was at the site renovating, so I'm not sure why the door should be closed, but I do it. Then wait. It seems to take a while.

"Draw the curtains."

I do, and since they were pretty thick, the room becomes quite dark.

Then I noticed her portrait in the curio is . . . glowing slightly.

I take it out and hold it, feeling warmth coming from it.

Out of the corner of my eye, I see another glow . . . this time coming from the casket.

The pink interior radiates softly.

"Come . . ."

Hesitantly, I step a foot in the coffin.

"No . . ."

Now I'm perplexed. Am I supposed to get in or not?

"Do not soil this . . ."

Okay, I get it. I slip off my shoes and step in again.

"*No . . . Do not soil this . . .*"

Alright. So I set the framed photo down and get undressed.

I know this sounds weird, and it is, but the allure of being able to hear Jill's voice—even if it is my imagination—is pretty strong. If getting naked and laying in a coffin is what I need to do, then so be it. I've been through a lot weirder lately.

I retrieve the photo and step in, laying down. I barely fit— the bottom of my feet were up against the end, and my head just touches the top.

"*Can we have some privacy?*"

In for a penny, in for a pound. I close the lid.

* * *

Sensory deprivation has both benefits and side effects. In the high school psychology class I took, it was said to have brought both a profound peace as well as hallucinations—with a chance of psychosis. But I figure that I've been hearing voices since I was a child and frequently have vivid dreams mixed with tormenting nightmares, so I'm well versed in hallucinations and psychosis.

I don't know how long I lay there in the total darkness before the first vision comes, but it starts pleasantly enough.

Summer, a field of bright green grass under a bright blue sky. Trees around the perimeter sway in the warm breeze. Nearby is a crystal-clear stream as birds chirp, flitting from tree to tree.

I walk through the field, seemingly alone. Then, behind an outcropping of stones that are neatly stacked at least six feet high, a little girl emerges. She is naked and it only takes a moment for me to realize it's Jill. Unlike the horror show of a nightmare I'd had, she smiles at me. I look down and see my body has trans-formed. I'm seven or eight, and naked.

"Collin! You found me!"

She runs up and takes my hand, leading me towards the stream. As we approach the bank, she runs, tugging on my arm before jumping in. I follow, and we're suddenly floating in the warm water.

It's too deep to stand in, so we just lazily drift, enjoying the—

Suddenly, there's screaming.

I look off towards the bank and see ten or twelve naked children running, looks of horror on their faces.

There is a popping sound, like a firecracker, and a boy drops. Another pop, and another, and two more children go down.

I suddenly understand they've been shot.

As we float down the river, I see several men in hunting clothes with rifles pointed at the running children, firing.

One of the men turns his head and sees us. I recognize him. He says something, then the President points his weapon in our direction.

* * *

"You must know by now that everything you have experienced is real, not imagined," Jill's voice says softly in the darkness.

"No," I whisper. "It can't be real."

"But it is . . . or was. It really happened."

"That stage with the glass around it?"

"Yes, Collin."

"No, please no."

"Now you know why they had to die. Because I wasn't the only one."

I stay silent, trying to comprehend.

I've felt guilt over the two men I killed, knowing that, even though they were trying to harm me, I should have done something else. But a rage in me had taken over, something I had never felt before, something that I can't explain.

But to think Jill had done the same . . .

In some ways, I believe it, understand it. She had been horribly abused, and had taken revenge on those that hurt her. On the other hand, this was Jill, a sweet, loving young lady who had a heart the size of Texas. Or Alaska. It was hard to accept.

"Do your research . . . return later . . . I will reveal more . . ."

I open the coffin lid and climb out. Time to get to work.

* * *

I go through my phone and through the photos I took in Henry's secret storage room of body parts. I make notes of the numbers on the jars and bottles. I turn on the laptop and start searching.

09 03 1658

I type in *September 3, 1658.*

What comes up is:

Oliver Cromwell, April 25, 1599-September 3, 1658.

Never heard of him. I click a couple more links.

English soldier and statesman who led parliamentary forces in the English Civil Wars; he was lord protector of England, Scotland, and Ireland from 1653 to 1658 during the republican Commonwealth.

Still, no idea who he is. But as I read more, I discover that while his body was buried, someone decided to dig him up and put his head on a pole. When it fell off after a storm, it got passed around for almost the next 300 years, until it turned up in 1960 and was supposedly buried again—although not with its body.

And now Henry has it.

04 18 1955

I look up April 18, 1955 and discover it's the date Albert Einstein died. The jar I had seen was part of a brain, and, sure enough, according to the Internet, Einstein's brain had been removed so it could be studied to figure out why he was so smart. Different pieces of it went to different places . . . and I guess one of those places had Henry Davis' address on it.

09 30 1888

September 30, 1888 was a little more disturbing—not that having heads and brains were all that normal.

There were two notorious deaths that day: Elizabeth Stride, and Catherine Eddowes. Both were victims of Jack the Ripper. I had to read that a few times to make sure I got it right.

Jack the Ripper.

A chill goes up my spine.

Reading about Stride's death reveals that while her throat had been slashed, her body was pretty much intact. Apparently, *Jack* had been scared away before he could finish what he really wanted to do.

Later, Eddowes was slaughtered. Her body sliced open and organs removed. The coroner wrote: *"I believe the perpetrator of the act must have had considerable knowledge of the position of the organs in the abdominal cavity and the way of removing them."*

That pretty much described Henry, who apparently has Catherine Eddowes' uterus on his shelf.

* * *

I head down to the staging area to check on the boys. Things are moving along nicely, so I take Ginger out for a long ride, and contemplate what I am supposed to do. Ginger seems quite sympathetic.

I'm told I'm now a Soulmadd, and I have a tattoo on my chest to prove it. I don't know what being a Soulmadd entails yet, but it seems to be a group of people who are out to save the world, and they want me to help.

I have a magical ring that glows and it gives me magical healing powers.

I have killed two men who tried to kill me.

My fiancée (or would have been my fiancée) is dead, probably killed.

I've spent time in her coffin.

She talks to me and shows me dreams. Sometimes nightmares.

In these visions, I have seen her kill three people. I also saw her get raped as a child and watched other children get shot like animals.

My adoptive father has death trophies, including body parts from famous people through history.

He has placed a spy camera in my bedroom—and who knows where else.

I'm sure there's more I could throw on the pile, but it's a bit overwhelming.

I take Ginger back to the barn, wash and brush her. She's being quite affectionate and alternately neighs or snorts, looking at me with an all-knowing eye. I brush her mane and ask her what I should do.

She snorts.

"Should I see a psychiatrist?"

She turns her head away and makes no sound. If *she* started talking to me, I'd have to check myself in, pronto.

I feed her and slip her a few treats. She looks at me again, and it's almost like she's smiling.

Chapter 19

"Minor things can become moments of great revelation when encountered for the first time." —Margot Fonteyn

July 26

I stand in front of the coffin, a bit leery to get in. The last time wasn't quite as pleasant as I would have liked.

"This time, we'll just talk."

I sigh and step in, sit, and lie down as I close the lid.

I take some time to relax and it's not long before her voice comes to me.

"There are things you need to know."

"Oh, I agree with that."

"Only some can be revealed now. Today will be about Henry Davis."

I only nod, interested in hearing what he might be about, but also wary of what I might hear.

"Mr. Davis bought 585 acres of property in 1784."

"I'm sorry—what?"

"Yes, Mr. Davis is a lot older than you can imagine. There is a lot you might not understand, but hopefully as the story is explained, you'll begin to comprehend."

I wonder if I will ever comprehend any of this. "Okay," I whisper. "I guess it's worth a try."

A long pause. It's long enough to make me wonder if she went away, not to return.. Then, quietly, I hear the voice:

"The Chicago fire of October 8, 1871 destroyed $192 million of prime real estate and left 100,000 people homeless and 300 dead."

Part of me speculates if I'm supposed to remember this, like some kind of supernatural history test, but mainly I'm thinking this is not the same voice that was speaking—it had changed. It wasn't Jill. It sounds familiar, but I can't place it yet.

"Mr. Davis helped finance the rebuilding of Chicago since the insurance companies were not prepared for such a massive calamity, and many were driven into bankruptcy. You have been reading some of his journals. There is one about this period titled Organized Chaos 10-8-1871'. You should seek it out to understand some of what he is capable."

I knew who the voice was. "Sylvana?"

"Yes, Collin."

"How . . . I . . . I don't understand. If you're with Jill, have you . . . passed on?"

"There are other levels than the one you are currently in. I am fortunate enough to have been given the ability to pass between them—and now that Jill is within you, you will soon be able to see what is beyond what your senses tell you."

"Okay," I say, not sure what she means, but like everything else, I'm sure I'll find out.

"Mr. Davis has deep connections not just with the government of the United States, but many countries around the world, dating back farther than some history books can say. But after the Chicago fire, he was able to utilize his connections to have a stone wall built by government employees around 700 acres of property that sat next to the original 585 acres."

"Let me guess—this is where the cemetery is located."

"Not just the cemetery. Mr. Davis used state and federal

*money to build the Meadows Polo Club and Resort as well—the
property that sits next to the cemetery. He was then able to secure
arrangements that protected the land in ways that only a few gov-
ernmental properties have been afforded."*

"Like what? Military security?"

*"That, as well as a 'no fly zone', and special connections
with the FBI, the CIA and the NSA that have given it the ultimate
secrecy."*

"For what purpose? What does he do?"

"He runs his operation, of course."

I pause, wondering what that meant. A cemetery wouldn't
need a "no fly zone"—unless, of course . . .

"His business is not about burying the dead."

No reply.

"He must be pretty rich, then."

"Beyond your comprehension."

"Billions?"

A long pause. *"Beyond your comprehension."*

I am, basically, speechless.

*"There is much that Henry Davis controls, beyond money.
But wealth is at the core of his being."*

I am trying to take this all in. My adoptive father, the creepy
old guy who seemed alternately scary and basically harmless while
I was growing up, sounds a lot scarier than I knew.

"Okay. But why did he adopt me? Why me? Why take me in
at all if he spent my life ignoring me? And now, why is he trying
to kill me?"

A long pause. A very long pause. Long enough that I almost
forgot the question.

"Wealth is at the core of his being."

Now it's my turn to pause. I try to let this all filter through.

"So he adopted me for money, and is now trying to have me
killed for money."

No reply.

I wait.

No reply.

"Who were my parents?"

"You have the answer to that."

I frown. "You'll make me work for it. Okay, fair enough. Are we done here?"

I'm annoyed because these little revelations are turning everything around of what—and who—I thought I was. And I have the feeling I'm not being told everything because it's worse than what I fear.

"One more thing," Jill's voice says softly. *"Be careful, Collin."*

* * *

So, after checking on the guys and making sure all is okay—and no one is trying to kill them—I go to the barn. Ginger, it turns out, has a calming effect that helps me to think things through. She doesn't talk to me like Jill does, but she is a good listener.

I give her some treats and brush her again. She neighs happily.

So, if Sylvana is right, Henry Davis adopted me for money.

My parents died in a plane crash. Money. Plane crash. Insurance? What other reason would there be? Maybe inheritance?

This assumes Henry knew my birth parents. Maybe they played bridge together and vacationed in the Hamptons.

And now he wants me dead. Again, presumably for money. Something tells me there's a life insurance policy floating around with my name on it.

After a few minutes, I am a bit overwhelmed. I go over to the corner and sit on the ground, feeling sorry for myself. It's all seems so transitory, since my life to this point has been one big lie. I try to think of one thing that might have been truthful, but it all seems suspicious.

The truth shall set you free.

I almost laugh. The truth seems as ephemeral as the lies that paved it over.

But, it is right.

I need to know what the hell is going on.

* * *

I type *Randolph Simon Graves* into the search engine, and basically find two hits—one for a man currently living in Australia who sells some kind of homemade spray for repelling mosquitoes. The other is a link to a news article—the same one I read in the lawyer's office. It doesn't mention anyone else on the airplane.

Was my father a pilot?

And where was I when all this was going on? I suppose there are parents who leave their kids with nannies while they go traipsing around Europe—one Henry Davis comes to mind—but generally not that many. Was I left behind?

Or was I on the plane?

As much as I love Jill and am endeared to Sylvana, I really can't take the word of a couple of voices I hear while laying naked in a coffin. I need to research this, if for no other reason than to verify that what I've heard is truthful.

In the article, there's a small picture of an airplane—probably a stock photo—but it says *Click for images*. I click, and a small gallery of pictures appear, one of the fuselage of a plane in the water.

Photography by Rocky Roberts, one of the captions says.

* * *

The next morning, there's a knock on the door. I open it and see a man in a gray uniform and gray baseball-type cap holding a clipboard.

"I have a delivery for Collin Graves."

"Oh. Yeah, that's me."

I sign for it, and he heads back out to his truck where he and his partner unload four small sturdy boxes about the size a dozen donuts might come in. They're placed on a hand truck and wheeled up.

"Where would you like them?"

"Over there." I point to a corner of the living room, and the boxes are carefully placed, and the men leave.

I open the lid of the top box and just stare at it for a while.

I hear Patrick walk up beside me.

"What was all that—*holy mother of tacos!* Where did you get that?"

"That's what Jill left me in her will."

We just look at it. Finally, Patrick kneels down and picks up a gold bar.

"Wow, that's heavy."

"There's six others just like it."

He shakes his head as he admires it. "Some guys have all the luck."

"Yeah, I wish it were that easy."

* * *

We take the gold to the Five Star Storage Facility. Since I have a few months left on the rental, I might as well use it until I can figure out what to do with the seven gold bars.

On the way home, Patrick drives so I can call the newspaper—which no longer prints newspapers, only publishing its material electronically. No one seems to have heard of a photographer named Rocky Roberts until I get transferred to an editor who remembers him.

"He retired ten, twelve years ago. I think he lives in Rockfield."

Calling information didn't turn up any Rocky Roberts, but did a Rutherford Roberts.

"Hello?"

"Mr. Roberts?"

"Yes."

"Were you a photographer for the Chicago Express?"

"I was a freelancer, and they often bought my work. Why?"

"My name is Collin Graves, and I saw an article from nineteen years ago of a plane crash in the Atlantic—a couple from Chicago died in the crash."

"Atlantic? I never took any photos of the Atlantic. I do remember a crash in Lake Michigan, though."

"Okay. What can you tell me about that?"

"Well . . . yeah, I guess it would have been about twenty years ago. There was some mystery surrounding it because the weather was not a cause, and it didn't appear to collide with any other aircraft."

"What about the pilot? Did he survive?"

"As far as I know, there were just the two adult bodies found, so I would assume one of them was the pilot. Certainly couldn't have been the baby."

"I'm sorry, what?"

"The baby. A little boy was found safely belted into a baby carrier in the fuselage. I'm pretty sure he wasn't flying the plane. Why do you ask?"

* * *

I guess I shouldn't be surprised. The media had misreported the deaths of both Jill and the TV anchor Russ Zorbo, so I guess it's plausible this story was mishandled as well.

Of course, that implies someone was manipulating the stories for their own purposes. And that implies someone who had a stake in how the stories were released.

When we get home, Patrick heads into the house—"Sandwich time!" he says—and I head to the barn to pay Ginger a visit.

As I come around the corner, I see Harold the groundskeeper kneeling at one of Ginger's legs. He's got her out of her pen, tied to a post, and has some kind of hypodermic that he's aiming to stick in between her forearm and knee.

I grab the wide-mouthed shovel leaning against the wall, and rush up, swinging it over my head as I come up behind him. He turns just as I get within striking distance, and thump him square on top of the head. He topples over backwards.

Ginger neighs loudly, and her front hoof slams down on the hand that held the hypo, the crunching sound quite loud, mostly from his bones being pulverized.

Harold lets out a half-scream/half-grunt.

I stick the blade of the shovel against his throat.

"What are you doing?"

His eyes roll around unfocused, looking a bit demented.

He wouldn't answer me if he could.

I raise the shovel, and feeling a mix of extreme anger and a great surge of power, I piston my arms down as hard as I can. The blade hits him square in the throat, slices through, and the head rolls away toward a pile of hay. Blood spurts out the neck like a hose being turned on and off.

Ginger snorts her approval.

I have to think this through.

What do I do with his body?

Chapter 20

"Naturally, one does not normally discuss plans to commit murder with the intended victim." —Robert J. Sawyer

July 27

I again awake to the sound of someone knocking on the front door. I go downstairs to find the door already open and Patrick talking to a man in a suit.

"A body?" I hear Patrick say.

"Yes, out by the edge of the cemetery, near the street. Could you come with me?"

"What happened?" I ask.

"They found a body."

I frown at the police detective, doing my best acting job. "Was it a grave robbery? Did someone get dug up?"

"No sir. It appears to be the recent victim of a homicide." The man studies me. "Are you a . . . caretaker here?"

"No, I'm Jacob Davis. My father owns the cemetery."

Immediately, the detective's face softens, almost smiling. "Then I hope you can help. We need to see if you can identify the body."

"Sure," I say. "Let me get my shoes."

* * *

Patrick and I follow the detective out to the far corner of the property, near where the Meadows, the cemetery and the chain link fence along the sidewalk meet.

"A young lady out for her morning walk found him," the detective says. "You didn't happen to hear anything, did you?"

"I didn't," I say.

"Me either," Patrick adds.

Up ahead, there are several people standing around in a semi-circle, staring down towards the ground.

We approach, a couple of uniformed officers stepping aside.

"Wow," Patrick says.

"Oh geez," I say.

The headless corpse is propped up against the back of a headstone, right where I left him.

"Does, um, he look familiar?" the detective asks, sounding like he knows it's a silly question.

"Kind of looks like the body of the groundskeeper," Patrick says.

"Yeah, it does."

"The groundskeeper? Would you have a name?"

"Harold Jopp. His place is over there." I point towards the glorified shack off in the distance.

"When was the last time you saw him?"

I pretend to think. "Yesterday morning. I saw him out my bedroom window getting into his truck. He was preparing one of the graves for a service."

He writes down a note in a small booklet. "Would you know of any reason why someone would want to do this to him?"

"Well," Patrick says, "he wasn't a very nice guy. I wouldn't be surprised if someone had . . . an issue with him."

The detective looks at me, expecting my two cents.

"Yeah," I add. "He was a prick. Excuse my language."

The man nods. "I hate to ask this, but did you have any run-ins with him?"

We both shake our heads.

"He would just scowl at me and spit," I say.

"He'd spit at you?"

"Not at me, just kind of . . . in my general direction."

"Yeah, he did that to me once," Patrick adds. "I spit back, and he really got mad. Turned all red and called me a—a nasty name."

"Did you react? Call him something back?"

"No. Look at the size of him. Dude is . . . was scary big."

The detective thinks about this, then nods. "Just to dot the I's . . . did either of you happen to see his head?"

We both shake ours.

"No, we would have called you," I say.

"We're going to have to search the property, if that's okay."

"Sure."

"We'll have the team go through the cemetery. I'll be checking out your place after I go through Mr. Jopp's."

"No problem. I'll leave the door unlocked."

He smiles and nods.

* * *

Patrick and I walk back, silent. I think he knows, but also knows better than to say anything.

I head upstairs and get in the shower, then I head to Burkfelt Jewelers.

The door is unlocked, but the place looks empty.

"Mr. Burkfelt! It's Jacob!"

I walk up to the counter and peer at the jewelry in the glass case. Quite a collection. I'd like to think I have a good eye, but I probably don't.

"Mr. Burkfelt!"

I wander from case to case, and finally, he comes out from the back.

"Hello," he says pleasantly. "How are you doing today, Jacob?"

"Good, and you?" I decide not to mention recently killing a man.

There's a stack of papers on one of the cases where I'm standing and as he collects them off the glass, one of them slips out and onto the floor.

I scoop it up and hand it over, noticing it's a flight itinerary. The one word that caught my eye was: *Nicaragua*.

"So, how can I help you today?"

I pause, debating whether I should say anything. I decide to wait.

"Well, I wanted to let you know that I have the money, and I'd like to proceed with our arrangement."

"Well, I've been thinking . . ."

My first thought is he has changed his mind about selling me his business, but his eyes twinkle, which might mean something else.

". . . In order for you to succeed, you're going to have to learn."

"Yes, I realize that. I was thinking that maybe there's a class I could take somewhere?"

He smiles. "You may know that I used to be a professor."

"No, I didn't."

"So, I have a little skill in teaching."

"That would be great. Were you an instructor for . . . what would it be? Geology?"

"Close. Gemology, but, no, that came later. No, I taught advanced world history and theology at the university."

"Theology? Really? That must have been interesting—but other than being a priest, I'm not sure what kind of career a student could have out of that."

"Actually, it's more practical than you think. Everything you do or say is based on your personal theology. Your morals, principles, decisions—good or bad—are theological."

"I always thought it had to do with God."

"It does, in many respects. But even if one doesn't believe in God, that's a theology."

I decide to take a chance. "I saw on that paper that you're going to Nicaragua."

"No, not going," he said, looking away. "I'll be staying here."

"I just wondered if that was something . . . theological."

"No, nothing like that. Now as far as gemology, I've had twenty years of experience, and I'll be glad to teach you."

"Twenty years? You could probably teach me in about twenty minutes," I say, smirking.

"I'm sure you're a fast learner," he says, smiling in return.

"Now, about the business, we never really talked money."

"How much do you have?"

"More than enough. I just have to figure out how to sell a bar of gold."

His fuzzy eyebrows arch upward. "Excuse me?"

"I have a bar of gold—well, a few, actually."

"An ingot?"

"I don't know. It's as big as my forearm."

Mr. Burkfelt's eyes twinkle again. "I think we can work something out."

* * *

He shows me the equipment in the back, including the Quintus Diamond-View machine he recently purchased that makes diamonds. There was also the more intricate hand tools to shape and create jewelry. Needless to say, I find it all quite fascinating.

"I'll tell you what," Mr. Burkfelt says. "The Quintus set me back . . . well, a good amount. If you are willing to reimburse me for that, I would be happy to make you a partner, teach you the ropes, and pass the business along to you once you feel ready."

"That sounds like a great arrangement," I say, sticking out my hand to shake.

After we seal the deal, he adds: "If you bring that gold bar to me, I can cash it in for you, and you can pay me from that."

"Sounds perfect," I say. "Would you have a bag?"

He frowns. "A bag?"

"Something I can put the bar in. I don't just want to carry it around."

"Ah, yes. Let me see . . . I think I have something that might just do the trick."

* * *

I return an hour later with the bar tucked neatly away at the bottom of the leather book carrying case—which looked like an expensive piece of property all by itself.

I give him the bag with the bar and he tells me to return in a couple of days.

I go home, feeling better than I had in days.

When I pull up, there's an unmarked police sedan parked out front, so I know they're probably searching the house. Fine with me. They won't find ol' Harold's head in there. Chances are, they won't find it at all.

I enter the living room, and Patrick is watching TV.

"Hey."

"Hey."

"How long have they been here?"

"About an hour. They asked why you have a coffin in the spare bedroom."

"Do they understand we live on a cemetery?"

"They asked if you sleep in it."

I smile. "They probably think I'm Eddie Munster."

Patrick squints at me. "Who?"

"Nevermind."

I hear shuffling from upstairs, so I take a seat.

"The good news is, I'm going into business with Mr. Burkfelt, and I was thinking . . ."

"Uh oh."

"How would you like to go into the jewelry business?"

"You mean *not* refurbishing caskets?"

"How about creating little works of art?"

"Do I get to keep them?"

There's the sound of shoes on the stairs, and a moment later, the detectives appear.

"We want to thank you for your time, Mr. Davis. Have a good rest of the day."

"Thanks, you too," I say as they go out the door.

We listen to them drive away.

"There's something I've got to show you," Patrick says.

"Uh oh."

* * *

The moment we walk into the staging area, my brain is inundated with sounds . . . those horrible screams of the children. It hits me so hard, I literally stop in my tracks and close my eyes.

I think of the "dream" I had of floating in the stream while naked children were being shot on the shore. The screams are similar.

"You okay?" Patrick asks.

"Yeah, migraine," I say as I rub my temples.

It begins to slowly subside.

He points to a stack of three caskets.

"We were pulling one off the bottom, and it was filled with urns."

"Ashes?"

He nods. "And then we pulled another, and it was full. And a third. I don't know how many more we'll find."

As the screams in my head turn to whispers and whimpering, I realize I don't know either, but I'm afraid it's going to be a lot more than I want to consider.

Chapter 21

"Catalogues of Sin" —Leinad Platz

July 29

I originally thought I was going crazy, but was able to internalize it. It got worse, in some ways, when I met Jill—not that she was to blame, but I figured my heightened emotions heightened my feelings of insanity. Could be the meaning of "Crazy in love."

Deep down, I didn't think I was crazy. I just couldn't rule it out. I may not have been normal, but I probably wasn't losing my mind.

Once Jill died, what I thought was heightened went through the roof. The vivid dreams were now lurid and incredibly intense. If I had wondered whether the passing of Jill had something to do with my seemingly unstable emotional and mental state, it then shifted to the Soulmadds—which, I was told, I was one. So I thought they were the reason for the changes I was going through. First meeting Jill, then her death, then the Soulmadds.

Now I understand my adoptive father, Henry Davis, is at the center of it all. Whatever it is.

I think back to the time at the restaurant when Jill asked me about growing up, and I realize I spent the time talking mainly about Henry. I think of her journal entry which mentioned Harold Jopp and another man watching her home—Henry? I now no longer wonder if he had something to do with her death. I'm sure of it. Just no way to prove it.

Yet.

And if what I was told in the casket was true—even if I was dreaming, hallucinating—then he's not only at the center of what's going on with me, but has been involved in a lot more scary stuff.

Faith is certainty in what we hope for and confidence about what we do not see.

Sylvana told me that—I hope I got it right. While she was talking about believing in God, I also apply it to what's going through my mind now when it comes to Henry Davis.

I have faith he is evil. I don't need to prove it . . . but I do want to know more.

I have to know what I'm dealing with.

I stand at the gravesite of Harold Jopp, listening to the priest offering his soul to God, and I wonder what God will do with it. Which leads me to wonder what God will do with me since I put Harold there.

The only other person in attendance is Henry Davis, standing two seats away, being very quiet.

We have not spoken in months, and do not speak now. Until the service is over.

He turns to me, looking younger than I remember.

"I need to catch a flight," he says when the priest has finished and wandered away. "Could you please see this is . . . completed?"

I nod. "Sure."

He considers me for several moments, looks like he wants to say something, then puts his head down and walks off towards the house.

I begin to put things away—folding the chairs, dismantling the canopy, before lowering the casket into the ground. I get the backhoe, and begin to fill in the grave.

I see the black car pull up, and Henry exits the house, opening the rear door. Before getting in, he pauses to look my way. One could say ours eyes locked, except we were a hundred yards apart. Then he gets in the car, and it drives away.

I finish burying the man I killed. Then I go home and take a nap.

* * *

With Henry out of town, and Harold not skulking around, I have the place to myself. It's after 10, and all is quiet. I really don't have to sneak into the house, but I do anyway.

I go into the "secret" office, not really sure what I'm looking for, but hoping I find it. I go through the drawers, and find some ledgers. Numbers and accounting are not really my forte, but I go through one of the books labeled "INSURANCE POLICIES" and see scores of listings. The first entry is 1923.

I begin to read down the names, people I don't know and never heard of, wondering what this is about.

Chandra Cloy, Marcia Porter, Donna McIlry, Jane Reese, Seinna Talbot, Renee Von Kamen, Jeanne Morse, Samantha Cribbs, Tabitha Doozle, Anne Kendrick, Susan Donnell . . .

I think of the dozens of urns filled with ashes. The empty caskets. And now, insurance policies meticulously detailed. I recall the "conversation" I had, supposedly with Jill and/or Sylvana while lying in Jill's coffin.

"He must be pretty rich, then," I had said.

"Beyond your comprehension."

So, he is cremating people, not burying them—which I don't understand—and collecting life insurance policies on them? Could that be possible?

Doesn't make sense.

I look over the names again, and realize . . . *they are all women.*

I check the dates. Some are a few years apart, others just months.

A quick tally of the amounts—just running the numbers

through my head as I go down the columns—is in the hundreds of millions.

I put the ledger back. I see others labeled "FIRE" and "PROPERTY" and "CASUALTY".

At the very back, I sense the drawer is deeper than the back of it implies. As if there's another compartment.

I pull all the ledgers out—stacking them carefully so I don't mix up the order—and feel a small hole at the back of the drawer just big enough for my pinky. I stick it in and pull, and it gives quickly, revealing a stack of more ledgers.

Once I pull them out, though, I see that some are ledgers, others are scrapbooks. Each is as meticulous as the ledgers.

I open one and see a marriage certificate. *Groom: Henry Davis. Bride: Mathilda Cummings. Date: 1912.*

On the next page is a black and white photo that is remarkably clear and well-preserved. The woman is pretty and smiling softly, but not anyone I recognize; the man pictured is undoubtedly Henry Davis. He looks pretty much as he does today, only with a mustache and old-timey clothes.

I turn the page and see a birth certificate. *Melba Davis. DOB: May 4, 1913.*

Turning the page, there is a death certificate. *Melba Davis. DOB: May 4, 1913. DOD: October 30, 1913.*

The next page, another death certificate: *Mathilda Davis. DOB: February 13, 1891. DOD: March 9, 1914.*

So the baby died at just under six months old, the mother, five months later. I flip through the scrapbook, and see page after page of marriage, birth and death certificates. I stopped counting after 25. All the wives, dead. All the children, dead. And all of the children were female.

And all the photos showed a man who looked exactly like Henry Davis.

I look up at the painting on the wall, the one labeled *Lord Harod Dunraven, 1875.*

Spitting image.

I still don't understand. He couldn't really be that old. Could he?

In another book, more wives, and deaths . . . but the birth certificates are all of male children. And there are no death certificates for the kids.

The last page is a marriage certificate for Henry Davis and Linda Gratano, followed by her death certificate four years after I was born. Her death is listed as *food poisoning*. My adoption paperwork is next, and it appears he paid quite a lot to have me become his son—$120,000. I'm not sure I should be impressed or disgusted.

Another book is labeled ORPHANS. That gives me a chill, but I open it and see pages and pages of names and dates and the names of the orphanages. Each page must list forty names, and there are over 200 pages. I flip to the back and see it's almost full, the most recent entry dated three years ago. I go back a few pages, wondering if I'm listed. Sure enough, there I am, *Collin Jacob Graves,* my birthdate, and an orphanage named *Bridgeworth*.

What stops me cold, though, is another name. Not an unusual name. Probably quite popular, as names go.

Patrick Aaron Williams.

The orphanage is also listed as *Bridgeworth*.

Could it be . . . ?

Patrick told me he lived with his father, a drug user, and his mother was a waitress who lived elsewhere. Did he make up that story? Or was he lied to? Or is the *Patrick Aaron Williams* listed there someone entirely different? Since the date of birth fits Patrick's time frame—I don't remember which day his birthday is—I have to assume they are one and the same.

I open another scrapbook and see a list of what seems like random male names, dates, and a third column of a mixture of male and female names. The last column is a series of numbers— ranging from 50,000 to 1.5. I'm guessing it's a dollar amount. The first column of male names is labeled *Beneficiary*; the second, *DOB*; and the third, *Insured*. The last column is unlabeled. I puzzle over it for a few minutes before I realize it must be a ledger of life insurance claims. Hundreds, and hundreds.

This is, apparently, in addition to the other book filled with claims.

Is this a list of beneficiary pseudonyms that Henry used over the years to collect on claims of . . . who?

One of the names catches my eye. *Tabitha Doozle*. A memorable name. I saw it in one of the other books. But which one and where?

I go back over them, trying to find the needle in the haystack. It's like the puzzle where you uncover the picture of an object and then need to remember where you uncovered it before to match it up. It takes several minutes, but I find it.

Two plus two is four, and a "Maurice Precius" was the beneficiary on a life insurance policy for Tabitha Doozle.

I pull out some other books, finding one marked *DC*. Opening it, I see they're death certificates . . . DC. I run through the pages, and about a third of the way through, I find the one for Tabitha Doozle.

I close it and put it on the stack, when another catches my eye.

SPOUSES

Below it:

CHILDREN

It never seems to end.

* * *

I go back home, trying to absorb. The *SPOUSES* and *CHILDREN* books looked, on the surface, to be more of the same. But I saw the *CHILDREN* book had a column listed *Agency*. More adopted children? He apparently had dozens of "natural" children, and then adopted dozens and dozens more—all of whom died?

Linda, who I grew up believing was my mother, was just an

insurance payout. And maybe I was meant to be as well.

But I wasn't. Why?

The only thing I can figure is Sylvana became my nanny literally the day after Linda passed. Did she protect me from Henry's plan?

I wonder what the dollar amount is on the life insurance policy that has my name on it.

* * *

"I had my first lesson today," Patrick says when I show up at the staging area.

"How'd it go?"

"It was pretty awesome. I took an urn of ashes, and Mr. Burkfelt showed me how to operate the machine. It takes a while, with all the heat and pressure, it's an interesting process."

"How did the diamond turn out?"

"Not good. It was a first one, so it was kind of lumpy, and then broke, but they'll get better. Where were you?"

"First, I buried Harold. Then I went through Henry's office and found more disturbing documents."

"Everything he has is disturbing."

I fill him in, but I don't yet mention the ORPHANAGE book.

"So, he cashed in on all those policies?"

"Looks like it." I pause. "Are you an Aquarius?"

He blinks at me, confused. "I guess, if I believed in that crap."

"January thirty-first?"

He looks even more confused. "Yeah. Why?"

"Your middle name is Aaron?"

The confusion turns to a look of anger. "What are you getting at?"

I realize I may be scaring him after talking about all the names I found in the books and ledgers. "You said your dad was a dealer/user and your mom was a waitress."

"Yeah. So?"

"There's more to the story, isn't there?"

He is fuming. Not mad enough to hit me or anything, but pretty pissed off. He's breathing hard and trying to keep it under control.

"I was in an orphanage," I tell him. "I think you were too."

"There's a lot of shit that happened that I don't want to go over," he says, eyes narrow and angry. "I don't believe living life in the fucking rearview mirror, and you shouldn't either."

And with that, he turns and storms away.

I stand there, feeling puzzled and awful. I didn't mean to hit that nerve. I didn't even know that nerve was there.

I'm such a stupid putz.

Chapter 22

"I am intrigued by inanimate objects. They're a piece of history, someone's statement and idea of life." —Mike Mills

July 30

Knowing Patrick needed some space, I hit the road the next morning to do some selling. I spent the three hours driving to Indianapolis thinking about what to do about Henry. If I should, or could do anything about him. I just had to wonder what he might be up to.

I figure it's like a game of chess, trying to play out the next three-to-five moves. Although his hands are clean, there was little doubt that Spencer Crais—the man trying to douse the staging area with gasoline—and Jerome Galway—the casket competitor/ county coroner—were sent to kill me, and sent by Henry by way of Harold Jopp, the groundskeeper. I would have to think any future attempt will be more sophisticated. Maybe something that will look like an accident? Or hiring a hitman perhaps? Chicago is not known as one of the country's safest cities, so a staged drive-by shooting or a home-invasion robbery gone bad?

I had to consider it could be more subtle. Poisoning comes to mind. Linda Davis, who I once thought was my mother, had supposedly succumbed to it. Could be a car accident. A hit-and-run. Or, like Jill, from some mysterious and non-existent ailment that, for some reason, no one would question.

Whatever it might be, it could take some time before another effort was made since I would guess Henry knows I was onto him, or at least suspects it.

* * *

The three stops I made were all productive. The sample casket I had in the back of the pickup helped seal the deals since anyone could offer low prices on non-existent products, but for the buyers to touch and feel and examine the item went a long way.

Two of the three ordered on the spot, while the third requested to try some on consignment—something I wasn't interested in doing, but I told him I would think about it. I could tell by the way he eyed my not-so-new truck that he probably considered I may not be on the up-and-up . . . although I doubt there are few people roaming around the country trying to sell hot caskets on the black market. Maybe I should invest in a new truck.

I knew when I got back home, I'd have to look into renting a warehouse, or maybe a storefront so I didn't look so much like a fly-by-night.

I checked into a reasonable hotel and after grabbing dinner, settled in for the night. I had brought Jill's framed photo and her diary, finding some peace and comfort in the words, even though I'd read them more than once.

Her voice, lately, has been quiet, and I miss it. I know, I know, I shouldn't get so attached to something that might not be real. But to me . . . well, it is welcome.

I eventually fall into a serene sleep—lights on, diary fallen off to the side—as I experience peaceful dreams of green fields and mountain air. There are no men with rifles, no screaming children, just me and Jill.

But ultimately, it changes.

A dark room . . . dank . . . what little light there is comes from an iron grate in the ceiling. On either side are hooks, and attached to them are chains. The other end are attached to a man's wrists. He is suspended mid-air, naked and, apparently, unconscious. His ankles are attached to another pair of chains anchored to the stone floor.

* * *

My cell phone bleats, waking me. I grab at it and see the time on the display—3:32 AM.

"Hello?"

"You've gotta see this!"

"See what?"

"It's a—no, you've just gotta see it."

"Patrick, the last time you said that—" I cut myself off, not wanting to try to explain hearing children screaming in my head. "The last time, you could have just told me on the phone. I'm three hours away. What is it?"

"If I told you, you'd say, 'Well, that's stupid.' But seeing is believing."

That I understand since many of my experiences over the last few months have been impossible to explain without sounding stupid . . . or insane.

"Okay, I'll leave in a little bit." I pause, not sure if I should bring up our last conversation. Instead, I only allude to it. "Are you okay?"

"Yeah, I'm fine." And he leaves it at that.

* * *

I pull in just before 8 AM and head straight for the staging area, which is empty save for the coffins in the midst of refurbishing. Since cell phones don't work in the tunnels, I grab one of the radios on the off-chance he was in one of the passages and not in the house sleeping.

"Are you still up?" I say into the walkie-talkie, then wait.

"Yeah, I'm down at the end of K-2. Bring a flashlight, we haven't gotten all the lights strung up yet."

"Okay." I know I'm supposed to say *Roger* or *Over-and-out* or something, but I was too self-conscious.

I get a mag-lite and do my best to find the K tunnel, which, if logic serves me correctly, would then apparently split into two branches—hence the K-2.

It was quite a walk, and once the meager lighting ended and I continue with just the flashlight beam pointing the way, I realize how eerie it would be to get lost down here.

I pass "I" that goes off to the left, and "J" which forks off to the right before I come across "K" on the left. Not far down, as logic predicted, it divided. I eventually see a faint glow ahead— probably an electric lantern or Patrick's flashlight. The tunnel curves gently to the right, and opens up to a kind of wide empty space where I find Patrick at the top of a ladder examining the top of tunnel's side.

"Whatcha doing?"

"Oh, hey," he says, coming down. "We ran into this dead-end." He jumps off and then taps the concrete. "It's some kind of impenetrable wall."

"What do you mean 'impenetrable'?"

He points off to the far side where some power tools, including a jackhammer, lay on the ground. "Well, first I tried to score it with the circular saw."

"Score?"

"Basically cut a kind of pattern in the surface where you want to jackhammer the concrete. I mean, I used a high-grade diamond-tipped saw blade, and nothing. The only mark it left was on the blade. So, I tried the jackhammer—I mean, really tried to brute-force the thing—and take a look for yourself."

I slide my hand over the surface, thinking it just looked like any other concrete wall. It feels like it. But there are no marks, no cracks, just a smooth face.

"What do you think it is?"

"No idea. Not concrete—at least not the usual stuff. It doesn't feel like metal, but I guess it could be some material I've never seen or heard of before."

I look up and point my flashlight at the ceiling. "This whole area is like this?"

"Just this wall, as far as I can tell."

"What is this under? What's above ground?"

"The best I can figure is we are right up against the property line of The Meadows."

I slide my hand over the wall, thinking. "Who are they keeping out? I mean, all the way down here, it's only dead people—or mainly ashes."

"Maybe it's not who they're keeping out."

I look at him, surprised. "But it's a polo club." Then I think of the "dream" of the "gentleman's area" and the "Madame" placing a shackle around one of Jill's ankles.

He nods. "That's what they say. From what I can tell, it's mainly a place to eat and drink. An awful big property for that. And what is that other building for?"

"It's . . ." I was going to say *the Theater*. But it's not. At least not if my dream/nightmare was correct. The "Theater"—where I "saw" Jill raped by a TV anchorman—is off to the side of the restaurant. The building he's referring to is on the far side of the property. "I guess it's the offices."

"Without windows?"

"How did you see it?"

He pauses, almost like he doesn't want to tell me.

"Last night, while you were wherever you were, I took a break, went to the house and thought I heard something upstairs. I went up there, keeping the lights out, but didn't find anything. I stood at that window up there at the end of the hall, just looking out. You can just make out the top of the building. I saw a guy up there—although I wasn't sure. It's kind of far away, it was dark, and the guy was all in black. It looked like he was carrying a rifle, like he was a guard or something. So, this morning, once the sun came up, I went over and scaled the wall."

I smile and shake my head. "You can't scale that—it's ten feet high and flat as a board."

He smirks. "Okay, so I took dumbass's truck and used its roof for a little help. Anyway, I got a look around."

"You jumped down there? How did you get back up?"

"No, I just scoped it out from the top of the wall. They have a lot of cameras."

I shake my head. "And for every one you see, there's probably three you don't. I'm sure they've got you on video."

Patrick shrugs. "I'm photogenic."

I frown. I doubt anything good would come out of it.

"I've been wondering . . ." Patrick says.

I wait for several seconds. "What?"

"I wonder if the wall above ground is the same material."

I nod my head. "I never thought to check, but I wouldn't be surprised if it is."

"It's like a fortress."

I wouldn't disagree.

"Aren't you curious about what's in there?"

"Sure," I say. "But if there are guys on the roof carrying guns, I don't see the point."

His face becomes serious, then he nods slowly. "Yeah, I guess you're right . . . but it sure is tempting."

I smile. "You might be good at picking locks, but I think getting into a secured, fortified building might be a different story. And getting out might be harder."

Again, he nods, but the slight grin says he isn't convinced about that.

Interlude 5

I open one of the leather-bound journals and turn to a page dated almost 50 years ago.

Finally, he is born. The child was nearly a week late, but he appears perfect in every way. The plan went off without a hitch. She will soon be disposable.

The man—surname Dieter, his first name escapes me—was a missionary with his wife in Kenya, and died in a traffic incident. It wasn't too difficult to arrange since they all drive like idiots over there. But it wasn't him I was interested in.

She had a heritage of pure blood—clean, without an alternate race in her ancestry to spoil it.

After the funeral, the distraught wife was given a sedative by a concerned physician. She went out like a light. The doctor then performed the insemination. When Greta later discovered she was pregnant, she naturally concluded it was a product of her late husband.

But the child is mine, as I provided the seed.

I have already planned the boy's days, from now until his grand ascension. I can hardly wait.

5 years later:
She has been dispatched. It took a little longer than I

anticipated. The cancer introduced into her system either wasn't as strong as the scientists estimated, or she hung on out of desperate love for her son.

My son.

He was there when she breathed her last, and though there were tears, he was brave.

5 years after that:

He is brilliant. He has been taught well, but he picks it up so quickly and adapts seamlessly. At the stealth school in Germany, the way he handles the other children is skillful, able to get them to do what he wants without them seemingly realizing how they are manipulated. He even has the instructors wrapped around his finger—though I have had to ask the coaches to assist him in paring it back somewhat. We do not need more attention drawn to him than there already is.

His past has been scrubbed clean, and he has taken to his new name like a bird to the air. He was fed the story that although the woman he believed to be his mother was a good and kind woman, he was actually kidnapped from the hospital when he was an infant.

I think he is ready for ideology training. I have brought in and begun consulting with one of Dymortis' theologians on the best course of action. He is working on a plan based on the boy's testing. We will need to depart for Buenos Aires soon. The immersion into that culture will be useful, the consultant says.

Five years later:

His fifteenth birthday, and he's already class president. His charm is magical, his personality addictive, his looks stunning. I have created well. That doesn't mean he is not without his weaknesses. His carnal predilections are evident. I have already had to pay off families of girls who he has tarnished. But even then his charisma has kept the worst of his exploits from damaging his reputation. I must work at having his training be better so he has the capabilities to plan and conceal his indiscretions before they transpire. In his future, planning will be not only key, but crucial.

Three years later:
His graduation was glorious. Valedictorian. A speech that was inspiring, humble and humorous. A standing ovation. Universities are falling all over themselves to have him attend. Harvard? Princeton? Yale? Whichever he prefers, as long as it is one of those.

Six years later:
Top of his class, both a law and business degree. Magna cum laude. *He will take the offer from Grupnik, Valle & Tighe, the top New York law firm. He'll need to cut his teeth there before he can test the waters for public office. Build a group of connections, learn the ropes, get a feel for the landscape. He may have traversed high school and college with effortless aplomb, but law and politics is cutthroat, unlike anything he has experienced up to this point. There can be no missteps. I have arranged a system to take care of his voracious sexual needs. There was a reporter from one of those independent hippy "newspapers" sniffing around some story that had apparently surfaced, but I had him dispatched before any story could be written, much less published.*

I need to keep a close eye on that young man. His penis will ruin him if he is not careful. Especially for his penchant for young boys and girls.

Ten years later:
Senator. US Senator MacNeill Quinn. The voting was close, but he pulled it out.

I set the journal down, surprised, but not exactly shocked.

MacNeill Quinn. Who would have known? Apparently, Henry did.

I pick up the photo album, chock full of pictures from the days when cameras still used film. Pictures of MacNeill Quinn clothed. Pictures of him naked. Pictures of him engaged in sexual acts with children who look to be five to ten years old.

I want to vomit. I flip through the pages and see hundreds more.

I close it and thought burning it would be the only decent thing to do. I don't care if Henry Davis realizes it's missing and thinks I had something to do with it. It's . . . it's . . .

Evidence.

That was when I realize I can't burn it. And I can't return it.

Henry Davis had a blackmail book against his own son, MacNeill Quinn.

The former Senator MacNeill Quinn.

The current President of the United States, MacNeill Quinn.

And now I have it.

And I know just where to hide it.

Chapter 23

"In the spider-web of facts, many a truth is strangled." —*Paul Eldridge*

In the dream, I am one of eight men, dressed in all black, running down a nondescript corridor.

"Regulator Team Lead Hawthorne," the man in front of me says into a radio. An earpiece directs the sound into my head. "Approaching Exit 12."

"Subject is twelve meters from building. Appears unarmed," a voice on the radio says in my ear. "Approach with caution."

We reach the end, my assault rifle pointed at the ground.

"Mark five . . . four . . . three . . . two . . . one," Hawthorne says, hand on the door before pushing it open. We all burst into the night air, weapons leveled at a male, shaved head, black t-shirt, jeans.

"Halt!" Hawthorne barks and the male immediately raises his hands. "Face down on the ground, now!"

The male complies, dropping to his knees, then laying on the neatly trimmed grass, arms out as if he had done this before as we rush towards him, about 50 feet away.

Two of the men descend upon the male, one at his legs, the other pulling his arms behind his back, snapping on handcuffs as the rest of us point our guns at him.

Then he is jerked up to his feet and pushed towards the door we had just come from.

The intruder is marched down the corridor to an elevator. The doors open and four of us step in with the prisoner while the others continue down the corridor and out of sight.

We descend four floors below ground, exiting and turning right. An unmarked door is opened by Hawthorne, and we lead the male into the mostly empty room. There is a white plastic table that looks like it belongs on a cheap patio, and a single white plastic chair.

The male is placed in the middle of the room.

"Proceed," Hawthorne says, and one of the men props his rifle against the wall, pulls a long knife from a holster strapped to his thigh. He quickly shears the black t-shirt off the male, revealing tattoos but no weapons.

The male's shoes and socks are removed, followed by the jeans and boxers.

The handcuffs are removed.

"Raise your arms," Hawthorne says, and the male complies. The handcuffs are put back on, bracketing the arms at the wrists.

A thick chain hanging from the ceiling is placed between the male's arms, then pulled up and secured by a padlock. The naked male is effectively chained to the ceiling.

The male stares at me for a moment.

"I should have listened to you," he says before we exit, the lights extinguished, the door slammed closed and locked.

* * *

September 26

I awake to a chilly afternoon. Fall has set in early. I head downstairs to find Patrick on the couch watching the news.

"Hey," he says.

"Hey."

"I was just watching a report that the Congress passed a bill outlawing Christmas trees."

"What?"

"It only applies to fresh trees. They say it's an environmental issue and any violators will be fined up to a thousand dollars and spend up to two years in jail."

"That sounds bizarre."

"Well, the President says he'll sign it. He looked and sounded serious."

I stare at the TV. The anchor is talking with an analyst.

"Will banning Christmas trees really help the environment?"

"Well, there are approximately 350 million trees being grown currently in the U.S., and more than 30 million sold each year. It has a huge impact on the environment."

"The President said in his remarks that this is one step we can take to help curb global warming. Aren't there more proactive things we could be doing instead of banning holiday tree sales?"

"It's something. The National Oceanic and Atmospheric Administration predicts that this winter will be the coldest in history, breaking records dating back more than 200 years. The current rise in gas prices will also help curtail automotive usage."

"Let's talk about this for a minute. The national average for a gallon of gasoline stands at $8.63—an increase of more than fifty cents since last week. Analysts are predicting prices to hit $20 a gallon by year-end, and some are suggesting this is being done through government manipulation, forcing motorists to drive less, improving CO_2 emissions. Is there any truth to this?"

"This government has been very proactive in championing environmental issues, but it would be a little farfetched to believe leaders are able to convince oil companies to be cohorts in what would effectively be an extortion plan."

"But the oil companies, with higher prices, would make more in profits."

"I would suspect it's a wash in the sense that consumption

is way down, offsetting any potential profits from higher prices."

"This sounds insane," Patrick says. "I can believe the government might raise gas prices to reduce use, just like they did with cigarettes, thinking that if they raise prices, then fewer people would smoke."

"It worked didn't it?"

"There were times I smoked less, especially when it hit twelve bucks a pack. But now that we've made some dough, it doesn't seem as bad."

"I can understand gas, or cigarettes—but Christmas trees? That just seems silly."

Patrick is quiet for a few moments. "Well, I guess I never understood the whole Christmas tree thing anyway. I mean, they were there growing up, but I didn't know why we brought a tree inside, then put presents under it." He pauses again. "Of course, some years there wasn't enough money for presents, much less a tree."

"Yeah, that must have been rough."

"I bet you had really fancy trees."

"Nope," I say. "Henry didn't believe in celebrating either Christmas or Easter."

Patrick is silent for a while, then asks in a somewhat shy voice: "What is the real meaning of Christmas?"

"It the celebration of the birth of Jesus Christ."

"I know that, but what's with the trees and ornaments and presents? It doesn't sound like it has much to do with Jesus."

I smile. "Yeah, I guess it seems that way, but it's all meant as a time to teach the children."

"Teach the children?"

"Look at it this way: They are symbols. The pure color of the fir tree remains green all year round, depicting the everlasting hope of mankind, the needles point heavenward, making it a symbol of man's thoughts turning towards Heaven."

"I guess that makes sense, but it doesn't seem obvious."

"Yeah, it does kinda get lost, doesn't it?"

"What about ornaments, candles and wreaths?"

"The ornaments represent the star that was the heavenly sign of promises long ago. God promised a savior for the world, and the star was the sign of fulfillment of His promise. Then, the candle symbolizes that Christ is the Light of the World, and it is to remind us that He displaced the darkness. The wreath it symbolizes the real nature of love, a real love that never ceases."

"And Santa Clause? What does he mean?"

"He symbolizes the generosity and good will we feel during the holidays."

"And that stuff about 'He sees you when you're sleeping, he knows when you're awake, he's knows when you've been bad or good, so be good for goodness sake'?"

"It does sound like an alternate Jesus, doesn't it? But he's just something, I think, that makes it easy for kids to understand."

"So what about all the other stuff—like holly and candy canes and giving each other presents? It all seems kind of random."

I nod. "The holly leaf represents the crown of thorns worn by Jesus. The red holly berries represent the blood He shed. A candy cane represents the shepherd's staff. The crook on the staff helps to bring back strayed sheep to the flock. The candy cane is the symbol that we are our brother's keeper. And presents represent the way God loved the world by giving His son, and that we should share that love with others.

"My favorite is the Angels—the ones who heralded in the glorious news of the Savior's birth. The Angels sang glory to God in the Highest, peace and good will towards men. And the bells symbolize guidance and return. The lost sheep are found by the sound of the bell."

"It sounds like a lot of the meanings got lost in all the traditions."

"That's why it's so important to not focus on the symbols, but be reminded of the truth behind them. Like teaching the children the true meaning of Christmas and not to put men in the center."

I pause and close my eyes.

"For I am but a humble servant of the One that is, and I bow down to worship Him, our Lord, our God."

When I open my eyes, Patrick has the innocent look of a child, then looks away, seemingly embarrassed.

"I'm sorry," I say. "I didn't mean to make you uncomfortable."

"No, you didn't. It's just . . ." Then he shakes his head.

"What?"

"You sound like you have something special."

I nod, understanding. "It's special, but not unique to me. Anyone can have it, if they choose."

Another pause. "So if you never celebrated Christmas, how do you know so much about it?"

"Sylvana. She told me all the stories and explained them. And she always reminded me to pay attention and stay true."

Patrick frowns. "Stay true to what?" But the moment he said it, it was like a light came on in his eyes. "To God?"

"Yes. To God."

"So if I pledge my life to God, things will get better?"

I slowly shake my head. "If you consider some of the stuff I've gone through this year, not really. But it gives me the strength to move on and know, in the end, I'll be okay."

"So why did God take Jill from you?"

"Who says He did? It's my guess that someone—not God—killed her."

"But He could have prevented it—or healed her."

"He could have saved His Son—Jesus—but He didn't. I believe He gave us free will, in part to show our character, but also because if He controlled everything, we'd all just be a bunch of robots."

"But doesn't He sometimes intervene? Like unexplained miracles. And people who pray for change, and it happens."

"Sometimes, yes. No one knows why He sometimes does, and other times doesn't. We can guess that because He sees the bigger picture, He makes changes for reasons we don't understand. Other times He chooses not to intervene and let things play out."

We are silent for a while. Then, as the talking heads on cable news try to explain recent events, Patrick says:

"It sounds like the best we can do is guess at a bunch of conspiracy theories. Who is manipulating gas prices? What's up with the Christmas trees? Why did Jill die? Who is trying to kill you?"

I only nod, remaining quiet. I had an idea that all those questions had the same answer, but I kept it to myself for now.

* * *

It is now obvious that Henry Davis hasn't used this old office in some time. I think he has moved his operations to the more sophisticated Meadows—probably in the armed building. I still approach the secret office with care. Thankfully, Henry is out of town again, off doing whatever he does, which he has been quite often lately.

This time, it was more than curiosity. I was on a mission.

But I ask myself once I snuck back into the eerie room: *Where to begin?*

I feel a sickness, not really a nausea, but like hard lump on my heart. As dramatic as it sounds, it's as if this mission haunted my soul. While looking around at all these strange artifacts of human suffering, I realize Henry is a very disturbed man.

I stand, wondering where to begin.

Organized Chaos 10-8-1871 is whispered in my head.

Okay. That was tied in to the Chicago Fire. It has to be here . . . but where?

I begin to go through drawers I thought I had been through before. But I'd been looking for other things then—now it's something specific.

A fly buzzes around my head, breaking the silence as I search. I swooshed at it, thinking *Shoo fly, don't bother me*. Eventually, it buzzes away.

I search row after row, journal upon journal. After half an hour, I pull one journal out and open the cover. *Organized Chaos.*

The first several pages are dog-eared. The beginning had some kind of weird unrecognizable handwriting that rambles on for 5 or 6 pages. Then, the more legible scrawl of Henry began.

12-4-1857

"J.P.", since his birth 20 years ago, has displayed unwavering nerves of steel. I will soon reward him by transferring him from the London Central Bank to the New York Central Bank. At first, I will put him in charge of overseeing the Detroit underwriting project, in order to prep him for his debut underwriting and redesigning the financial Chicago project. I will have a sizable yacht awaiting him in the New York Harbor. Unlike most, named after women, the yacht will be named after a quote: If you have to ask, you cannot afford it. I'm sure my well-groomed son will be pleased. It will be fitted with all the amenities to fulfill his extravagant and influential lifestyle. It will be also be well supplied with his signature Havana cigars—Hercules' Clubs.

Second, at the right time, J.P. will be the one to hand the POTUS the 3.5 million ounces of gold necessary to aid the U.S. Treasury surplus, in exchange for 2 empowering deals.

The first, upon exchange, the POTUS will sign the binding Executive Order between the U.S. Government and my Dynasty. This Executive Treaty will place me and my organizations into complete obscurity. Thus setting forth to burn any undesired votes at will. Permanently closing our doors to public view and opinion. Allowing me full control to create political and domestic conspiracies that I will implement into motion at will, causing disinterest upon the growing undereducated U.S. population. Placing a strong "mirage shield" around my media and all my branches of the U.S. Government. I am pleased, at the general unaware U.S. population is falling easily into my guidance. As it will be my ideology shaping future economic and social developments. I have agreed to all future U.S war efforts will be supported with favorable but messy financial outcomes. Impending bloody wars will be necessary to advance my cause. As I am charting out many of these killing fields.

And second, the implementation of the Federal Reserve Act.

I am currently working out all the financial calculations. Dymortis instructs me bullets will have to fly before a POTUS will be agreeable to sign this bill into law. Plans and arrangements for such will come when required. This bill must and will be signed into law!

A chill runs up my spine as I look over to see Abraham Lincoln's skull sitting on the corner of Henry's desk. Apparently, the 16th president mustn't have been so agreeable.

I find this all very puzzling and hard to understand. But, again this has become normal for me lately.

The fly returns, and I swing my arm at it, missing wildly, wondering how it even got in here. Did I let it in? Did it follow me?

Then, I open the second dog-eared section.

10-6-1871

Dymortis is questioning my loyalty. His instructions and pointed words are sharp. Chicago must be burnt down in order for me to gain full control. I have had the new plans of the city already redesigned, as I did for Detroit before their fire of 6-11-1805. Dymortis is exercising his authority over weather, making the climate several months prior unseasonably hot and dry. I have never questioned Dymortis's Universal abilities. Until now. Is it possible Dymortis can hurl a fiery comet from deep within the Dark Universe and hit a precise mark on earth untold miles away?

Only one more day. I will be prepared. The plans have been well rehearsed.

I will not fail him.

Then the next:

10-8-1871

I stood on the roof, grasping the chimney against the nearly gale force winds. Dymortis was at his best. My gaze followed the comet streaking across the sky as planned. Then with my telescopic eye, I look off to the east towards downtown Chicago as the glow began to quickly illuminate the night's sky.

10-9-1871

Success. Both the Great Chicago Fire and the Peshtigo Fire were the perfect firestorms, the latter being blamed by some astronomers on possible fragments from Comet Biela—despite the fact it hasn't been seen since 1852. But if they want to speculate to that, I will not correct them. Up to 2,500 deaths were estimated during the fiery event in Wisconsin. It was beautiful. Dymortis will never be questioned again. As his mighty Universal powers have regained my focus. The extreme heat agitated the atmosphere into a flurry of super-heated tornadoes and hurricane-force winds. A scorching hail of embers, white hot sand, and debris peppered both areas. Rooftops were blown off houses, and chimneys crumbled. These winds were certainly felt in Chicago as the flames swept across the vulnerable wooden city. Dymortis hit his marks with pin-point accuracy and precise timing.

I then notice a newspaper article with a smiley face drawn by it. I'm assuming drawn by Henry. I question the smiley face. What kind of man would be delighted over such massive devastation and loss of human lives?

There is an article from the *Peshtigo Eagle* slipped between the pages.

"The frenzy of despair seized on all hearts, strong men bowed like reeds before the fiery blast. Women and children, like frightened specters flitting through the awful gloom, were swept away like autumn leaves. Crowds rushed for the bridge, but the bridge, like all else, was receiving its Baptism of fire. Hundreds crowded into the river, cattle plunged in with them, and being huddled together in rise general confusion of the moment, many who had taken to the water to avoid the flames were drowned. A great many were on the blazing bridge when it fell. The debris from the

burning town was hurled over and onto the heads of those who were in the water, killing many and maiming others so that they gave up in despair and sank to a watery grave."

I notice another account spoke of the horrific deaths experienced by the victims:

"By now the air was literally on fire, scattering its agony throughout the town. She said the fire came so suddenly that the only way she could describe it was that the heavens opened up and it rained fire"

I read these accounts with surprise that Dymortis is a powerful "Universal Force." And Henry was deeply involved with him, whatever their plans. I wonder what Henry had to gain control of and why? I now realize I had more to worry about than Henry.

I now am beginning to more deeply sense the heartless evil that lays inside both of them. I walk over and studied the map on the wall of the redevelopment of Chicago, 1868. Then, I look down to the wooden bins with other rolled up maps. I notice the one labeled Detroit. I pull it out and unroll it. Sure enough, it is titled *The Redevelopment of Detroit: The Woodward Plan 7-4-1803*. About two years before the fire. I carefully study the map, then roll it back up and replace it back in its bin.

I return the journal to its place, but I want to learn more. In the drawer, I go back to one journal and find it is labeled *Detroit*. I tuck it under my arm, then leave, sneaking back across the cemetery.

In my room, I open the journal. Again, it begins with several pages of strange hand writing. Then I recognized Henry's writing, dated 7-11-1805.

The ground work has begun. The area has been leveled. This city will be spectacular with its Paris like architecture and Washington Boulevard. The progressive era and industrial complex will soon be the benchmark of the new Ideology. Soon, this city will grow into a thriving hub of money and metal. Detroit will serve me well as many future racial riots are already planned. Financially, this will prove to be one of my wealthiest achievements within the United States to date. I will soon gain full control over many union and government resources. More government agencies will soon follow.

My sons will each be properly groomed, prepared and placed well within city governments and banks. However, Chicago will be a grander prize, though a much more difficult task to overcome. I will rely on Dymortis foresight and guidance.

I need to take a shower.

Chapter 24

"Today is a new day. Hiding from your history only shackles you to it. We can't undo a single thing we have ever done, but we can make decisions today that propel us to the life we want and towards the healing we need." —Steve Maraboli

Standing in the bathroom, drying off, I feel pain over the tattoo/branding on my chest when the towel runs over it. Although it doesn't hurt on its own, when I allow my fingers to feel it, the scar is both tender and warm—almost hot—to the touch.

I wipe the steam off the mirror and see nothing unusual . . . at least not more unusual than the strange design that has been on there for months. I consider somewhat wryly if this isn't like some type of Bat-signal, like the light scanning the sky of Gotham City, broadcasting to Batman that his help is needed.

And then I wonder if that's exactly what it is. A warning. An alert.

I get dressed quickly and head downstairs, half-expecting to find an intruder trying to burn the place down.

Instead, it's eerily quiet.

The light is on in the living room, but the TV is off. Everything else is dark.

I stick my head in Patrick's room, but he's not there.

I grab a radio from off the counter, turn it on, and press the button. "Hey, Patrick—are you there?"

I wait for a reply.

Nothing.

"Patrick, come in, over."

Silence.

I keep the radio in one hand and pull out my cell phone, hitting speed dial for his number. As it rings in the earpiece, a tinny piece of music blurts out from the living room. The Blues Brothers, "Peter Gunn Theme." Patrick's ringtone.

I walk in and see his cell phone sitting on the coffee table, lit up and vibrating. I end the call.

Okay. That's weird. Like me, he rarely went anywhere without his phone. And yet, here it is.

I look over at the bathroom, but the door is open and the light is off.

I sit on the sofa and think about this, closing my eyes, trying to concentrate.

Help me.

It's very faint, and not the female voice I've been used to.

I sit and wait for more, for something else, but nothing comes.

Instead, what crosses my mind is the strange dream with the "Regulators" taking a man into custody and chaining him up naked in what could only be called a cell.

"I should have listened to you."

Of course it was Patrick. Match that up with our discussion of the building on the grounds of The Meadows, and his smug little smile, and I'm pretty sure where he is.

My problem is figuring out how to get in there—and get out—without getting caught. Or shot.

I put the radio and my cell phone down, lean forward, hang my head, and try to think.

Although it seems like an hour, it's probably only a couple of minutes before an idea comes.

I go to the dining room and start to go through a pile of

papers, mostly maps of the underground tunnels. I pull out a pair that shows the way through to the far side of the property. I head for the front door, open it, then pause.

What else would I need?

A gun would be nice.

Then I think of him being strung up in the cell.

I'm going to need something to break the handcuffs or cut the chain.

I run to the barn and go through the various tools and the best I could find was a pair of bolt cutters. I hope they will work. I grab a flashlight on the way out.

I then run to the staging area, then into the tunnels, pacing myself, not rushing too hard, checking the maps every once in a while to make sure I was on course.

Eventually, I come to the large, impermeable wall Patrick discovered that would mark the border between the cemetery and The Meadows.

There's nothing here that would indicate any type of entrance or way in.

But there had to be. It just seemed there wouldn't be tunnels or a wall if there wasn't a way through.

I go back out to the next tunnel, seeing it ran roughly parallel to the wall. There were a few off-shoots to the left, but nothing on the right. The lights strung up along most of the passages had ended and I turned on the flashlight, hoping it would have enough battery.

After going what seemed to be a quarter mile—and wondering if I was even still under cemetery property—I come to a dead end.

I point the flashlight around, not seeing anything obvious like a door, and start to get a little frustrated. Maybe I ran past it. Maybe I need to go back, and go slower.

First, I check the hard-packed dirt of the walls, feeling for anything that might be out of the ordinary, but there's nothing. I shine the light on the ceiling, hoping that there'd be a hole or latch or chain—something—that would offer an exit.

I kneel and check the floor both with the light and my hands, though I don't know why anything would go farther down than I already am . . . but I recall the elevator in the dream went down four floors.

And then I feel a lump. Not much of a lump, not terribly obvious, kind of round and flat, as if a coaster or hockey puck was buried in the earth. I dig using the tip of the bolt cutters and after a minute of gouging the ground, a black iron rings appears.

Bingo.

The trap door was not just covered with well-packed dirt, but seemed sealed. It took fifteen or twenty minutes of work to get it open, and when I did, it creaked like an old door in a horror movie, only about ten times louder.

I let it fall, then grabbed the flashlight and point the beam into the dark hole. At least there is a ladder. The floor below—it looks like cement—is only about ten feet down.

I toss the bolt cutters into the void and hear them clatter. If there are guards on the prowl, I figure they'd be alerted to my presence by either the cutters or the creaky trap door.

I stuff the flashlight into the waistband in the back of my jeans, and start down the ladder, counting the rungs. Fifteen. I reach the bottom and pull out the flashlight, collect the bolt cutters and start down a corridor.

I have no idea where I'm going, but after roughly five minutes, I can see light up ahead. It was a T intersection, and I pause trying to get my bearings. Which way goes towards The Meadows? If I had my directions correct, the corridor off to the right would go under the cemetery, so I turn left. I don't know what I'm looking for, but at this point I didn't need to worry about that since there is nothing but an empty, concrete passage—no doors, and certainly no windows.

I soon come to another T section—left or right? I look each way, and a feeling of *déjà vu* comes over me. This is the hallway in the dream. At least it looks like it. Plain, with nothing but a series of lights and nondescript doors running the length in either direction.

I turn right, trying the knob on the first door I came to. It's unlocked, and show a dark room with only a metal table and a folding chair. I close the door and go across the hall to the next. Empty—not even a chair. The next has nothing but a pile of chains. The one across from that only has a large sheet of plywood leaning up against a wall.

In the sixth room, there is what at first looked like a pile of clothes—but then I realized it was a body. Not Patrick, as this corpse is all bloated and decomposing. Impossible to tell, though, if it's a man or a woman. The odor is overwhelming to the point of making me nearly retch, so I close the door and quickly head to the next room. It has a stack of white sticks, which I quickly understand are bones. There are a lot of them, and based on a few of the skulls I saw, human. And small, like they were not adults.

I think of the whispers, screams and cries of children that I heard many times before, and a chill goes through me.

I close the door, and go to the next. Opening it, a fluorescent light flickers on, and I see what I had come to find.

Patrick is hanging by his wrists from a pair of handcuffs attached to a chain. He appears to be unconscious, his chin resting against his chest. His naked body has several lacerations and welts, as if he had been whipped. Fresh blood covers his left leg from a huge gash that seems to have taken out a large chunk of flesh in his thigh. Perhaps worst of all, his genitals have been mutilated, the organs sliced and hanging only by small bits of skin. A testicle dangled outside the scrotum, suspended only by what looked like a thin tube. Blood drips down onto the floor.

This just happened, I think, knowing I have to act to save his life. If he was alive. I haven't even checked.

Hoping to feel a pulse, I put my palm directly over his chest where a long but shallow cut had sliced from his sternum to his left nipple. The moment my hand touches his flesh, the ring starts to glow. The slash grows warm, and then begins to mend.

Underneath it, I can feel a distinct heartbeat.

I slowly slide my palm along the cut, feeling the healing warmth beneath.

Okay, so that is working.

I then bite my lip and put my hand on the gash on his thigh. It was like touching raw meat—which, I guess, it is. It too grows warm, and I feel it begin to fill in beneath my palm. My skin becomes uncomfortably hot, and I withdraw, shaking my wrist as if I had just touched a stove. The wound has been replaced by a shiny red oval of skin that looked more like a third degree burn, but better than a seeping laceration.

I wait as my hand cools off, and—

Clink.

I hold my breath.

It sounded as if it had come from somewhere outside the room, down the hall.

I move as quietly as I can to the open door and listen.

Nothing.

I better get moving.

I step in front of Patrick and whisper: *"Pardon my touch."*

Grimacing, I take both my hands and place them over his genitals. My stomach rolls over—not from the thought of me touching another man's sex organs, but that they were bloody, maimed, and just gross. The work they had done on him had nearly brought a new meaning to the word "dismembered."

My palms and fingers grow hot. The blood is cauterized and the smell made my stomach do another roll. I don't know if it makes things worse, but as the tissue is healing, it *moves* under my skin, like I was holding a living thing . . . which, I guess, I am.

Again, my hands become too hot, and while I hold them as long as I can, I finally have to pull away, or else I imagine they would literally catch on fire. They sting horribly, as if dunked in boiling water, but slowly the pain begins to subside.

I look at Patrick's crotch to see if I had been able to make it any better. I can't say I've stared at many naked men either at a distance or this close up, but while it was apparent my laying on of hands had helped bring the tissue together and stopped the bleeding, it didn't look right. Without trying to seem lascivious or juvenile, it just appears swollen (and not the way it otherwise should), red and . . . well, just not good. Better than it had been, certainly, but "healed" would not be the right word.

I pause again to listen to any sound that might be coming from outside, but hear nothing.

I pick up the bolt cutters and train them on the thin links between the handcuff bracelets. I stop, thinking. If I cut them apart, Patrick will collapse to the floor. I just didn't want his head to smack on the concrete.

I awkwardly lift part of his torso onto my right shoulder as I lean back with the cutters and snip at them. It takes me a few times, but the handcuffs break apart, and Patrick's body comes free, with both of us tumbling to the ground. At least he lands on me, although I get a bit of the wind knocked out of me.

I manage to get up, wrestle Patrick up and over my shoulder, then carefully walk to the door, listening once again.

Silence.

I stick my head slowly out the door and look to the right.

Nothing.

To the left, nothing.

I enter the hall, close the door, and head back the way I came, carrying a bare-assed Patrick, hoping I could not only handle this weight for the long walk that is ahead of me, but that I can find the ladder up and into the catacombs under the cemetery.

* * *

I don't know how long it took me. Hours, probably. It was light when I make it to the surface. Patrick is still out. But I find I not only have the will to get him to safety, but the strength.

Laus Deo.

* * *

I lay Patrick on his bed and cover him up, wondering if he had lost too much blood. His breathing is shallow, his heartbeat soft but regular. I'll just have to keep an eye on him.

My palms are very sensitive, radiating a small amount of heat, and they ache. Nothing compared to what Patrick had gone through, but annoying nevertheless.

I stand at the window and watch, wondering if the Regulators would make an appearance once they figured out their hostage was missing.

Patrick sleeps. I watch. It will be a long day.

Chapter 25

*"Strength is nothing more than how you hide the pain." —Ritu
Ghatourey*

September 30

By dusk, I have convinced myself they would be coming under
cover of night. I think of hiding in the basement, but they'd find
us. No gun. Other than some kitchen knives, no weapons. I decide
to do the only thing I can think of.

I get some clothes on Patrick, ignoring the pain in my hands.
I wiggle some sweat pants and a t-shirt on him, then carry him to
the truck. Fortunately, the seat belt holds him in place, somewhat.

I know they'll be watching the place. It's pretty dark, though
not as dark as I'd prefer. I start the engine and drive out, lights off.
I wait a couple of miles before turning those on.

I go out to the suburbs where I know there are hotels. I don't
pull into the first one, or even the fourth. The eighth—a Harvest
Inn—looks good. But instead of turning there, I drive into the one
across the street that looks better, an Atrium Inn. Leaving Patrick
buckled in—he looks like he is passed out drunk—I go inside and
ask for a room facing the street. The clerk gives a brief look of what
is either curiosity or annoyance, but sets me up on the third floor.

After he gives directions to the shortest route to the room, I go back out, get Patrick out and, with him flung over my shoulder, I make my way to the stairs. I would have taken the elevator, but that would have increased the chance of running into someone else. I could laugh it off as helping out my inebriated friend, but it would be one of those things people don't forget.

Although I'm getting very adept at lugging his body around, going up all those steps wears me out. After reaching the second floor, I have to wait a minute to try and catch my breath. I lean up against the wall, readjusting my grip on his body as best I can. Then I continue up the final flight of stairs, get the door open, then make it down to room 312. I manage to get the door open, shuffle both our bodies in and plop Patrick as gently on the bed as I can before turning around and going back down to the truck.

I drive it across the street to the Harvest Inn, and park, locking it, then hurry back across the street. On the way, I turn off my cell phone, then pull out the battery and put them in separate pockets. I'm pretty sure they can't track the cell signal when it's off, but removing the power also removed any doubt. Electronically, I'll be invisible.

Once in the room, I partially open the drapes and check the vantage point. Perfect.

I get a glass from the counter, and fill it with tap water from the bathroom, then go back by the bed and wait.

* * *

I didn't have to wait long.

At 8:30, a nondescript Roto-Rooter van pulls into the Harvest Inn lot and parks next to my truck. A pair of men dressed all in black get out and check the pickup while another pair goes in the direction of the front office.

I figure if Henry Davis had put cameras in my bedroom, he wouldn't be above sticking a tracking device on my truck. Or using the GPS on my phone to follow me around. Unfortunately,

I was right.

Soon, the pair that had gone to the office are back. I can imagine the conversation.

"Did a tall young man, about 20, check in within the last hour?"

I watch to see what the answer might have been—and apparently, it was "Yes" as they run up the stairs to the second floor, knocking on a room door.

I have to say I feel a little guilty that some other poor sad sack would be harassed by these goons, but it's not like I had a choice. Well, maybe I did, but this was the best I could come up with on short notice.

The door opens, and while I can't quite make out who the guest is, it didn't take long for the men to nod their heads before turning around and leaving.

They reconvene between the van and truck, probably discussing their options.

If I were them, I'd consider two scenarios: One where they knew Patrick and I were nearby, and the truck was left there as a decoy. The other scenario was that it's a decoy, but someone came by and picked us up.

Frankly, I wish I'd thought of the second one.

I close the drapes and wait, making sure the door is bolted. Not that it would matter.

* * *

By midnight, I was nodding off in the chair.
So far, so good.

* * *

At 2:45, I am startled awake by yelling from outside. My heart goes from zero to 600 in two seconds.

I hear *"Hey!"* And then a bunch of unintelligible stuff that sounds half-angry but mostly drunk.

I stand by the door, eye to the peephole. Can't see much of anything. I wait. More mumbled talking. Close, but not close enough.

I decide it wasn't the all-in-black Regulators, but some college kids who got kicked out of the bars and made it back to the hotel. But I wait anyway, to make sure.

Finally, I watch a pair of young men stumble by, one holding up the other, though it could have been the other way around.

I go to the drapes and very carefully—and very slowly—part one side just enough to peek out.

My truck is still there. But so is the van.

They are waiting, and watching.

None of the men can be seen, but that didn't mean they aren't there.

I slowly step back and settle again in the chair.

I have to do something. I'm just not sure what.

* * *

My bright idea of taking a room that overlooked the parking lot across the street also had the disadvantage of being seen from the parking lot across the street.

Dawn came, and with it, what looks like an icy rain.

And, yes, the van is still there.

I do have an idea, I'm just not sure how to carry it out.

There is moaning from the bed.

I get up and sit on the edge.

His eyes are half-open.

"Hey, punk," I say with a smile. "Good morning."

He groans, but his eyes open a little wider. His mouth opens and closes—either he's trying to say something, or he needs something to drink. Probably both. I go and fetch a glass of water, setting it on the nightstand.

"Where is this?" he says thickly.

"A hotel—a safe place from the goons."

He frowns.

"Can you sit up and drink some water?"

He seems to think about this, then his tries to prop himself up on his elbows. I help him up, stacking pillows behind him.

"How are you feeling?"

He grunts. He's too manly to actually tell the truth. But his eyes are wide open and he looks alert.

"How long have we been here?" he asks, taking the glass from me.

"About twelve hours. They're across the street, but don't know we're here."

His eyebrows go up and he takes a drink. Then another.

"Go slow," I tell him.

He hands me the glass. "What happened?"

I shake my head. "You got caught, you dipstick."

He frowns again, but then a light comes on in his eyes. And then he closes them.

"Yeah," I say. "It was pretty nasty."

He looks at me. "I remember them . . . Did they . . . ?"

I nod. "But I did what I could."

He blinks a few times. "I don't want to look." His tone is dark, the words are slow, the voice scratchy.

"You don't have to," I tell him. "But . . . I don't know . . . In some ways, you might be a little better than you remember."

His expression is somewhat wry. "How do you improve on perfection?"

I laugh.

"So, what are we going to do?"

"I have an idea. But I need to think it through." I pause. "I think I'll take a shower first. You need to use the bathroom?"

Patrick frowns, then sighs. "Yeah." He throws back the covers and I help him out of bed. He makes it to his feet and seems a little shaky, but I help him around the bed and to the bathroom door.

"Thanks, man," he says. He hobbles inside and closes the

door.

I go back and turn on the TV, taking a seat in the chair. A news channel.

Eventually, Patrick comes out, but I don't take my eyes off the screen. He limps to the bed and climbs back in.

A few minutes later, I head to the bathroom to take a shower.

* * *

When I come out, and Patrick is pointing at the TV.

"You just missed it. They had a commercial on—Phillip's Furniture is closing!"

"What? Why?"

"It just was one of those 'Everything-must-go' things."

"Wow."

"Yeah. I don't miss that place, but I didn't think they would close."

"My first job—if you don't count grave digging."

"Me too—if you don't count . . . Nevermind."

"You started the year before me?"

"Naw, I was sixteen."

"Seriously? You were there five years?"

"Yeah," Patrick says, sounding sort of wistful. "Chauncey was an asshole—and he got pretty good at it—but he also took a chance on me when I needed it. I mean, I had dropped out of school, was living on the streets, not sure how I was going to eat, but he hired me and taught me how to repair furniture. Not that he took it easy on me, but he kept me on even when I fucked up and didn't deserve it."

"Yeah, I guess there was a nice guy somewhere inside the creepy candy coating."

We sit in silence for a few minutes.

"So what are you going to do?"

I shrug. "I'm going to confront him head-on."

"Confront him? You think that's a good idea?"

I sigh and check the time. "I don't have another one."

Then I stand up and pick up the phone.

* * *

It's an hour before there's a knock at the door.

I get up and check the peephole. Then I unlock and open the door.

"Hello, Jacob. Hello, Patrick," Mr. Burkfelt says, stepping inside.

"Thanks for coming," I say, relieving him of the laptop he's carrying and closing the door.

* * *

After Mr. Burkfelt was kind enough to go downstairs and get us continental breakfasts, and I work on the laptop for an hour, and I am ready. Well, as ready as I'm going to be.

I pick up my cell phone, put the battery in, and turn it on. When it was booted up, I dial.

"Hello?"

"Mr. Davis, please."

"I'm sorry, he's in a meeting. Can I take a message?" the man says dismissively.

"This is his son. I think he'll want to be interrupted and talk to me."

A pause.

"Hold please."

I wait.

"You sure this is wise, Jacob? I mean, Collin," Mr. Burkfelt says.

I give him a small smile to hide my nervousness. "No, I'm not sure. But I'm open to other ideas."

Mr. Burkfelt just looks sad, not saying anything.

It's another minute before someone comes on the line.

"Are you still on the line?"

"Yes."

"Here is Mr. Davis."

A pause.

"Jacob?"

"I need you to call the goons off."

Another pause.

"I'm sorry? You need me to what?"

"Call them off. Now."

"Jacob, I think you are mistaken. I do not—"

"The Regulators. The men dressed all in black. Sitting in a van. Call them off."

A longer pause.

"I am still not understanding what it is you are asking."

"I thought you might want to play dodge ball. So, let me put it in a way you'll understand: I know that you cheated thousands of people on their cemetery plots. I know Mom didn't die from food poisoning. And I know what goes on at The Meadows. Now, listen carefully—I have put up a website with the evidence on it. I have an email prepared to go to the media to expose it all."

On the other end is laughter. *"If you think you know so much, you would realize the media will not be helping you."*

"Yeah, you think they're in your back pocket. But there are other channels, other outlets you don't have control over. They'll have this posted and distributed in minutes. If you don't believe me, you should check out the *Cymbolism News* website. Go ahead. I'll wait."

"Jacob, you cannot blackmail me. You know that."

"It's not blackmail if I do it. Check the site."

A pause. *"Alright. If it will amuse you."*

I wait. It's a couple of minutes before he comes back on the line. I'm sweating as if it were 100° with 90% humidity.

"I see," he says. *"Those photographs could be doctored."*

"Yes, but they're not, and you know it. Oh, and one other thing—I have more. Not just the Senator from New York, but two

Supreme Court Justices and a high-level cabinet official."

A very long pause. I close my eyes and probably hold my breath.

"So, what is it you would like me to do?"

"Quite a few things. But for now, tell the Regulators to go away."

"So you are nearby. So close." A little chuckle from him. *"I think you and your friend will not be troubled by those men any longer. I wish you a pleasant day."*

And the line goes dead. I can finally breathe.

I get up and go to the window, peeking through the curtains. Less than a minute later, I watch the van back out of its parking spot, pull out of the lot, and drive away.

"They're gone," I say. "Let's go home."

Chapter 26

"Will you step into my parlor?" said the spider to the fly.

Mr. Burkfelt and I get Patrick situated in his bed, and I'm just glad his room wasn't upstairs.

"Thanks, guys," Patrick says, looking quite pleased that I had brought the TV in.

I toss him the remote. "I'll make you something to eat after I see Mr. Burkfelt out."

He offers a small smile, then pushes the power button.

I lead Mr. Burkfelt to the living room. "I really appreciate you helping us. I couldn't think of anyone else I could turn to."

"I am glad to do what I can." His bushy eyebrows furrow, and he looks at me seriously. "You know what you're up against, don't you?"

I blink a few times in surprise. I had only given Mr. Burkfelt very vague information on what had happened, so I'm a little startled that he's taking this so somberly. "Yes, I do. A little too well."

"It's bad magic, Collin," he says, shaking his head. Is that the first time he's called me that? "There are forces at play here that can hurt you more than what's happened to Patrick—especially if you don't remain on course and keep alert."

I stare at him for several moments, as realization dawns on

me.

"Stay true and pay attention," I whisper.

He nods and his eyes twinkle. "I wish I could be more helpful, but all I can say is that you watch your back. Dun—I mean Henry will retaliate. It's just difficult to know where and when."

"You were going to say 'Dunraven,' weren't you?"

He purses his lips, but his eyes still twinkle. "I must return home. I'm not sure I can help you very much, but I can offer advice. If you have questions, please call me. I'll answer the best I can."

He pats me on the shoulder, then turns to the front door, opens it, and leaves.

I stand there for a minute, letting this sink in.

I turn to see Patrick shuffling out of the bedroom towards the bathroom. I hope he doesn't need my help, but I wait in case he does.

There's a pause, and then:

"Holy shit," he shouts. "All my junk is bright red!"

I go to the doorway. His back is to me.

"I did the best I could."

"I know." He pauses. "I apologize for not sending a Thank You card."

I don't reply, not sure if he's only being sarcastic, or is just angry. Probably both. I tell myself he's not angry at me, just the guy who tried to take his tallywacker off.

He flushes but just stands there, not moving.

"You okay?"

"Yeah. Just . . . damn."

"How is the little firecracker?"

He turns with a smirk. "You mean 'Mr. Dy-no-mite'?" He shuffles to the sink to wash his hands.

"There's some aloe vera lotion in the cabinet—that might help."

He nods. He looks tired.

I go to the kitchen.

* * *

"Okay," I say, carrying a tray into his bedroom. "Time to eat."

"Smells like . . ." He pauses, pretending to sniff the air. ". . . Brinner!"

"You are correct, sir!" I set the tray down, and he looks like a child on his birthday, grinning from ear-to-ear. "Blueberry pancakes, eggs over easy, bacon . . . and there would have been toast, but it was moldy."

"The best!" he says, beaming. Then he suddenly flinches and winces in pain.

"You okay?"

He has his eyes closed and head turned to the side. It is several moments before he can say anything.

"Headache," he whispers.

"Want some aspirin?"

He doesn't answer. Dumb question, on my part.

I hurry to the bathroom and return quickly with a bottle. I tap a couple out onto his tray. He's holding the heel of his hand against his eye.

"Make it stop! Make it stop!"

I do the only thing I can think of, and put my palm on top of his head. The ring glows slightly, and immediately, he begins to relax.

I wait.

His breathing returns to normal, and he pulls his hand away from his face, blinking.

"Hoo wee," he says, shaking his head slightly. "That came out of nowhere."

"Take the aspirin anyway," I say. "Let me get you something to drink."

I come back with a glass of orange juice.

He pops the aspirin and drinks.

"Thanks," he says. "That was particularly bad."

I frown. "There were others?"

"Little things. Short bursts. But . . ." He pauses, looking a little embarrassed. "They come with images."

I don't reply, though I could easily say *I'm right there with you, Brother!*

"They . . . they've been sick."

"What kind of images?"

He pauses, thinking, as if he were trying to put it into words. "Dream-like. Or nightmare-like. That last one was children running, screaming."

I nod, knowing.

"But they then were falling. Someone was . . . was shooting them."

"Yeah. I've had similar."

He looks at me, then smiles slightly. "I thought you were just psychotic."

I grin. "Who says I'm not? Now you better eat before ice cubes form on your eggs."

I leave him to his food, and go to get my own, bringing it back to sit in the chair next to the bed.

I point a fork at the TV screen. "What's the ruckus all about?"

"They're protesting the Christmas tree ban. They're burning presents, even have a doll of the President hanging from a Christmas tree."

The protestors are obviously very angry. One is dressed as Santa with a machete sticking out of his back. A sign reads *What next? Banning Birthday Cakes?*

The anchor comes onscreen with the word *Scandal* in large red letters over her shoulder.

"New York Senator Max Durlston is under fire tonight after photos surfaced on the Internet that allegedly show the three-term politician engaged in sexual acts with children. While his office did not return calls for a comment, there are reports Durlston is in hiding with his family, including his wife of nearly thirty years. Gerald Reed has our report . . ."

"Did you really upload those pictures?" Patrick asks around

a mouthful of pancakes.

I nod as I chew. "I didn't know who he was. There was just the word 'Durlston' in pencil on the back. I searched the Internet, and he was the first name that came up."

The screen displays the photos, heavily pixelated, but clearly showing Durlston's face.

"Man, that's sick."

"Not as sick as the actual photos. I've wanted to burn them."

"Maybe you should."

We finish eating watching the weather report—snow on the way.

Out of the corner of my eye, I see Patrick wave his arm.

"You okay."

"Fucking fly."

"I had one buzzing my head a couple days ago. Or was it yesterday?"

He waves again. "Flies in this weather? What's with that?"

I pause, wondering. A fly in autumn is not the weirdest thing I've run across lately, but it just makes me consider it's not some random thing. But more importantly, the fly reminds me of the barn, and the barn reminds me of a horse.

I get up and grab Patrick's dishes. "I've gotta take care of Ginger. She's probably frantic."

"Thanks for Brinner."

I put the dishes in the kitchen, grab a jacket and head out to the barn. The air is crisp and clean and a little too bracing. Winter is a couple of weeks ahead of schedule. I'll still enjoy my ride with Ginger. It would be hard—

I stop, my eyes having a hard time believing what I am seeing.

That Ginger is dead isn't the issue. That she had been slaughtered was horrible, but even that is not the worst. The blood that coats her and pools like a small pond on the floor is literally sickening, but still not the most appalling. What makes me retch, sending my breakfast out in front of me, is that she was hanging by the feet from the rafters.

* * *

"Oh, dear God—no, not Ginger too!"

I fall to my knees, my fists clench, I grit my teeth as tears pour down my face.

"You rotten bastard!" I scream, slamming my fists into the ground. Over and over.

Finally, I stop and stand on wobbly legs. I turn and walk out of the barn, pulling my phone out of my pocket.

"You son of a bitch," I said, nearly screaming. "You're a sick, sick man."

"You did not actually believe I was going to allow you to blackmail me, did you?"

I pause, breathing hard, nearly hyperventilating. "Blackmail? You want *blackmail*? I have pictures of your son—the President of the United States—*raping* a six year old girl. You want me to bring down the government? I will. And I'll bring you down with him, you revolting pervert."

There is no reply. I look at the phone to see if I am still connected.

"You there?"

"Yes. Are you?"

"I have the contact information for the *New York Times, The Guardian, CNN,* and about fifty other news organizations."

"I am sure you do. But they will not publish or broadcast anything you send them."

"Of course they will. I just handed them a U.S. Senator. They're falling all over themselves."

"They will not publish it because . . . you do not have it."

"What? Of course I do. Are you delusional? Haven't you seen the news?"

"You should return to the house."

"What? Why?"

"Your answers will be at the front door. Goodbye, Jacob."

And the line goes dead.

I turn and storm out of the barn, angrier than I have ever been. I was nearing a blind rage, when suddenly I realize there are cars parked in front of the house that I don't recognize. Then I see the three men on the porch, and one standing near the cars.

I run up, and quickly notice that while they were in jeans and polo shirts, they were wearing holsters with guns.

"Can I help you?" I say politely, though I could have just as easily took a swing at one of them.

They turn to face me, one of them holding papers. "Jacob Davis?"

"Yeah. Who are you?"

"We're with the Chicago Police Department. I have a warrant to take a laptop computer."

"Why? Are you on an errand for Henry?"

The bulky man has a mustache and a hard policeman's face. He frowns. "I don't know anyone named Henry. This was requested by District Attorney Sliever, and signed by Judge Tomlinson. I need you to open this door, please."

I consider saying "No" but think better of it. They will get on the other side one way or the other.

"Before I open the door, can you tell me the reason for taking my laptop?"

He holds out the paper. "It's all detailed there. Please open the door, and you can read through it."

"It's unlocked. You'll find the computer on the kitchen table. Please take it and go."

All three men march in and the fourth stays by the cars, watching me while I stand in the pitiful glow of the porch light and try to read the search warrant. It doesn't take me long to find the relevant wording.

"*. . . the notebook computer is suspected of containing child pornography.*"

Chapter 27

"Chaos is a name for any order that produces confusion in our minds." —George Santayana

"What was that all about?" Patrick asks after the men leave.

They had gone through the rest of the house, making sure I don't have any other computers lying around.

"Ginger's dead," I tell him flatly.

"What?"

"Hung from the rafters and slaughtered."

Patrick looks as confused as I feel. "The cops? How did they do that?"

"No, the cops didn't do it. Dear old dad—or rather, the Regulators. And I'm not sure how they did it."

Mr. Burkfelt's words comes back to me: *"It's bad magic, Collin."*

"I can't believe the creep had Ginger killed like that," Patrick says.

"Me either . . . but he's clearly sending a message."

"Yeah, an inhumane message."

"That's what worries me."

"I don't understand why he is doing this to you. Just because you uploaded those pictures?"

"He's a cold hearted bastard . . . but I don't know why yet."

"Well, I'm really sorry about Ginger, I know she meant a lot to you. I'm not into horses, but I could tell she was special."

"That's the problem, she meant something to me."

"So why were the cops here?"

"To take the laptop. Henry arranged for them to confiscate it for containing child porn."

I watch Patrick as the gears turn in his head. "You uploaded those pictures. They're going to find them. You'll get arrested." He licks his lips, looking nervous. "Maybe we should . . . be somewhere else . . . in case they come back."

I nod slowly. "Maybe we should—but not because of the cops. They won't find any child porn on the computer."

He blinks, trying to understand. "But you scanned the photos. Even if you delete them, they're never really deleted. I read that."

"True, but only if they were on the hard drive. I knew it was dangerous having that stuff on there, so I uploaded them directly to a secure website, then scrubbed the folders using a high-level erasure algorithm. The most they'll find are links to the website, but they won't be able to get in."

"You sure?"

"Yep. The U.S. Government has been trying to crack the website for years, and can't."

"So you're not getting arrested?"

"Not for that. I'm sure Henry will figure something else out."

A long pause while he thinks this through. "Where do we go?"

"I've got a couple of ideas."

* * *

I lay out the maps of the underground tunnels on the bedspread.

"So, these are all the passages, and I think we've been through most of them."

"I think I've been through all of them," Patrick adds.

I point to the edge of the map. "This is The Meadows. We know there are tunnels there, we just don't have a map of them."

"And they'd be too dangerous to wander through."

"To the north is Bertrand Avenue. On the west is Langston Avenue. But look here on the south, by Portage Avenue."

He picks up the map and looks closer.

"More tunnels."

"And they go somewhere off the edge of the map."

"But there doesn't seem to be a connection."

"I bet there is, though, or they wouldn't be on there."

He sets the map down. "And that's where you think we should go?"

"It's the back-up plan." I pull my phone out and dial.

"I'm not in the best shape to go through a bunch of tunnels," Patrick says as if he hadn't heard me. "It's hard enough making it to the bathroom."

"Hello," I say into the phone. "It's Collin, Mr. Burkfelt. I was wondering if Patrick and I could come over. I think we need to talk."

"That is fine, Collin. I will call a taxi to pick you up. You shouldn't be driving. Can you make it off the property without being seen?"

"Yes, no problem. And I'll turn off my phone. Oh, and if you can have the cab meet us down the street, at the little shopping center, that would probably be safer."

"I was thinking the same thing. I look forward to seeing you."

*   *   *

I pack a few things for us, putting them in the gym bag I had used when I'd workout with Jill.

Upstairs, while getting some of my stuff, I went to grab the framed photo of Jill, but it wasn't in the curio where I had left it. I take a moment to think, making sure I hadn't put it somewhere else, but I know the answer.

No, I hadn't.

I'm not sure if the cops took it—and I had no idea why they would—or the Regulators came through and took some stuff on the orders of Henry.

Nausea develops in my stomach, feeling not only violated that they had been sneaking around my home, but that they had taken something very precious to me. It feels like Henry Davis is going after the very core of my being, attacking the things that mean the most to me—Jill, Patrick, Ginger. Two of them are dead, and Patrick had come close to it.

I will not let Henry Davis defeat me. *I will not.*

* * *

We step out onto the porch, the bag slung over one of my shoulders, my arm supporting Patrick with another. He is leaning on a baseball bat, using it as a make-shift cane.

I lead him to the barn and tell him to prepare for the worst.

"I'm not even going to look."

I go to the corner, also doing my best not to look, and pull up the trap door. I consider the ladder.

"I'll just go real slow," Patrick says.

I drop the bag down the hole, then his baseball bat. I think for a minute. It might be a good idea to have something between the barn door and the trap door. My eyes fall on the little red wagon I had used for carting Ginger's food around. It wouldn't hide the trap door very well, but it could give us an extra minute. I roll it into place.

I go down the ladder first, standing at the bottom, only able to offer encouragement as Patrick makes his way down. It takes him a long time since his left leg has trouble bending at the knee. Eventually, he gets to the point to where he could pull the trap door shut. All goes dark. I fumble for the bag and rummage blindly for the flashlight.

"Sorry this is taking so long," Patrick says. "I'm like an old man in slow motion."

"Take your time, Grandpa. No hurries."

He is on the third rung from the bottom when we hear voices above. They are muffled, but one I can make out:

"Over there."

I look up at Patrick, who purses his lips, then jumps. He does his best to land on his good leg, and I'm able to half-catch him to keep him from falling over. He grunts, but otherwise stays quiet. I grab the bag, kill the flashlight beam, and drag him deep into the shadows. Then I hurry back and fetch the baseball bat before slipping back.

We wait.

Five minutes later, after no sound or sign of them coming down, I hand him the bat, pick up the bag, and we begin hobbling deep into the tunnel.

* * *

We finally make it to the staging area. From here, we can make it to a gate in the fence. I hunt in my pocket for the key to the lock, get us on the other side, then lock it up again. A homeless man sitting on a bus bench watches us, but says nothing.

We wait for the light at the corner, with me constantly looking around for a van that might contain a bunch of Regulators. We cross at the green, and continue down the street, heading for the shopping center, which is really nothing more than a burger joint, a convenience store and a laundromat. As we finally arrive there, I look around the parking lot, but don't see a taxi. There is, however, a Lincoln Town Car with tinted windows. We limp to the car, but the driver is not behind the wheel. I open the back door and help Patrick in, getting him into the seat belt. I hope it's the right car.

He's quiet and sweating profusely. Then I go around the other side and toss in the bag and bat.

I close the door and look around for where the driver could be. I go to the store, and see a white man with a beard in black slacks and white shirt holding a cup of coffee, talking with the clerk behind the counter. I open the door and stick my head in.

"Are you the driver?"

"Yep. You ready?"

"Yeah, sorry we took so long."

"No problem, partner. I'll see you, Tito."

As we walk to the car, I ask: "Do you know where we're going?"

"Absolutely. You just sit back and relax, it's all been taken care of."

I get in the back next to Patrick, who has his head back and eyes closed.

The car pulls out onto Langston and we head south—not the best route to Burkfelt Jewelers, but it puts the cemetery behind us.

I'm finally able to relax. The question crosses my mind if I will ever go home. Maybe not. Maybe it would be better to move away, get away from the place once and for all.

"I don't want to alarm you," the driver says, "but I'm going to have to make a few evasive maneuvers. I hope you're buckled in."

As he says that, he hits the accelerator, and we are quickly zipping down the road, until he comes to a light that is just turning yellow. He makes a tire-squealing left turn, fishtailing slightly, but he quickly corrects.

I turn around to look out the rear window, and a few moments later, a familiar white van skids around the corner, nearly taking out a pedestrian. The van is only on its right-side wheels for a second before landing heavily and then continuing to speed after us.

The driver gains even more speed, and the van falls behind.

We make a right turn at another signal, and he guns it again.

I glance at Patrick, who seems oblivious.

We make another left, then a quick right into a residential neighborhood. The van hasn't made it around the corner two signals back, so it seems like we lost them. The driver isn't taking that chance, and while he isn't driving as crazy-fast as he had on the bigger street, he is making good time.

We reach an outlet onto a boulevard, and he pauses, looking each way, then speeds across.

"So, I take it you're not a typical taxi driver."

"You could say that. I started my career as a cop, then went to Hollywood and became a stunt driver. Moved here five years ago, but still go to L.A. for work once in a while. I mainly work for the Challengers now."

"The who?"

"Challengers. We're the counterpart to the Regulators. Hold on."

He makes another left, then a quick right. He slows to a reasonable speed, then pulls into an alley.

"So you're with the Soulmadds?" I ask.

"The Soul what?"

"Okay, nevermind."

Near the end of the alley, he pulls up behind Burkfelt Jewelers.

* * *

I help Patrick to the backdoor where Mr. Burkfelt nervously stands. The driver brings the bag and baseball bat.

"Thank you, Derrick," Mr. Burkfelt says.

"You're welcome. I'll hang around back here for a bit to make sure our friends don't make an appearance."

Inside, I lead Patrick to the backroom. There's a simple card table set up in the middle of the room with four fold-up chairs. I get him seated in one as Mr. Burkfelt locks up the backdoor.

"Can I get you some tea?"

"That would be great—and maybe some water for Patrick?"

"Of course. Be right back."

I take a seat and watch Patrick. He seems to be half-asleep, still sweaty, but doing better.

Mr. Burkfelt returns with the tea and a large plastic tumbler filled with water.

"Here you go. Would you like any sugar?"

"No, this is fine. Thank you."

"So," he says taking the seat across from me, "it looks like you're kind of in a corner."

I nod. "Henry killed my horse, and he has . . . something of value of mine."

He looks slightly pained. "I doubt it will be retrievable."

"I know."

"What is it you are thinking of doing?"

"I don't know yet. I think . . . I know this may sound strange, but I think I may be entering my destiny. Sounds stupid, right?"

Mr. Burkfelt shakes his head. "Not at all. The timing is right." He pauses. "You've heard the saying 'The stars are aligning'? It's not that trite, but there are elements moving into place that feels like the time is coming. Your father has been making arrangements that don't portend well."

I let this sink in. "He's not my father."

"Technically, that's true."

"His real son—"

"—is the President. I know."

"So, you're a Soulmadd?"

"No, I haven't been so blessed. I'm more of a consultant. I believe your—I mean Henry and some of his minions can sense a Soulmadd's presence, but I'm able to slip around that."

"How do you consult then?"

"I advise them on the political implications. As I am about to advise you."

I take a sip of tea. "Advise me how?"

"You were considering leaking the photos of President Quinn to the media."

"Yes. How did you know?"

"The Soulmadds tell me what I need to know."

I sip more tea, thinking. "So they spy on me as well."

He looks uncomfortable. "I . . . I don't know all that they do, but I wouldn't be surprised."

"I have a red penis," Patrick suddenly says. "Bright red." He turns towards the old man. "Like a fire hydrant."

Mr. Burkfelt frowns. "Maybe he needs to lie down and rest."

"No, I'm fine," Patrick says, leaning forward, putting his elbows on the table. "You're just talking about not having any privacy, so I thought I'd contribute. Collin here has a glowing tattoo on his chest." He pauses. "I need to pee."

"That door over there," Mr. Burkfelt says, pointing towards a corner.

Patrick slowly stands up and I rise to help him.

"No, no, I got it. One man job." He is on both feet, not the least bit wobbly. Then he turns and shuffles towards the bathroom. "Dy-no-mite."

"He's not been completely normal since the . . . thing," I say.

"Nor should he be. He's very strong, but no one can walk away from a situation like that unscathed."

"You don't think I should release the photos."

"No, I don't. It will not gain what you think. You can bring down Quinn, but his replacement is as much a pawn of Dun . . . I mean Henry."

"Dunraven."

Mr. Burkfelt nods. "His true name."

"And Dymortis?"

The bathroom door opens and Patrick wanders slowly out. "Now I itch," he says. "I guess that's a good thing, but it's going to drive me crazy. Just so you know, if you see me grabbing myself, I'm not a perv." He takes a seat in his chair.

We both stare at him.

"Sorry," he says. "TMI?"

Mr. Burkfelt looks at me as if to ask *What's TMI?*

I shake my head to say *Nevermind.*

"Anyway, I asked about Dymortis."

"There's not much I can tell you."

"But he's bad magic?"

"He created it."

"So Dunraven works for or with Dymortis?"

"All will be made clear soon enough."

"Dunraven, from what I've found, dates back decades—even centuries."

Mr. Burkfelt nods. "He has been involved in tragedies and torments that have plagued the world for a long, long time."

I think about all I've read. *The Titanic.* The Great Chicago Fire. Abraham Lincoln.

"What should I do?"

Mr. Burkfelt pauses. "As I said, all will be made clear soon. I have arranged a room for you two at a motel down the street. It's not a Hilton, but it's safe." He reaches in his pocket and pulls out a plastic key card. "Derrick will take you over there. We'll meet again tomorrow."

I help Patrick up, and we go out the back door. Derrick has the car waiting.

Interlude 6

I am sitting on the grass in a park or clearing of a forest. Everything is peaceful and quiet, and the colors are unnaturally rich. Tall, stately trees surround the area, and the sun peeks through the leaves, spackling the ground with twinkles of light as the breeze passes by.

Out of the trees on the far side of the clearing, a shadowy figure appears. I stand, unsure if it is friend or foe. It seems to be cloaked in a robe, much like the Soulmadds, and slowly moves forward. Once in the clearing, I sense it is a female and wonder if it's Sylvana. I can only wait as she approaches.

Twenty feet away, I realize it's not Sylvana.

Jill.

"Hello, Collin."

I rush towards her, my arms in an open embrace.

Her hand comes up as if to tell me to stop.

I step in front of her and hold my palm up to touch hers . . . but it only passes through me. I feel nothing. It is as if she is not there. But yet I see her.

"What is this?" I ask.

"Our destiny is not yet complete. I cannot tempt you, or distract you, so you may focus on your calling."

"So what is this?"

"I am here to bring you background and knowledge for your

journey."

"My journey?"

"Lord Dunraven will not rest until he corrects his mistake. You have the free will to run away, or challenge him."

"Are you saying I am a mistake?"

"To him you are. You were chosen by him to follow in his footsteps as he thought he could change and manipulate you as he does others. He was intending on introducing his high level of evil into you, but discovered you were not a candidate for his purposes. He could possibly taint you, but not take you over as he intended. That was his mistake."

She pauses, and smiles.

"But you are not a mistake to us. To us, you are perfect."

I shake my head. "I'm not perfect. I've made many mistakes, and have often chosen poorly."

"True. But your intentions were unspoiled. You have a clear heart." She gestures towards the ground. "Please, relax. I will answer some of your questions."

I sit on the ground, Indian-style, and she does the same. I feel the need to argue about their impression that I am perfect. I think of my occasional hurtful thoughts towards other people, my judgmental feelings, my sexual fantasies. As if reading my mind—which she probably did—she says:

"But you kept them to yourself. You did not harm or demean other people. You did not defile yourself or others."

I can't say I'm convinced, but I wasn't going to argue.

"Henry Davis—Lord Dunraven—intended for me to become his heir apparent?"

"Yes, your adoptive father is Dunraven the XIV, and he executes the instructions written for him to carry out—the orders of Dymortis."

"Yes, I've come across that name. Who—or what—is he?"

She seems to ignore the question. "You are now the only remaining living being from the Royal families. Your natural parents were of Royal blood and were the last two from the pure lineage. That means you are the only one left."

"Royal blood?"

"It is not the best word, perhaps, but the closest. It should not mean to imply that you are of better quality or higher rank than anyone else."

"But it does imply everyone else has tainted blood."

"Not tainted. There is nothing wrong with mixed blood. I suppose the best way to put it might be like water. Some like to add a difference, to change or enhance its flavor."

"So, I am boring."

She smiles. "You are anything but boring." Her smile fades. "Your adoptive father has become impatient as he knows he cannot reproduce any more children of his own, and it will break the Dunraven family line—and knowing this has infuriated him, reacting and over-reacting like a madman in his quest to carry out the final orders.

"The Dunraven's created the fiat empire known as the Red Shield Society, a sinister organization, and they have infected grave pain and suffering on the Earth."

I pluck a blade of grass. "How did this all happen? Was it all allowed?"

"Dymortis descended to Earth and pronounced upon the youngest Dunraven the cruelest black curse of all—greed. It has empowered him, given him the grand reward of Blacksoul, and the prearranged protection necessary to fleece the flock of humanity for centuries. This addictive greedy genetic flaw now lies among many on earth today, a poisonous noose around mankind's throat—with the exception of the Royal families only because they are secretly shielded and protected by their blood from this evil greedy spell.

"Throughout time, Dymortis—through the Dunraven's—is responsible for throwing the first sharp stone, igniting religious wars that still burn in the world today. Dunraven has intentionally fertilized the seedlings that created the wealthiest bloodlines, collecting over half of the total world's wealth—over five hundred trillion dollars residing within this single family today.

"The Dunraven's have obtained this position through lies, manipulation and murder. They exploit the weak and tempted to serve their real evil master. The Dunraven's spent centuries dismantling your family's legacy by burning down villages and taking control of the monetary systems. Over the years, they slaughtered your bloodline, with their aim to victimize, confiscate and eradicate all of your family's cherished ancient scriptures. Their goal was to erase the Royal footprints by sweeping them out of the history books.

"The Dunraven's also controlled the media, building a massive communication network through TV, print, radio, Internet, cable and satellite companies. They could—and did—control the news. Their goal was to sway the people to believe a one-world government was the only solution.

"Lord Dunraven has begun to seize control of as many publicly owned assets worldwide as he can. They are collecting industrial and military technologies. The Dunraven's alone are in position to be the ultimate adjudicators of ethnic targeting, financial aggrandizement, and the individual frailties of the world.

"But at the right time, the true light will call upon enlistments and forces orchestrated by the Soulmadds—and by you!"

I try to absorb this—it's a lot to take in. I'm not even sure what some of it means.

"What is the emblem on my chest? What does it mean?"

"It is the ancient Royal seal—you are the last remaining living soul representing the wealthiest Royal family. It symbolizes transition, balance, honor, faith, unity, order, patience, stability, creation, longevity, protection, hope, freewill, endurance, life and navigation. He who bears the seal has complete immunity, exempted from all society laws."

"So I can't be arrested?"

"You can't be convicted. Your conviction comes from elsewhere, not the laws and authorities of Earth. You are the highest ranking Soulmadd, which means you are the Monarch ruling over all nations, presidents, prime ministers, kings, queens and all heads of governments—and even the Dunraven's."

"I'm sorry—what?"

"You are the Monarch above all on Earth."

I frown, not sure I understand. "You mean I get to tell everyone what to do?"

"You have that power. But power diminishes the more it is used. The less you use, the more you have."

"So I can tell you to go away?"

"And I will."

"Or remove your clothes and make love to me?"

"And I will."

"But I shouldn't ask you."

A voice comes from behind me: "You are aware of what you should and should not do."

I turn and look up, seeing another figure in a hooded robe. It is Sylvana.

"You understand you must remain focused," she says. "Your greatest foe is Dymortis. He has incredible powers that only you can challenge. No one knows we have found you or Jill—although Dunraven may suspect it. We still have a lot of planning and work to do before the rest of the world loses their freedom."

Sylvana stands to my right, looking down at me.

"I found a lot of documents," I say. "Birth certificates, death certificates. I'm not sure what their significance is, but for me to find them must mean something."

"Some are altered birth certificates of cast-away orphans, signed by fraudulent doctors. The orphans were given new names, fake adoption papers and social security numbers created by unlawful attorneys. They are sold to high-bidding families through an embezzling adoption agency.

"Orphans are considered 'subjects' and referred to only by their market number, embedded with microchips. Some are sold for millions to pharmaceutical companies to test experimental drugs, medical testing facilities for new surgical techniques, technology companies to test neurological devices, or to rogue military agencies to experiment on biological warfare. Some orphans are sold to the pornography industry, high-society escort services to play out their sexual fantasies. Others are brainwashed and become the tools of terrorists to inflict mass casualties, and some used at games called Run For Your Life, and indiscriminately shot for sport.

"Other documents are laundered life insurance policies showing 'natural' causes of death when they were not, signed off by coroners on the take to grant large sum payouts to elite beneficiaries. You may have encountered one of those charlatans."

Jerome Galway, who I killed.

"Jill Stone—under her birth name Jessica Sloane—had been one of the orphan children, and was one of only three who had escaped the Meadows Club. Another was a child named Parnell Wilson. You may know him as Patrick Williams. The third you will soon meet."

I am not surprised. "Does anyone use their real names?" I ask with a smile.

"Names are but a passage, a label. From this time, you should revert to your birth name, your Royal name."

"Collin Jacob Graves."

They both nod.

"We will not rest until the evil towards all humans is extinguished," Jill says.

Sylvana adds: "Using children for objects of greed or pleasure cannot be tolerated any longer."

"What is this 'Run For Your Life' game?"

Sylvana reaches down and places her palm on my forehead.

My eyes close, and I am transported to a dull landscape. Snow on the ground, grey dull trees without leaves, a stone-grey sky.

I turn to see a dozen naked children, muzzled, with their hands bound. They are locked in place to a chain wrapped around their waist. Some men approach and begin to remove the bindings on their wrists, and the muzzles on their heads. Then the shackles chaining them together are dropped, and the children scatter, running hopelessly wild into the open woods. I can see that half the children had fluorescent orange numbers, the other half lime green ones that looked like they had been hand-sprayed on their bare backs.

Then the gunshots start.

Two men behind rifles quickly took down twenty of the children.

The marksmen are given only ten bullets and ten seconds, Sylvana's voice tells me. *There are high-stakes bidders sitting in secret shelters, viewing each round of the competition.*

I watch as the surviving four children are collected into a holding pen.

They will be targets for the final round.

I recognize Harold Jopp, the spitting groundskeeper, driving around, picking up the small corpses, throwing them in the back like they were dead deer on the side of the road. Blood runs out of the tailgate, over the bumper.

As he pulls up to one corpse, the body moves—wounded but not dead. Jopp takes a tire iron and strikes the girl in the head.

"That's only worth half a point!" he yells toward the snipers.

Another round begins, another 20 children gunned down.

The distinguished older man I recognize from dreams that seem so long ago moves to the center of the field to crown the champion marksman.

His name is Edwin Graybill, and he is the supplier of the children.

More children appear. White hoods are placed over their heads, then are led to the trees, to which they're chained.

From what seems to be a great distance, the two competing marksmen take aim.

Ten points for the head. Five for an extremity. One for the torso.

The men do not miss, and each gets perfect scores.

The groundskeeper will take the bodies to the mortuary,

empty them into the incinerator, placing the ashes in caskets, and then randomly bury them throughout the cemetery.

"Is this what I'm up against?"

"No. But I think it is fair for you to see. Lie down and close your eyes."

I pause, not really wanting to be that vulnerable. But I trust Sylvana, and lie down. My eyes close.

Nothing happens for a long time . . .

I try to shake myself of the vision and run, tripping over a low headstone. Standing over me is the old short man wearing a white jacket, white pants and black shoes—the man from a vision that made me dance naked with him. I can only refer to him as The Dancing Man.

Then I feel something pressing on my chest.

I open my eyes.

He leans over, grinning, foot firmly on my chest.

Then smiles wide with crooked yellow teeth. "To be are not to be. Not really a question, but more a choice—a rather complex thought, isn't it, my Chosen One?"

"Who are you?"

"Some refer to me as Lucifer, The Prince of Darkness, or Satan. Some believe me to be the spooky Devil with horns growing from my head and sporting a long, pointed tail.

"But my real name, my true name, dear Chosen One, is Dymortis."

His breath is rancid, and his eyes bore into me.

"And I will kill you," he says before dissipating into a big puff of smoke.

Chapter 28

"We experience moments absolutely free of worry. These brief respites are called panic." —Cullen Hightower

October 1

I wake up to the sound of screaming—but not from me.

Patrick is sitting straight-up in bed, eyes open, emitting an ear-splitting shriek that should have be in a horror movie.

I push his torso back down on the bed, and he stops, his wild eyes staring at me, confused.

"You're okay, dude."

He begins breathing heavily, but is calming down. He closes his eyes and rubs a hand over his face.

I didn't know Patrick to scare easily—I thought of him as the one *giving* the scares—so whatever crept up on him in his sleep was truly terrifying to him.

It makes me wonder if our friends and foes have some kind of access to our dreams. I would have to think they do with me, but it worries me that someone, or something, is terrorizing Patrick. It's bad enough they tried to castrate him, then kill him, but this mental torture could be worse in some ways.

"You alright?" I ask.

"Yeah."

"Sounded pretty scary."

He pauses, licking his lips. "It was. I woke up to a man in my bed. That ain't *never* happened before."

I laugh. "Better someone that looks like me than someone that looks like you."

His eyes roll. "Someone's been looking in the pretty mirror again."

I get up and stretch. The hotel room is old and small, but clean. A king size bed that's more comfortable than it looks, a faux-leather lounge chair, a desk chair at a "desk" that is about the size of a nightstand.

I turn on the TV, and the WGN local morning show is on, the weatherman predicting dire cold for the next few days. I don't think either of us have a jacket.

Patrick makes his way out of the bed, and to the bathroom.

We need to consider what to do. We can't keep running. Or more accurately, limping. The only card up my sleeve—the photos of the President of the United States—was something I've been advised against using. On an intellectual level it makes sense, dovetailing with the warning Jill gave me in the dream: *Power diminishes the more it is used.* If I use it, I can cause a lot of damage, but then I have nothing left.

On an emotional level, though, my sense of right and wrong is screaming at me to do *something*. I recall a quote I learned in high school, if I remember correctly, by Edmund Burke:

"All that is necessary for the triumph of evil is that good men do nothing."

I can*not* do *nothing*.

Patrick comes out of the bathroom. "Well, things are looking better, if you know what I mean."

"I'll alert the media."

He is quiet for a few moments. "You know, I don't think I was able to thank you."

"For what?"

"Saving my life."

I shrug. "It's what we're supposed to do. You would have done the same for me."

"Touch your junk? I don't know 'bout that!"

I smile, shaking my head.

He steps up to me, his hand extended. "So, anyway, thank you."

"You're welcome," I say as we shake.

"So now the question is: What do we do now?"

"I was just thinking about that. And I think our next move is . . . for me to make coffee."

"Brilliant!"

He hobbles over to the stiff-looking desk chair and sits. I notice his hobble doesn't seem as stiff and painful as yesterday.

I grab the tiny coffee carafe from the tiny coffee maker and fill it with water from the bathroom tap. I bring it back and poor into the reservoir.

"So are the Soulmadds a kind of cult?" Patrick asks.

I pause, deciding how to answer. Especially since I don't really know the answer.

"That's the million dollar question."

"So you've thought the same thing."

"I've been told I am one.. It seems to be a high circle of spiritual . . . I don't know what they'd be called. What brought this up?" I put the pre-made filter with coffee sewn into it in the coffee maker and press the "on" switch.

"Sylvana. She was in a robe with a hood and tried to explain that you were special and were chosen to lead a movement against the forces of . . . I think she said 'Dunraven'." He pauses again. "Wasn't that the name of the guy in the painting that looks like your ex-Dad?"

I laugh. "Ex-Dad—that's a good one! Yes, Lord Dunraven is Henry Davis, or vice-versa."

I consider his words. *Chosen to lead a movement.* I feel goosebumps pop up on my arms. It brings a few questions: Who chose me? Lead who? To what?

"What else did Sylvana tell you?"

"That they tried to kill me once, and they'll try again—and that I should not go off on my own. And then something like 'Keep real and stay alert.'"

"Stay true and pay attention."

"Yeah. And then she disappeared. And some ugly guy in like a top hat and tails tap danced and . . . then he . . ."

He looks uncomfortable.

"It's okay," I tell him. "You don't have to tell me."

Patrick nods and stays quiet. But he looks like he is about to cry.

* * *

Collin . . . you must go . . .

I look around to see if Patrick had said something, but he was only blankly gazing at the TV.

A shooting . . .

I feel a little like I am a radio picking up signals only I can hear.

Burkfelt . . .

I stand up. "I gotta go. There's trouble at Mr. Burkfelt's."

"What? Wait—how do you know?"

"Not now, I need to get there," I say, moving towards the door.

"I'm going with you."

I turn to look at him. "Don't take this wrong, but you'll slow me down."

"Just go, I'll catch up."

So I leave, running.

* * *

The motel is only a couple of blocks from the jewelry store, so

I get there quickly, but find the door locked. I was going to pound on it, but then thought if Mr. Burkfelt is hurt, he can't open it.

I run around the back, just in time to see a white van speeding away down the alley.

I go to the closed door but it's unlocked. I rush into the darkened backroom.

"Mr. Burkfelt! Mr. Burkfelt! Where are you?"

No reply, but I hear a gurgling sound off to my right. I fumble around for a light switch, find one, but only a dim desk lamp comes on. It's enough, though, to see his body lying on its side a few feet away.

I go down on my knees, seeing a dark puddle spreading out from his torso. I roll him on his back and press my hand to his chest, feeling the blood pulse out of a hole near his heart.

The ring begins to glow and my palm heats up.

You stupid bastard, I think, mentally cursing Henry. *Are you too chicken to come after me?*

But I know the answer: If the great Lord Dunraven couldn't find me, he'd go after whoever he could.

Weirdly, I can see the blood . . . unpooling. It was as if it was flowing *back* into his body.

That's kind of a relief, telling me it's working.

His eyes are closed, but he starts wheezing, then lightly coughing.

"Mr. Burkfelt, it's Collin. You're going to be okay."

His eyelids flutter, then sort of half-open.

Behind me, a shadow fills the doorway, and I turn my head to look. I don't need the jerks in the van to come back.

"How's he doing?" Patrick asks.

"Better, I think. He's starting to come around."

The glowing stone in the ring begins to pulse lightly, then starts to dim. The warmth in my hand seems to cool. But he still seems unresponsive.

"Is there a couch in here?"

"No, but there is what looks like a rollaway bed."

I slide my arms under his limp body and do my best to gingerly lift him up off the floor.

"Where is it?"

"Over in the corner," he says pointing.

I look, and see the mattress. I guess he spent some late nights here.

I carefully carry him over and lay him down—only then do his eyes open. They are pained, and his mouth trembles.

"You'll be okay," I repeat.

"It . . . hurts . . ."

"I know, but it will go away."

His breath is raspy, but even.

I turn to go into the bathroom to wash my hands and hear him whisper something.

"What?" I ask. "What did you say?"

"We have to go . . . they'll be back."

* * *

Patrick finds the car keys, and I carry Mr. Burkfelt to the old Buick sedan, laying him in the backseat as Patrick starts the engine.

"Where are we going?"

I pause, hoping a whispered voice would instruct me. But there is nothing.

"I guess back to the motel."

Snow is coming down at a good clip, but Patrick drives carefully and we make it back to the room in one piece, and not followed by a white van.

I again carry the old man while Patrick opens the door to the room. I lay Mr. Burkfelt on the bed. I go to the bathroom and run cold water on my hands. The one that had been pretty much scorched when healing Patrick is still tender and sensitive, and performing the trick on Mr. Burkfelt had re-ignited it. Drying blood begins to wash off and down the drain. I use some soap and carefully wash them. It's unnerving to think that over the last few months I've had way too much blood on my hands—either killing people, or healing them.

I look at my aching palm and think: *Physician, heal thyself.*

* * *

Mr. Burkfelt is alert and sitting up when I return. Despite the blood that had seeped magically back *into* his body, his gray suit jacket and light blue shirt underneath are a mess. A small hole shows pink skin underneath.

He doesn't look great—pale, pasty, and pained—but his eyes are attentive, and he tries to smile when he sees me.

"Dumb question," I ask, "but how are you feeling?"

"There's a knot in my chest that feels like a fist, but all things considered, I'll take it."

"It gets better," Patrick says from the desk chair. "I still have a little limp, but there's a lot less pain."

"Thank you, Collin," Mr. Burkfelt says. "If you hadn't gotten there at just that moment, I would have died."

"I know. And I have to admit that if Jill hadn't told me, I'd still be sitting here watching some stupid talking-head football show with Patrick."

Mr. Burkfelt nods, but Patrick looks confused.

"Jill?" he asks.

"Well, it *sounded* like her voice in my head."

"You hear her voice?"

"She was supposed to be Collin's guide," Mr. Burkfelt says, "but . . . I think Dunraven got to her first."

"Guide?"

"The Soulmadd thing," I say. "So are you my guide now?"

Mr. Burkfelt nods again. "Reluctantly, yes. Not because I don't want to, but because I'm old and not as nimble and spry as a guide should be." He pauses, coughing lightly. "But I'll do."

"So what happens next?" Patrick asks. "What do we do?"

Mr. Burkfelt takes a while to answer. "It may be time to show you your new home."

His eyes twinkle.

"I hope it's a mansion in Malibu," Patrick says. "Huge, with dozens of rooms that have every toy a man would want."

"Oh, it's that alright," Mr. Burkfelt says. "Just not in Malibu— and more amazing than anything you could ever imagine."

Chapter 29

"The supreme art of war is to subdue the enemy without fighting."
—Sun Tzu

We pack the few things we have and step outside, Patrick first, followed by Mr. Burkfelt—and immediately, both of them have guns to their heads.

A pair of Regulators have the men by the collars, handguns pointing at their skulls. Both men are bulky, wrestler-sized. In the parking lot, the side door of a white van opens and three more men jump out. Two of them have assault weapons, the third appears to be the leader.

Mr. Burkfelt looks terrified. Patrick just looks pissed.

"Mr. Davis," the blonde-haired leader says. "You need to come with us."

I stare at him, thinking. I feel stupid. I should have looked out the window.

Dumb.

Tell me something I don't know.

I say the only thing that comes to mind: "Why?"

The blonde man looks away, out towards the parking lot, smiling slightly. "Because we'll kill your friends here if you don't."

I think some more, again. Not much is coming through.

"If I go with you, will you let them walk away, unharmed?"

Blonde Man smiles again. "Of course."

I look at Mr. Burkfelt, and then Patrick. "Go," I say.

Patrick reaches out and takes Mr. Burkfelt by the elbow, then leads him down the walkway, towards the motel lobby.

"Nice seeing you again, Professor," Blonde Man says, and Mr. Burkfelt, looks back, confused.

"Okay, in the van."

I make the men wait as I watch my friends go. When they're out of sight, I take a deep breath and start walking to the vehicle.

Before I get in, they stop me, and ask me to hold out my hands. I'm handcuffed, then told to get in the back. I hunch over and climb in, stepping around a metal box and a couple of extra assault rifles. I sit on the hard metal floor, back against the side, near the rear door as two other men position themselves to keep their weapons pointed at me.

The van is started, and we head off to . . . somewhere.

* * *

I can see a little of the outside world through the back window, but only enough to really see only sky and the tops of trees. It doesn't really matter. I know where they're taking me.

A few minutes later, we pull into a driveway and I can see the sides of buildings that we pass. Then the van stops, and the men get out, one staying behind to follow me out.

They march me into the big slab of a building—the one Patrick spied on and was probably tortured in. We walk down one of the long, plain hallways, past many closed, plain doors.

At the end, we get on an elevator and go down. I stand there, trying to think of the possibilities, but none of them are good. The best scenario I can come up with is to get them to shoot me, and I play dead while I bleed onto the concrete, hoping they leave me to die. Unlikely. They probably won't make the mistake they made with Patrick and leave me alone.

The doors open onto another plain hallway, and a thought rumbles through me: *Why do they need so many empty rooms.* Of course, not all the rooms are empty, but there's nothing living inside them.

We come to a room about halfway down, and I'm pushed through the doorway, stumbling and falling onto the cement.

"Get up," the Blonde Man barks. "Get the cuffs off him."

I make it to my knees, looking around. This could be the same room that Patrick was in, with chains hanging from the ceiling. If it was, they cleaned up the blood.

Two men approach, one on each side, and jerk me to my feet. One of them pulls out a key and removes the handcuffs.

My brain is still searching, thinking, but nothing of value is coming.

"Take off your clothes."

I don't move, except to raise an eyebrow. I feel a smirk on my face.

"I said take off your clothes."

"You don't need me naked to kill me."

"No, but the clothes get in the way of the knives."

I consider this for a few seconds, leaning towards not cooperating, making them do all the work. I'm not really interested in helping them torment me. But then the thought of these men taking my clothes off is even less appealing, and I realize I need to choose the lesser of two evils. I kick off my shoes.

He turns away, stepping to the wall. He points at a nail sticking out of the concrete. "See this?"

I don't bother replying.

"This is where I'll hang your balls after I cut them off."

Although I feel my skin grow tight and cold, I manage to smile. Half a dozen retorts pass across my mind, from *You must be fun at parties* to *I hope you'll frame them.* But I decide to change the subject.

"We really don't have to do this. We can make a deal."

"I already made a deal, and I keep my word," Blonde says.

"I have gold," I say as I pull my socks off. "Bullion. Bars. You can have it if you let me go."

"We'll take it anyway, but thanks for the offer."

"It's not in the house," I say as my coat comes off.

"I know. Five Star Storage." He pauses, watching me closely. "We've been following you for a while."

I try not to show any reaction. Not sure I succeeded. I undo my pants and push them down. These could be the men who killed Jill, but I don't think so. I think that was solely a Henry Davis/ Dunraven endeavor. I slip out of my underwear.

"I have more money than just the gold. A lot more. I could give you a billion dollars, and my financial advisor wouldn't even notice."

I see the slightest twitch in his face, as if this struck the tiniest nerve. Then he smiles again.

"Then why do you live in a fucking cemetery?"

"I just inherited it. Seriously." I'm standing there pantless, men with guns surrounding me as if I'm the world's most dangerous man. "My birth parents had some kind of royal trust, and it just got transferred. I have so much money, it's ridiculous. You could take half, and there'd still be more."

The smile falters, then fades. He waves his hand at me. "Finish."

I shrug and pull my shirt off, throwing it off to the side with the rest of my clothes.

His eyes slide down to my chest, and he flinches.

"You bear the seal."

I know it's glowing. I can feel it.

He stares at the tattoo, mesmerized. The men on either side of him are staring at it too, but more out of curiosity of a radiating brand shining on my chest.

He knows, the voice tells me.

I feel a shift has occurred, though I'm not sure why. I decide to take advantage of it.

"Now, we can do this your way, or my way," I say.

He's still hypnotized, not even blinking. But I can tell the gears are turning in his head. No, it's more than that. I'm a little stunned as I can actually *hear* his thoughts.

That's the Royal Seal, he thinks. *Dunraven warned us he is dangerous, and now I see why. He has the powers and authorities of the Royal Dominion. This is the Rescuer discussed in theology class.*

He steps forward hesitantly, eyes still fixed on my skin. His hand raises, index finger extended, and he gently touches the brand on my chest. But only for a second when he feels its heat. His hand jerks back as if shocked, and he looks up into my eyes.

"This is supposed to be a myth," he says.

"Do I look like a myth?" I decide to play it up and hold my arms out as if I'm going to do a jumping jack. "I am not *of* the Royal Dominion. I *am* the Royal Dominion."

I lower my arms.

His tongue comes out to moisten his lips. "The Professor said there is no proof you exist, but that there was evidence. He used the Royal Brand as an example. He even had a rudimentary drawing of what it might look like. We all thought he was . . . foolish. But here it is."

My brain is racing in ten different directions, trying to come up with the best way to handle this.

I decide to try something. I raise my hands and place them on his shoulders.

"You know the truth," I say.

"I can kill you, but you cannot die."

I don't know if this is true, but I'll go with it.

"And what happens then?" I say this with my best scholarly voice, if I have one.

He goes ghostly pale, as if he's going to be sick. The tongue comes out again.

"According to . . . legend . . . you have the power to heal . . . and to un-heal."

"Your weapons are useless."

He closes his eyes, and nods.

"You really buyin' this?" the man on his left says. "Sounds like some kind of religious voo-doo mumbo jumbo."

I turn towards the man, putting my arms out again. "Go ahead. Shoot me." I smile.

The man's eyes narrow, as if this is a trick he's trying to figure out.

I feel an energy building up in me, like the healing power, only much more intense and concentrated, emanating from my chest. It grows quickly, and the two men in front of me both take a step backwards.

The one with the rifle suddenly raises it in one swift, practiced movement.

The blast is immediate, and deafening.

* * *

I thought I knew pain, bad pain, but this is . . . indescribable. It feels as if my entire body is on fire. When I first got the tattoo, that burned. This is an inferno, from head to toe, every inch of my body.

If I was shot in the head—which was where the barrel was pointed—am I imagining this? Why am I even conscious?

There is no peaceful feeling, no white light, no warm arms to hug me and welcome me into the embrace of God. There is only pain.

I open my eyes, but even that hurts. And it doesn't matter because I don't see anything. Only darkness.

Is this hell? Darkness and pain?

Then I can feel my tongue inside my mouth, and something tells me I haven't passed on, just passed out.

Get up.

I realize I'm lying on my side. I take a deep breath, and decide to follow instructions. It can't hurt anymore than it already does. But even as I think this, I can sense the pain has lessened.

I roll forward, onto my stomach and get on my hands and knees. Still nothing to see. The agony is subsiding, fading slowly like a fog gradually receding.

I manage to get to my feet, a bit wobbly but manageable. I don't know which way to go. I stick my throbbing arms out and shuffle forward. I eventually come into contact with a wall. I feel around it, but find nothing. I follow it to the right and come to a corner. Then I slide along that and after a few feet, my toes touch something. I pause, then lean down to feel what it is. Clothing. A face. A body.

I step over it and continue my blind journey. I reach another corner. I move to the right again, and quickly find the frame of the door. I locate the knob, and turn it, pulling the door open. Light floods in from the hallway, and again, I'm blinded. I try to blink it away and turn around to look inside the room. One, two, three, four, five. All dead. Or at least not moving.

I stand there for a few minutes, still shaken, still in pain, but can now feel it drain away slowly like a backed-up sink.

I better get out of here.

\# \# \#